Charlotte Grimshaw is the author of three critically acclaimed novels, *Provocation, Guilt* and *Foreign City*. In 2000 she was awarded the Buddle Findlay Sargeson Fellowship for literature. She has been a double finalist and prizewinner in the *Sunday Star-Times* short story competition, and in 2006 she won the Bank of New Zealand Katherine Mansfield Award. In 2007 she won a place in the Book Council's Six Pack prize. Her story collection *Opportunity* was short-listed for the 2007 Frank O'Connor International Prize, and in 2008 *Opportunity* won New Zealand's premier award for fiction, the Montana medal. She lives in Auckland.

D0233624

BY THE SAME AUTHOR:

Provocation

Guilt

Foreign City

Opportunity

SINGULARITY

Charlotte Grimshaw

Published by Jonathan Cape 2010

2 4 6 8 10 9 7 5 3 1

Copyright © Charlotte Grimshaw

Charlotte Grimshaw has asserted her right under the Copyright, Designs
and Patents Act 1988 to be identified as the author of this work

This book is sold subject to the condition that it shall not,
by way of trade or otherwise, be lent, resold, hired out,
or otherwise circulated without the publisher's prior
consent in any form of binding or cover other than that
in which it is published and without a similar condition,
including this condition, being imposed
on the subsequent purchaser.

First published in New Zealand in 2009 by
Random House New Zealand

First published in Great Britain in 2010 by
Jonathan Cape
Random House, 20 Vauxhall Bridge Road,
London SW1V 2SA

www.rbooks.co.uk

Addresses for companies within The Random House Group Limited can be found at:
www.randomhouse.co.uk/offices.htm

The Random House Group Limited Reg. No. 954009

A CIP catalogue record for this book
is available from the British Library

ISBN 9780224088930

The Random House Group Limited supports The Forest Stewardship
Council (FSC), the leading international forest certification organisation. All our
titles that are printed on Greenpeace approved FSC certified paper carry the FSC logo.
Our paper procurement policy can be found at www.rbooks.co.uk/environment

The Random House Group Limited makes every effort to ensure that the
papers used in our books are made from trees that have been legally
sourced from well-managed and credibly certified forests.

Text design: Kate Barraclough
Cover illustration: Getty images
Cover design: Stephen Parker

Printed by Griffin in Australia

To my parents, and to Oliver and Margaret

LONDON BOROUGH OF WANDSWORTH	
9030 00000 8834 5	
Askews	25-Mar-2010
AF GRIM	£12.99
	WWX0006146/0014

THE YARD BROOM

It had started to get hot as soon as the sun rose. Angela got up early and went out onto the deck. A few stars hung on the horizon, but the sky was turning to pale blue and the air was thick with a haze of dust and seeds. The plants and trees were motionless. There had been no wind for a week, just the heat and the cloudless sky, the land burned brown by the drought. The skin of the bay was smooth and glassy. In the distance the dunes of the White Beach seemed to hang in the air above the dried-out swamp and the hill, recently burnt by a scrub fire, stood out black against the banks of pure white sand. A truck rumbled by along the road, raising dust. A dog wandered along under the gum trees. Angela went to the bathroom and looked at her face in the mirror. There was the sunburned skin, the straw hair, blue eyes, and the black shadow that had risen in the night under her right eye, dark and ugly as the burnt hill in the distance. She touched it, and felt it throb. A phrase came into her mind. 'The last straw . . .'

Nathan was lying on his side, asleep, his muscular arm with its tattooed circle of barbed wire resting along his body. He had a small, neat boyish face, even-featured, with a tidy, curving mouth. His head was shaved; he wore a bone carving round his neck. His hand, the fingers loosely curled, was black with tattoos, and there was a small star tattooed on his cheek below his eye. His fingernails were broken and black from work, as were hers. They couldn't get the grease and grime out of them, and after a while they gave up trying.

Last night they'd gone to a party deep in the pine forest. Angela hadn't wanted to go; the people who lived in the forest were like bandits, they lived in tumbledown shacks surrounded by dead cars; they made their money by growing dope and trading drugs. They were Nathan's cousins but Angela was afraid of them. She'd tried to make excuses but he'd persuaded her to go, and she'd driven there with him in the ute and sat out on the deck with toothless Hineana, who rolled joints on her knee while slapping away the howling kids who tottered around her, crying for attention. 'Get off, I'll give you a hiding,' she threatened, whacking their heads, grinning, smacking her lips. She looked demented, though there was an intelligent, malignant gleam in her eye. Angela offered to put two of the smaller children to bed. Hineana shrugged and went on rolling her joints. When Angela took the two stinking toddlers inside she couldn't find where they were supposed to sleep. She put them in a double bed. Outside, people were already drunk and stoned. She lifted up the blind. The house lights shone across the clearing, making shadows of the hulks of dead cars, and beyond that the trees rose like a black wall. The trees crowded around the house, suffocating it, shutting out the light. Anything could happen out there.

Nathan had been shifty all evening — he was up to something with Hineana's husband Huru Wright. There was a man called Brad Richards who'd come up from Whangarei, and he and Huru and Nathan were cooking up something, Angela could tell. She couldn't stand Huru. When he looked at you, it was like being watched by an animal. His expression was intent and cold, also blunted and damaged, as if all feeling had been beaten out of him. He was long-haired and short and squat, and his shoulders sloped like an ape's. When he smiled, it gave you a shock. He looked as though he were thinking over some horrible, pleasurable, secret idea.

She glanced down at the two kids. They were silent, staring, not moving. She thought, they'll be just like their parents. Little killers.

As she got up, one of them started to cry and reached out a hand. He had no choice being here, but why was Angela here? She heard Nathan calling her. She pulled the boy's small hand off her arm and went out. She sat on the deck and drank beer.

There was a fight — two men squaring off, their shadows playing on the ground, until one struggled free from the other and ran straight into the blackness of the trees. His opponent stumbled back to the deck and went on drinking. The other man stayed out there, watching perhaps, just outside the circle of light. That was what bothered Angela about the place, people huddling in the light and the blackness all around, so that everything was compressed into a hellish little space, and always the feeling that something cold and immovable was watching. She put her hand on Nathan's and said, 'Let's go, before . . . '

It was hours before they went, and when they did he was so drunk and stoned he could barely keep on the road. Dust and pine needles and insects whirled in the headlights. He hit a bank and stalled and she sat while he cursed and struggled to start the engine. She saw shapes just outside the lights. He began to accuse her of crazy things, keeping secrets from him, spying.

'Huru says you sit there just looking at people,' he said. 'Staring at them, like you're taking notes.'

Something he'd talked about with Huru and Brad Richards had made him paranoid. 'It's freaky out here,' he said, setting off too fast, so that they crashed and bumped on the rough surface, risking another stall or a crash into the clay bank.

They drove out of the forest. Now they could see the sky and the blazing stars, and the dry, barren scrubland in the moonlight. The moon was shining on the sea down at the bay, and there was a boat going out, sending a beam of light across the water. The camping ground was full of caravans and tents and there were torches on the beach — people fishing or going for a late night swim.

'You don't like Huru, do you?' Nathan said unpleasantly.

'You know I don't. What's to like? His good looks?'

He said quietly, 'He's my cousin.'

'I don't have to like him. Anyway, you don't like him either.'

'So I can't trust you then.' His voice took on a self-righteous whine. He drummed his fingers on the wheel. His expression, when he glanced at her, was very bad.

'Come on,' she pleaded. 'You're paranoid. You can trust me.'

'I might have things I need to keep to myself.' He gulped and cleared his throat, as if his mouth had gone dry. The ute swerved.

'Hey, you idiot. Watch it!'

'You watch it. *You* watch it,' he shouted. He slammed on the brakes and slapped her on the side of the head. Stars exploded in her eyes.

He looked stunned. 'Sorry,' he whispered, and reached out his hand. She pushed him away. They sat in silence. There was a fire down on the beach and they could hear people singing.

It was early morning, but she could tell it was going to be hot. Wavy lines of heat rippled up from the dry, brown land. There were little tornadoes of dust in the distance as cars drove along the main road. She put on her shorts and boots and reflector jacket and walked down to the dump. This was the only place for rubbish disposal in the settlement. There was no collection; people had to bring the rubbish in themselves. There was already a pile of bags at the gates, left by those who couldn't be bothered waiting for the dump to open. She collected as many as she could, dragging them along to the office, a shipping container, where they sheltered from the rain and the heat, and kept their gear. The dump had been overhauled — people used to throw everything into a single large container, which was then taken away by truck. Now it was called a recycling station, and the rubbish was sorted into types, and people had to pay to deposit their loads. Nathan and Angela worked fulltime sorting the rubbish and taking fees. In the summer the baches and camping grounds were full and there was a huge amount to be sorted; in the winter they dealt with the rubbish from the permanent residents.

Nathan turned up in the ute. Angela started on the bottles. She could tell when a car was approaching by the clouds of dust, and when it drove onto the site she came out of the shade of the office and took the bags and the fee. The locals arrived in their beaten-up cars and were lazy and messy, and tried to avoid paying. The holiday people had good cars and were conscientious about what they handed over. These shiny city people — even their rubbish was tidy. It was always the same: the kids, grumpy and hot from being in the car, would open the door and she'd hear the chorus of reedy little voices, 'Pooh!' 'It stinks.' 'Oh phwoar!' and then the giggling and the squabbling between those who wanted the window open, and those who couldn't stand the pong. It was bad all right. Not only did the bins give off a terrible reek but the land itself, especially in summer, was soaked with layers of rubbish, so that the stink came up in waves from the ground and hung on the hot air. The few trees were decorated with paper that had blown out of the bins, and the land around was so barren and dry that it increased the sense of dreariness and squalor. The men avoided Angela's eye, paid their fee and jumped back in the car. The women sat in the passenger seats and stared.

She used to hate the smell. Now she didn't notice. The fact that she'd stopped noticing it bothered her for a while; she thought she might smell bad after work and not realise. But she and Nathan led the same life here as everyone else, going to parties and hangis and tangis and to the pub in town, and no one had ever given her any trouble (or told her she stank). But the stares of the holiday women — Angela minded them. They took no notice of Nathan. A Maori rubbishman. Poor Nathan, they assumed he was where he belonged.

What they saw: she was nineteen, with blonde hair and blue eyes. She wore a filthy sleeveless reflector jacket over shorts and a T-shirt, and heavy boots with short thick socks. She had crude blue tattoos on her forearms, a bracelet tattooed on her wrist. Her hands were dry and filthy, her fingernails broken. No make up. Her skin was streaked with dust. Her eyes were bloodshot and one of them was blackened and swollen nearly shut. Her co-worker, and, since he was the one she was seen with in the settlement, the probable deliverer of the black eye, worked nearby looking hung-over and shame-faced, casting miserable looks her way and hoiking into the bins. A fine pair they were.

The morning dragged on. The cars drove up in a whirl of dust, unloaded their bags and drove away. Nathan worked without talking. Angela could tell he felt bad about what he'd done, but there was something secretive in his expression that worried her.

A couple arrived in an SUV. She was holding a map. He got out and went round to get out the rubbish.

Angela took the bags. 'You off home?'

'Back to Auckland.'

'I used to live in Auckland.'

'Really.' He was backing away, with a prissy little smile. The woman stared.

'Yeah, bugger off then,' Angela said under her breath. They drove away.

'Go and get us some lunch,' she told Nathan. He slunk off. She had always been able to tell him what to do. He might break out and lose his temper, but he loved her and was afraid she would leave. She had that power over him.

But lately Nathan had been spending a lot of time in the forest with Huru. Angela had asked him about it but he'd only worked himself into a state and told her to mind her own business. Huru had it in for her. He whispered in Nathan's ear, spooked him. Nathan was nervous and susceptible; he believed in ghosts and spirits and tapu. As far as Angela was concerned Huru was just a low-life and a criminal, but he came on like a black magic priest, like a tohunga. And she had one specific worry: that Huru would get Nathan hooked on all the drugs he was said to deal in.

Nathan came back with the lunch. He thought for a moment. 'Huru says . . . '

She took the food and said coaxingly, 'Nathan, you shouldn't go out there. They're bad. Stick with your own.' She meant the other side of his family who lived around the bay. They were respectable; they took diligent care of their marae. They all had jobs.

He gave her a sour look. He said, 'You think I want to spend the rest of my life in a dump?'

Angela's great-grandfather was Dutch. He was from Indonesia, where he'd been a rich landowner and a specialist in tropical horticulture. Her grandmother was born here and became a schoolteacher. Her mother, Maria, grew up in Auckland and went to university, but before she'd finished her degree she met Angela's father, who was doing a degree in fine arts. He'd come out from Germany in his early twenties and decided he wanted to stay here and be a painter. Maria got pregnant and dropped out of university. She worked in a bookshop. At some stage she and her friends started experimenting with drugs, and by the time Angela was about seven, Maria was an addict.

They lived in a flat in Grafton. Angela's father stayed home and painted and Maria went to the bookshop. She was fired one Christmas for being stoned at work and falling off her chair. She got addicted to speed, and soon she was paranoid all the time. Angela's father tried to get her to stop. He also threatened to leave, taking Angela with him.

One weekend Angela's father drove out to Piha with a friend, intending to take photographs for his work. They went for a swim at low tide. The surf was dangerously rough, and a wave picked him up and dumped him on his head on the sea bottom, injuring the vertebrae in his neck. He wasn't able to get out of the water and he drowned.

Maria began to lose control. One day she arrived at school at lunchtime, very agitated. She insisted Angela must go home with her. A little scene developed. Summoning the teacher, she pointed at the sky and confided in a hoarse whisper, 'See that helicopter? It's been following me *all day*.' That exchange set the teachers thinking, and Angela was taken away from her while she went into an expensive rehabilitation programme that Angela's grandmother paid for. Angela lived with her grandmother until Maria came out.

Some time later Maria found herself a boyfriend. He got a job in a law firm in Australia, and she and Angela went too, supposedly to follow him. They never did catch up with him. They lived in Sydney until Maria answered an advertisement for a job in a hotel at Ayers Rock.

They flew in over the great rock, the land around it dry and red, like, Angela imagined, the surface of Mars. She remembered the sense of isolation, after flying over the immense desert, and the heat that struck them as soon as they walked down the steps of the plane. At Ayers Rock there was a tiny settlement: four linked hotels, a camping ground, a small shopping centre and a few houses for the staff who worked in the hotels.

Angela thought she would see some Aborigines but she soon discovered they were kept out of sight. There was a tourist show, where they had a didgeridoo and talked about the rock, Uluru, and its spiritual significance to the local people, but the brown guide and the brown man who played the didgeridoo were Maori from Otara. Pamphlets in the hotels told guests they were paying a tax to protect the 'fragile community' of indigenous people. It made them sound as if they were creatures, exotic animals. The workers in the hotels regarded the Aborigines with contempt. They wouldn't work, they said. They were too drunk. When they did appear they usually *were* drunk, poor things. But you hardly saw them. Maria said New Zealand was a much healthier scene, as far as race relations went.

Maria tried to keep away from temptation. She worked on the reception desk at one of the hotels. She had a fling with the guide from Otara, but he was working his way through all the women in the place, and she got sick of that. Then she met Travis, who drove the bus that took tourists to and from the airport and out into the national park.

They had a small house in the residential area. It looked like a bunker, with a low curving roof, round windows and a concrete back porch. Angela could never get used to the stillness and quiet. In those few little roads nothing moved, no cars went past, and all around the vast desert stretched away into the silence. At sunset Uluru was lit up with blazing red light, its sides striped with soft, rippling black shadows, and when night came the sky was filled with big bright stars. Angela was supposed to be doing correspondence school but she spent a lot of time outside, exploring the red paths that ran across the hot, dry landscape. She was in a daze most of the time. Out in the national park there were lizards, dingoes, spiders, snakes. The heat was ferocious. She missed her school at home, her friends. She was lonely, had a sense of unreality. She stood outside the bunker in the vast, black, silent night, dreaming about home. She would have done anything to get away from her mother, and Travis.

Maria stayed clean, but it was hard. She was a gentle, nervous person. Travis started to be irritable and to push her around. When they'd finished their shifts he swaggered over to the house and behaved as if he owned it. He had a deep harsh voice and a square jaw; he lifted weights and boasted about his strength; he was relentless, charmless. At least Angela thought so. She urged her mother to stand up to him, but Maria would pace and tremble and often she would turn on Angela. 'You're just like your father,' she'd say. 'You've got a will of iron.' She looked at her daughter coldly, as if she was just another oppressor. Or she would throw things and scream, 'Why doesn't everybody leave me alone?'

After these scenes Angela would go outside and push a yard broom up and down the length of the porch, shifting the red dust, counting the steps to herself, ten steps forward, ten steps back. She remembered it as a strange, compelling ritual: the broom, the red dust, ten steps forward, ten steps back. She would keep it up for a long time, until everything merged and nothing existed but red earth, silence, heat shimmer, shadows on the red rock.

Maria started taking sips of Travis's beers. He egged her on. She moved to drinking wine, and then spirits. It wasn't long before she was sacked and they flew back to Sydney. She worked in the Ascot Hotel in King's Cross, and when she was fired from there she started working in a brothel. (She insisted she was a 'receptionist'.) After that fell through, they went back to Auckland.

Angela came home with the idea that something significant had happened to her at Uluru. On those silent afternoons, as she was pushing the yard broom up and down the concrete porch, she'd lost her grip. She finished school by some miracle and embarked on a vague attempt at university, but she had an affair with a married man that went badly wrong, and one day after an argument she hitchhiked down the Southern motorway and finished up in Wellington, which ended her university career.

Back in Auckland she moved into a flat with a group of people who were busy, she soon discovered, setting the record for the most armed robberies performed in a year. The papers ran a series for a while, *Today's armed robbery*, which was a way of needling the police about their failure to make any arrests. Angela's flatmate, an outwardly respectable blonde called Amanda, was the getaway driver. This Angela learned later, when the police kicked down the door. Her flatmates were arrested, and the landlord threw her out. Maria had gone to try her luck in Australia again. Angela's grandparents were dead. Her father's family was in Europe. She had no one.

She moved in with Hemi, who lived in a tinny house. She didn't work. She applied for the dole. She cut tattoos in her arms. Hemi was feckless, sweet-natured, and extremely kind. He was the leader of a local street gang that had a ferocious reputation. It used to amuse Angela, travelling about with this lot who affected the mannerisms of American gangsters and frightened everyone they met. She soaked up Hemi's kindness. But she was disgusted with herself. They were idle, directionless; they stayed up all night and slept all day. They never saw the sun.

Hemi and Angela and some of his gang drove up north for a tangi. In the car she listened, tranced with boredom, to their inane chatter. They stopped at a café in Kamo that backed onto a Christian camp. The camp advertised hot pools, and Hemi decided to try them. He and Angela went in, and he wanted to have sex beside the bubbling spa pool. It was a wet, ugly little room, with mouldy concrete pipes roaring in the walls. After a while she left him in there and came out into the car park. It was hot and bright, the cars flashing past on the open road. She had a crushing sense of inertia, disgust and squalor. She saw a man standing in the doorway of the Christian camp, carrying a backpack. She asked him, 'Where's the nearest bus station? I want to get away from here.'

His name was Pastor Kyle Sendells. She got into his car without a word to anyone. Pastor Kyle drove her up to the Far North, where she met Nathan, and where she'd been ever since, at the dump. She never saw Hemi again.

Angela's great-grandfather's house in Indonesia was large and grand. He was rich, well educated, by all accounts handsome and suave. His wife was 'delicate' and had only one child, Angela's grandmother. She never recovered from the change of country, and died relatively young. Angela thought about how they'd made their way out here after their home was taken from them, how they'd tried to make a new life, and where the lines of their family had ended — in her case, in a sea of rubbish bags at the far end of the world.

And yet she believed she'd reached the lowest point of her life that day at the Christian camp at Kamo. The shame and weariness were overpowering. She had faith that she would never feel that low again, and that faith started when she was sitting in the car with Pastor Kyle Sendells, leaving Hemi mile after mile behind.

Pastor Kyle started his religious patter as soon as they were on the road. Angela had been brought up an atheist and didn't pay any attention to it, but some of the things he said were useful, she had to admit. She was so low and depressed that she told him everything. It came out in a stream of despair. He was an intense, thin, wiry man, aged in his fifties, with deep lines down his face, blond hair and pale, sly eyes with fair eyelashes. He had on a faded, checked shirt, nylon trousers and cheap shoes with zips. She told him about her mother, her father's death, about Travis who'd pushed her mother around and turned her back to booze and drugs, about trying and failing to live a decent life. She even told him about pushing the yard broom up and down the porch at Uluru, and how she believed that was the point when she'd lost her mind.

He listened, and whenever she paused he chipped in. 'If we invite Jesus into our life,' he said, 'if we accept that he died for our sins . . . ' He must have thought she was the ideal person for him to practise on — people do turn to God when they're low — but Angela was absolutely immune to the Lord.

When they stopped at a café he sat down and stared at her, calculating, with his sly eyes.

He said, 'Number one. You feel your mother's addiction has tainted you.'

'I don't,' she said.

He spread out his freckly hands and looked at them.

'Was your father an addict?'

'No.'

'Addiction can be inherited. But if you had inherited that gene, you'd be an addict by now. So the taint hasn't attached to you.'

Angela stared.

'You're free of it.'

'You don't know anything about me,' she said.

He took dainty bites out of his hot pie. 'Point two. Those tattoos on your arms. They can easily be erased. Simply go to a doctor, who will refer you to a surgeon. With new techniques there will be no scars.'

She put her arms under the table.

'Point three. On the question of your mother,' he went on.

'Oh yes?' She gave him a dark look, and took her arms out from under the table.

'You tell me she was a woman who allowed herself to be overborne. When this Travis pushed her, she gave in. Isn't that true?'

'Yes.'

'Are you like your mother?'

'No. She says I'm like my father. Tough-minded.'

'You need to stop copying her then, and become yourself.'

'Christ,' she exploded.

He smiled. 'Yes. And then there is Christ. The fourth point is that you must take Christ into your life. When you accept that he . . . '

He ran on. She tuned out. She was annoyed, but very much struck by what he'd said.

He ordered extra coffees, sausage rolls and two pieces of cake. He told the girl he would pay when they were finished.

'Will you be finishing that pie?' he asked.

She shook her head.

'Then perhaps I may . . . ?' He ate it in a few efficient mouthfuls. He looked around. The girl who had served them was taking off her apron. A boy came into the shop and they left together.

'Have you got any money?' he asked.

'I've got twenty dollars.'

'We need petrol. And I need to ask you where you're going. I'm going to a settlement in the Far North. I have an errand there, a mission. I serve God, and I have my own private cross to bear. There's been sorrow in my family life, my church family — it strengthens me to love and serve Jesus.' He looked sly suddenly. 'Mine is a secret sorrow.'

'You might as well tell me,' she said with a bleak smile. 'I've told you everything.'

'And I've told you that you're free.' He held up his hand. 'Say no more. Think. There is nothing to hold you back. Four points. You're free.'

She followed him to the counter.

'Twenty dollars you said?' He nudged her. She gave it to him. He asked the girl, 'Have you got change for a twenty? Two tens?'

She gave him the change. 'God bless,' he said. They walked out, and he gave her ten dollars.

'Take it all,' she said.

'But you've got nothing else.'

'I've got a bank account.'

The girl called, 'What about paying for the extras?'

'Oh, we paid your colleague for those,' he sang out.

'Awesome,' she called, dopey.

He looked around edgily. 'Perhaps we should get on?'

'You didn't pay for the extras,' Angela whispered.

'They were your share to pay. And the Lord tells me you need a bit of kindness. He has mercy on people who have suffered, and sometimes he likes to give them a little freebie.'

They sped on.

At Mangonui, Angela was car sick. Pastor Kyle went into the shop. He came hurrying out, jumped in and drove off fast, unloading his pockets.

'Take these.' He handed her a tube of antacids. 'I assume you're not employed. You mentioned a bank account?'

She said, ashamed, 'I've been getting the dole.'

'You have to cancel it. You have to work. The Lord says if we are to serve him, we must honestly toil to help ourselves.'

She was silent.

'Besides, how much do they give you these days?'

She told him.

'Chicken feed!'

He took her to a tiny bach way out at the end of the White Beach. It was a wild, empty, beautiful place on a hill above the dunes. No one could approach without being visible a long way off. The front windows looked out over the rolling surf. He told her he often saw sharks cruising just beyond the breakers. There were islands on the horizon, and the land rolled away up the coast as far as you could see. From the garden there was a view of the swamp land behind the beach, reaching as far as the burnt hill. The garden was sheltered by the house and by a windbreak, and he had a healthy, well-tended vegetable patch. He lived there in the summer, when he wasn't giving sermons in evangelical churches, and when he was away a friend borrowed the place and looked after the garden.

He slept in the bedroom, and she had a couch in the sitting room. There'd been a woman in the place at some stage. Angela found some dowdy dresses and shoes. One day when he was out she found a pile of child's drawings in a drawer, and a letter written in felt pen in a child's big, uneven handwriting.

> I like my new toys. I miss my mum. I have fun and go on walks. I play with toys and ride a bike. I have nice things to eat. I do some lessons and do maths and learn to read. What I wish for please is to live with my mum again.

She closed the drawer. She supposed he must have had a grandchild to stay, but the letter was strange. She couldn't quite see how it fitted. It was a sort of report, and an appeal, but to whom? She wondered whether Pastor Kyle was up to something, and imagined some scam involving his church and a charity — fake begging letters that purported to be from African orphans, but were actually penned by a diligent Pastor Kyle.

At night she listened to the surf booming down on the shore. She swam in the sea and took long walks, all the way to the burnt hill. She got fit. They fished off the rocks every day, and their diet consisted of fish, tinned food and vegetables from the garden. He didn't drink or smoke. One day he drove her into town and got her to cancel her dole. She took the money out of the account and gave it to him; he thanked her and said, 'Now you are truly free.' They celebrated with a big meal. For such a thin man, he ate an enormous amount.

Angela met Nathan in town, and started to go out with him. He'd been a senior rugby league player; he was fit and good-looking, with a sweet smile. His family — the respectable side that is — were handsome people who owned a lot of land in the area. Nathan was the lazy youngest brother of eight children, the bad boy of the family. He'd avoided school and never learned a trade like the others, and ended up working in the dump. His family loved him and indulged him; he was a real favourite.

When Pastor Kyle decided he had to go down to Auckland, Angela didn't want to live in such an isolated place by herself, so she moved into Nathan's little house on the main road. They shared with Nathan's friend Brad Richards for a while, before he left to find work down south. (Angela liked Brad. She was sorry to see him go. She didn't know she would meet him again, much later, in Auckland, and discover that he had a different name. That she would end up living with him for most of the rest of her life.)

She started working in the dump with Nathan.

She often thought about Pastor Kyle's advice. First, she wasn't an addict. Second, she could, if she chose, have her tattoos removed. Third, she didn't have her mother's soft, scatter-brained nature, and therefore she should stop behaving like her and become herself. Fourth, the Lord — well, she chose to forget about Him.

When she'd first started going out with Nathan she hadn't shaken off her shame and self-disgust. During those aimless, sensuous, idle months with Hemi, a kind of sweet decay had seeped into her soul. Now things were changing. As time went by she felt the old layers falling away and a new self hardening up — her own true personality. She began to be sharp with Nathan, to be bored by him. Sensing the change, he hit out. He was losing something. She knew what was going to happen: he loved her and she was going to hurt him. Those holiday women who stared at her from their cars, at her black eye, and at the glowering tough guy who'd beaten her up, would have had a firm idea who was the victim. But Nathan had a look of bewilderment and dread after they'd been fighting. When she was sitting on the deck after work he would lie down beside her and rest his head on her knee. He clung to her. And she stroked his hair and stared out over the bay, silent, cold, unyielding.

Huru could see she was changing. He was stirring up trouble, whispering in Nathan's ear. Perhaps he wanted Nathan to kill her, just for his own evil entertainment.

After a stint in Auckland, Pastor Kyle came back to his bach at the end of the White Beach. Angela took to driving to the estuary around the coast from his place, and walking the tracks through the bush. He worked in his garden in the mornings, and when she turned up he stopped and put the kettle on, and served up fresh fish and corn cobs for lunch. They ate out in the garden, looking over the beach. Afterwards they went fishing.

It was another hot day, the bright light striking off the flax. Angela climbed Pastor Kyle's hill, intending to tell him about her latest row with Nathan. He wasn't in his garden. She went into the house and put the kettle on, then heard him dropping his boots at the back door.

He came in and looked at her steadily from under his pale lashes.

'You have a black eye.' His tone was flat. He looked hot and irritated.

'It's your fault,' she said, smiling.

'What?'

'You told me to become myself. Nathan doesn't like it.'

'Yourself? Oh, I see.' He took out a packet of cigarettes, lit one and eyed her impatiently. He'd never looked at her like that before, as if she were a nuisance.

'I'll come back another day,' she said, and then burst out, 'I didn't know you smoked.'

He didn't take his eyes off her. 'Want one?' he said.

She took one. He lit it. There was a silence. The wind whistled over the iron roof, a fly buzzed against the window, and the sky in the square of the glass glowed an intense, unclouded blue. She saw that Pastor Kyle had not shaved.

'Is something wrong?'

'No,' he said mechanically. 'I'm going fishing. Want to come?' There was no encouragement in his voice.

'I'll see you later. Nathan's waiting.'

He watched her go. He waved, and she didn't wave back, wanting him to know she was a bit hurt.

She turned off the track and lay down under a tree. It was Saturday, and since she didn't have anything to do she thought she might turn back and have a swim at the White Beach. She lay in the shade, looking up at the sky through the leaves, too lazy to move. After half an hour she heard someone on the track. She saw Pastor Kyle walking quickly, carrying a pack on his back and a large box in his arms. The box was criss-crossed all over with blue and black packing tape.

She lay in the scrub, waiting until he was a distance off, still visible through the trees. She followed. He left the track that led to the coastal settlement and turned down a steep slope, then disappeared from view. She hurried to an outcrop of rock and looked down. He was making his way through the trees to a sandy path that followed the coast just above the rocks.

Angela sat on the rock. The sun blazed down, and the sea glittered. The sandy path he'd taken must lead round the coast to the jetty where she'd left Nathan's ute. She decided to follow him, and if he caught her, to say that she'd seen him come down that way and thought it might be a good shortcut. The only thing that made her hesitate was his expression as he'd passed. There was something so fixed, so coldly intent in it, that she didn't like the thought of getting in his way.

She skidded down the slope and onto the path, which wound between rocks, under clay banks and over tangled pohutukawa roots. Below, the dark blue sea, deep here, washed in among the rocks, and further out gannets circled and swooped and dive-bombed, surfacing with fish in their beaks. The hot wind flipped the shiny leaves and the pohutukawa flowers blazed red against the sky. There was the iridescent sheen in the air that you get on very hot days. She passed under trees laden with straw bundles of shags' nests, the birds clacking their beaks and shitting down onto the white-streaked rocks, the air pungent with the smell of fish. She was heading out onto a small peninsula. The path went around an outcrop and then there was no more path just white sand and a long, lonely, beautiful stretch of coast fringed with bush, out of sight of the jetty, which lay behind the curve of the land inside the estuary.

Pastor Kyle had walked in the hard sand near the water. His footprints were visible. Where the beach met the trees the sand was smooth and cool, and behind the small dunes the bush made a thick, sheltering canopy. The sand was bone white and the estuary water was very clear, with a fast current in it. The tide was going out, the water running between the shore and an island. She stuck close to the edge of the bush, following the footprints until they crossed the beach and entered the forest. Near the shore she came to a sunny clearing in the trees.

There was a tiny weatherboard house, a boat pulled up on the sand below it, and a long fishing line strung out on poles into the estuary. Beside the house, in a clearing striped with sunlight, the air warm and still and dusty, was a wooden picnic table, at which a fat woman was reading a book. A small boy in yellow togs decorated with skulls and crossbones waded out of the water and ran towards her, cannoning into her side. She dropped her book and pushed him away, saying in a lazy, good-natured voice, 'Get off, you, you're soaking wet.'

She watched them. The boy lay down under the long line and covered himself with sand. The woman went back to her book. Angela decided to walk past them along the shore. She turned, and Pastor Kyle was standing behind her.

He was holding a bucket. In it was a mess of scraps and bones and blood.

'I followed you,' she said.

'I see that.' His gaze was steady.

'I thought it would be a shortcut to the car.'

'I'm going to feed the pig,' he said. 'Come with me.'

She followed him into the clearing.

'This is Mrs Sendells,' he said. The woman closed her book and sat back. She had a massive face and forehead, large eyes, wiry, curly hair and a small, thin-lipped ugly mouth. Her eyes were grey. She looked at Angela without expression, her massive arms folded. The boy came trailing over, covered in sand, and leaned against her. He was about seven years old, with close-cropped brown hair and freckles on his nose.

'This is Joseph.' Pastor Kyle patted the boy's head. The boy smiled shyly and looked away.

'I'll show you the track back,' Pastor Kyle told her, and walked off.

'Nice to meet you,' she said to the woman.

'God bless,' she said. Her eyes followed them. Her expression didn't change.

Angela hurried after Pastor Kyle. A short distance from the house was a smelly enclosure made of wooden boards. The pig stuck its hairy snout through a gap, grunting and squealing. Pastor Kyle emptied the slops.

'She's your wife?'

He sighed and put down the bucket. 'Mrs Sendells usually lives in Auckland. She's having a holiday. There's no room in my little shack.'

'Who's the boy?'

'A member of my church.' He faced her. 'Any other questions?'

'No. Only you never mentioned . . . '

'You've stayed in my house. That doesn't mean you're part of my family.' His eyes were cold.

'No.' She looked away, stung.

'I'll show you the track.'

He led her up a slope to a headland above the beach. They climbed across rocks, crashed through a bit of bush and came to a track that led to the jetty where she had left the car.

She set off but he called her back.

'Angela. I've helped you, haven't I? You've stayed in my house. We're . . . friends.'

'Yes.'

'I should explain. There are issues in our church family. A young woman, one of our community, had a divorce that, well, that was very sad. She's needed a refuge for her son, Joseph. Mrs Sendalls and I have agreed to help her.'

'A young woman?'

'Yes, it's a bad domestic situation. There's a difficult, violent, cunning ex-husband, who mustn't find out where his son is. Young Joseph needs safety and privacy. Do you understand?'

'I won't tell anyone.'

'Absolute privacy.'

'I understand.'

'God bless you,' he said.

She drove home, thinking it over. A woman had got Pastor Kyle to hide her son from his father. She remembered the letter in a child's handwriting that she'd found in Pastor Kyle's drawer. The letter had said, *What I wish for is to live with my mum.* Who was the letter addressed to? It was all very strange. Angela went round and round it and didn't know what to think.

Nathan was in a better mood when she got home and she forgot about Pastor Kyle. But she woke in the night and thought of it again. Pastor Kyle's manner had been odd, strained. And yet there could be a perfectly good explanation. In any case, Pastor Kyle was right. She owed him, and she would have to mind her own business.

A month later she came home from the dump, turned on the TV and there on the six o'clock news, was a picture of the boy she'd seen that day with Pastor Kyle.

Nathan had mates over. They were rowdily drinking beer. One of the cousins, picking at a guitar, broke into scraps of melody that were strikingly sweet and true. They were crowded into the sitting room and Angela couldn't shut them up, nor watch the late news. The little party went on for longer than she could endure. She lay in bed seething with frustration. At four in the morning a string broke on the guitar, there was a brief spat followed by reunion: loud oaths of allegiance hoarsely sworn under the bedroom window, under a bone-white slice of summer moon. Angela lifted the blind and saw a speckled streak of moonlight glittering across the bay. Four battered utes roared into life and the cousins sped off. Nathan came scraping his way along the hallway wall, towards bed.

The next day she went straight to the shop for a paper. The story was on the front page. It was a child custody battle that had taken a striking turn. Pastor Kyle had lied: the boy's name wasn't Joseph, it was Samir Jarrar. According to the paper, the boy's mother, one Karen Lot, had been accused of serious child neglect. The Family Court had taken the boy from her and awarded full custody to the father, Ramzi Jarrar, who was a Lebanese New Zealander, a pharmacist. Karen Lot, the article said, had then colluded in a plan with her father, a Mr Bryan Lot, to kidnap the child and hide him away from Mr Jarrar, in defiance of the court order. Bryan Lot had abducted the boy and disappeared, and Karen Lot was refusing to say where he and the boy were. The father, Mr Jarrar, was appealing for information. The police were searching for the boy. How had Pastor Kyle and his wife ended up with the child? The only clue was that Bryan Lot was a pastor in an evangelical church.

In a side article she found this: Letters have been received, purporting to be from the child, Samir Jarrar, saying that he is well and happy, and asking that he be allowed to live with his mother, not his father. The authenticity of these letters has been questioned by the boy's father, Ramzi Jarrar, who says his son, aged six, does not have the skill to write them.

Pastor Kyle and his wife must have agreed with the Lots that they would take the boy and hide him from Mr Jarrar. But the Family Court had decided Karen Lot wasn't a fit parent and that Mr Jarrar was. Surely the court would know best?

Angela drove back to the estuary that afternoon. She parked the ute back from the road in a layby where she hoped it wouldn't be seen. She walked past the jetty, along the track, over the rocks and down the slope through the trees.

She hid and watched. There was no sign of life. She went further into the clearing. The house was empty. The windows were closed, the door was locked and the long line had been reeled in. The pig was gone from its pen.

She walked along the shore. The tide was sluicing out towards the mouth of the estuary. Shadows slanted across the beach. She walked around the curve of coast until she came to the sandy path. She set out with the uneasy fear that someone might be watching her from the hillside above. She hurried past the gannets around the rocks. There was rain out at sea, great curtains of water sweeping in, and the sea had a metallic sheen. A shower dripped down through the branches and the wind sighed in the treetops. She reached the bottom of the hill below Pastor Kyle's bach. Instead of going up the path she clambered through the scrub, and arrived on a section of bank behind his house, looking down on the garden. There was no sign of him or his wife or the boy.

She stayed in her perch for a long time, until the shadows grew long and spiky on the dunes, and the thought of darkness began to bother her. She left her lookout and retraced her steps.

She drove home. What she'd seen a month ago seemed remote now. Perhaps the boy in the clearing wasn't the one pictured on the news. The fat woman with her ugly, curly mouth and her level stare, the little boy covered in sand, Pastor Kyle with his bucket of bones: the scene took on the flavour of a fairy tale or dream, touched with faint, sensual menace: the golden, dusty light among the trees, sunshine and shadow, the murmur of the sea.

Nathan was sitting on the deck rolling a beer can over his forehead. Angela sat down beside him. 'Nathan, don't tell anyone this. Promise.'

He shrugged. Nodded.

'I've seen that boy. Samir Jarrar, the one in the news whose grandfather kidnapped him.'

He didn't say anything. He stopped rolling the can over his face.

'You know the one I mean.'

'Yes,' he said.

'I saw him.'

'Where?'

'In a house over at the estuary. Only he's gone now.'

'They said on TV they think that boy's in Taupo.'

'Well, he's not,' she said, looking sharply at him. She was

surprised he knew what she was talking about. 'I only saw him once, but it was him all right.'

He stood up. 'I don't believe it.'

She threw up her hands.

He said quietly, 'Are you trying to stir up trouble. Do you know how many police would come crashing through here if you spread this.'

'No.'

'Then maybe you should keep your mouth shut.'

She said, 'Pastor Kyle's got him. It was his house.'

'Pastor Kyle. He's your friend. He's everyone's friend up here. If you get him into trouble, for no reason . . . '

He put his arms around her. 'Don't make trouble. We have to live here. I love you.' He pushed her back and looked into her eyes. 'Do you know how much I love you.'

She pushed him away impatiently. Hurt flashed in his eyes. She leaned against him, and he held her tight, pushing his face into her shoulder. They sat like that, in silence, while the last of the sunset lit up the hillside and the shadows darkened in the dips and gullies above the bay.

Weeks went by. They worked in the dump. The weather grew cooler and the settlement emptied out. Now there were days of rain, soaking the brown land, making rivers of red mud at the sides of the roads. The bay was calm and still, the water silvery. They fished from the rocks in the early mornings, in the salty silence under the pohutukawa trees. Stingrays glided under the water, rippling their wings, fish jumped, rain dimpled the water. Nathan slid off the rocks wearing a mask and snorkel, gathering kina, diving and surfacing like a seal. Under the white sky the bay, ringed by black wet rocks, seemed to be holding itself in check. All was calm, the only sound was the patter of the rain.

One afternoon Nathan gathered a sack of kina and loaded it into the ute. They drove along the dirt road towards the pine forest. There was mist hanging over the tops, the camping ground was deserted, and in the forest the air was cool and damp. They both shivered at once, and looked at each other and laughed. Once they got stuck and Nathan had to rock the ute backwards and forwards, until they shot out of the bog with a roar and a spray of mud.

Huru came across the clearing to meet them, taking the sack of kina. Three women brought chairs onto the deck and began to take the innards out of the kina with spoons. The children tottered around, the toddlers wearing only nappies, despite the chill.

Huru took Nathan aside and talked in his ear. Nathan nodded and chewed his nails, and occasionally broke out in a false little chuckle. They walked away into the trees.

Hineana offered Angela a spoon for the kina. There was a lot of clutter on the deck, clothes hanging on lines above their heads, stacked tools, a yard broom.

Angela looked at a pair of boy's yellow swimming togs, decorated with skulls and crossbones.

She spooned out the messy kina and tipped it into a bowl. One of the women started singing, low and tuneful and sweet.

'Seen Pastor Kyle lately?' Angela asked Hineana.

Hineana rolled her eyes and smacked her lips and laughed, 'Oh, he never comes out here. No never. He doesn't come here.' She grinned at Angela, toothless, shaking her head. 'Not him, oh no.'

The rain drifted against the dark wall of the trees. Hineana offered her a beer. They worked, listening to the low singing. Hineana looked at Angela again, chuckling and shaking her head. Her eyes were very bright. Angela put her hand on her arm. 'I'll just go to the toilet.'

She went quickly through the musty bedroom; there was nothing but the bed and a pile of clothes. In the lean-to laundry, under a pile of coats, she found a large box striped with black and blue tape — the box she'd seen Pastor Kyle carry from his bach.

Outside, Huru and Nathan were shaking hands. They left, driving out as the last patches of light were gleaming in the sky. Angela pretended to have a headache, and went to bed as soon as they got home.

At first light next morning she took the ute. On Pastor Kyle's track the bush sparkled with dew and the ground sent up a wet earthy scent. The surf was rough at the White Beach, the waves booming. She knocked on Pastor Kyle's door. He opened it, wearing pyjama trousers and a holey grey jersey. The place smelled of cigarette smoke.

She walked in and said, 'You've given that boy to Huru.'

He stood very still. He lit a cigarette, never taking his eyes off her.

'Sit down,' he said.

Slowly, he went to the kettle and filled it. He cleared his throat. 'You're upset. You don't know what you're talking about.'

'The police are looking for him. If you don't send him back I'm going to tell someone.'

He faced her. 'Angela. Think about what you're saying. You want to make trouble for your friends?'

'I won't get anyone into trouble if you send him home.'

'Home.'

'He's supposed to be with his father. He's got a custody order. You can't leave him out there.'

'You will let me down. And others.' He pursed his lips, studied his fingernails, considering. 'You might like to think about this. Nathan drove the boy out there. He's involved in this. And so are you, that means.'

He looked at her steadily. There was a silence.

'I don't care,' she said.

'Think. You had nothing before you came here. This is your home, your community. Huru . . . '

'How can you have anything to do with Huru?'

'Huru understands what's right. That boy was being brought up without his church family. Without God.'

'And he's with God now? That place is evil. If you leave him there, you're evil.'

'You're going to betray Nathan,' he said.

He paused, and then added softly, 'What will Huru think about that?'

She snatched up one of his cigarettes and lit it. Her hand trembled. 'If you don't send him back in three days I'll ring the police.'

He put the kettle carefully down. 'Is this the new self, the new you?'

'I'll give you three days,' she repeated.

His expression was dreamy, strange. He mouthed a couple of words, smiled, shook his head and said, 'I took you in.'

She faltered, 'That's not the point.'

He came towards her, his voice toneless, mechanical. 'You're faithless. Disloyal. You are the slut daughter of a drug-addicted whore.'

She ran out and fled down the path. She stopped on the track several times, thinking he was following her. Panicking, she couldn't start the engine. Finally she got it going and drove towards home.

She pulled over on their road and looked at Nathan's little house with the beautiful, misty bay spread out before it, the water crossed by cloud shadows, the gannets circling and plummeting, hitting the water like bombs. A squall disturbed the calm; the water broke into a million glittering ripples. Pastor Kyle was right; she couldn't go home. This was the last time she would sit here, looking over the bay.

She turned the ute around and headed for the main road. The sun was rising higher over the brown hills; the eastern sky was pink, the light glowed softly at the edges of the clouds. A hawk flew up from the road and circled lazily away. A feeling rose in her, so reckless, so happy . . . She nearly drove herself off the road.

She made it to Auckland in the evening and found a room in a cheap motel in Greenlane. She abandoned Nathan's ute in a car park. She waited. Pastor Kyle was cunning and he wouldn't want trouble. He would know she was serious about telling someone. Sure enough, after three days, the TV news reported that the boy had turned up at a small police station outside Whangarei. He was returned to his father.

The following month it was reported that Nathan and Huru had been arrested in the settlement. There were drug charges. They were to be questioned about Samir Jarrar. Pastor Kyle's name wasn't mentioned; his role in the affair stayed a secret between him and his God. As far as Angela knows he's managed to keep it that way. No one talks to the police up there.

Two weeks after she got back to Auckland she found a job in a restaurant and a room in a flat. She tidied herself up, wore long sleeves to cover her arms. One day the man she had known up North as Brad Richards came into the restaurant. They talked. He came back regularly. He started to ask her out. She took her time. She didn't want to go out with anyone for a while. She was working hard, earning good tips, preparing for the operation to remove her tattoos.

THE OLIVE GROVE

Larry told Emily, 'The universe is expanding.'

In the hours before dawn, when thunder cracked in the mountains and still there was no rain, Beth's voice came out of the dark, 'Per, are you listening? Have you heard a word I've said?'

Sometimes Emily could hear her parents laughing. Beth would sigh in the morning, 'Per makes so many jokes, I can't get to sleep.'

Long nights. Forked lightning through a crack in the curtains. There was heat and distant storms, no rain.

The darkness was gigantic and had size and weight. Emily felt she was pressed into a tiny space. Everything was in the ear. Voices. Silence.

She lay in the dark, thinking. Before Beth and Per there was no Emily. Emily was Nothing. Then there was the Big Bang (ha ha, the big old double bed creaking in the night) and Emily began to be. Before Beth and Per, there was no family. No Emily Larry Marie. The family began: a small, tight nucleus, full of packed energy. Years passed, eons of notimetime, of crowdedtime, of allclamouringatoncetime. And everything moving out across the vast emptiness, always spreading outwards. One day there would be no Beth, no Per . . .

The Big Bang was not an explosion, Larry explained. It was a slow, cold expansion.

The card had arrived last week — a postcard of three dancing figures by Matisse. Emily brought it to her mother, who was sitting as usual on the balcony admiring the garden. 'It's from Javine,' Beth said, turning it over. 'She's coming to stay for three days. Do you remember Javine, Milly?'

Emily thought. 'No. Yeah.' She made a face.

In the garden by the olive grove, sunlight on grey stones. Emily, hiding in the long grass, spied on her mother through the wire fence. Beth held Marie by the hand. And she said, 'Marie, pick those ones. They're fresh. No, those ones have had it.' (The petals overgrown and limp.) 'Chuck them away. They're going to go brown.'

Funny little Marie, with her blonde hair. She threw the dead flowers in the air and watched them scatter. Petals stuck to her hands.

Perhaps the universe was like a flower. Starting from a bud, losing its tightness as it spread outwards. Would it wither and die? Emily went to Larry, who turned the pages of his book with one finger. He sighed importantly.

'When the universe is ready it will start to shrink again, back down to the first pinpoint.'

'How do you know?' she asked.

'I just do.'

'How will it know when it's ready?'

Was the universe like a balloon, blowing up, deflating? Was it like lungs?

'Go away,' Larry said, propped in bed with a stomach bug, his head in a book. He burped horribly, to make her leave. The sun made a dancing white star on his bed cover.

Emily slouched down to Madame Olivier, who let her feed the two elderly sausage dogs that lolled on grimy cushions in her kitchen. Madame Olivier gave Emily greasy snacks that did strange things to her stomach.

'I'll have to start boiling the drinking water,' Beth said.

In the flat Emily had her own bedroom with a window that looked over the olive grove. She sat on a table on the balcony, playing ludo against herself. Beside the building the path ran down the slope, through a tunnel under the railway line to the harbour. The waterfront was beautiful; it ran along the bottom of the Old Town and around the shore towards Monte Carlo. The town lay in the curve of the coast, its orange buildings and tiled roofs rising up the slopes of the steep hills. In the marina were lines of boats — launches and yachts, their tall masts clinking and jinking. The sea was blue and sparkling with a milky haze on the horizon, the beaches were sheltered by stone breakwaters, and along the seafront the palm trees whispered and clattered in the breeze. Behind the town rose the grey mountains and, way up high, were the twin tunnels of the autoroute that ran through the ranges into Italy. In the winding lanes of the Old Town the houses were ancient and crooked; the paths between the houses ran steeply up the hill to the graveyard; in the dead hours of the siesta, under washing strung on lines beneath the buildings, there was shade, silence, sometimes the strong waft of primitive drains. Emily and Larry walked to the graveyard and watched the funerals; in the bright air under the cypresses the tiny black-clad widows, their absorbed, inward faces.

They lived in a large, ornate white block of flats. There was a white gravelled courtyard and a grand front entrance. In the mornings the courtyard blazed with colour: bright flowerbeds, palms, rock gardens sprouting with spiky cacti. On one side of the building was the path that led to the school, a large old house with green shutters and bullet holes in the walls. There were two class-rooms — one for Emily's class, one for Larry's. The playground was a shaded circle of concrete with a tree in the middle. The toilets were in a wooden outbuilding — little cubicles with a round hole in the concrete and two footprints to stand on, on either side.

Beth sent Emily to school in new clothes, a skirt and a matching tartan jacket. Emily was furious. She hated skirts; she hated anything that matched. The girls in the playground asked, '*Tu veux jouer?*' She nodded but dropped out at first, unable to understand the rules. There were red beetles in the stone walls. After school Emily collected some and stuck them alive to a piece of cardboard. They waved their legs, drowning in the white glue. Ashamed, she hid the murdered beetles down the side of her bed.

That night there was thunder, and in the morning, in the tunnel under the railway line, she and Beth and Marie came upon a gulping mass of toads. All morning in the classroom Emily wanted to go to the toilet but was too embarrassed to ask. Instead she drummed her feet on the floor, tap tap tap. The teacher told her to stop the racket. '*Pas bon point*,' she frowned. If you earned enough *bons points* you got a prize, usually a pretty little card, *une belle image*.

That week, let out the gate early, Emily turned to go home, thinking it was lunchtime. But the teachers laughed and pulled her back, and led the children down the path to a bus. They drove to a medical centre and were stripped to their underwear. They stood in a line and were pushed forward, one by one. A doctor poked a cold metal stick in Emily's ears. He covered her eyes one at a time and asked her what she could see on a coloured chart. She knew the French words for all the pictures, but wouldn't say.

'How old are you?'

She whispered, '*J'ai cinq ans.*'

The doctor splayed his fingers. 'Yes. You are *fife*. Good girl.' He laughed kindly, reached out his finger and pinged the elastic on her underpants. She backed away. She felt what he had done was terribly wrong.

They rode back on the bus, and this time she was allowed to go home for lunch. But in the afternoon she was caught scribbling in pen on her hand. The teacher grabbed her blue and red paw and held it up to the class. '*Pas. Bon. Point.*'

That evening she fished up the cardboard card from the side of the bed. The red beetles had turned brown. There was a faint smell. She pushed the card back down. Next time she went to look the card had gone. No one said anything about her crime.

Larry went on being sick. He refused to get up.

'Perhaps it's culture shock,' Beth said. She boiled water and set pans of it on the bench to cool. She told Emily to drink from the pans only, not from the tap. Emily drank from the tap anyway, when no one was looking.

Larry lay reading, or staring at the ceiling. Beth called Per into his room, 'Look at this.' She held up Larry's hand. The skin on it had begun to peel.

'How weird,' Per said, perplexed.

'I'll have to get a doctor,' Beth said.

The doctor came, breathing fumes of garlic and wine. 'A virus,' he said.

'And the peeling hands?'

'A side effect. Give him fresh air.' The doctor sniffed. 'Try boiling the drinking water, Madame.'

Per came home for lunch. Emily got a great surprise when she saw him. His front tooth was missing. He'd bitten a piece of French bread and felt a jolt ('like being socked in the jaw') and when he'd looked down his false front tooth was stuck in the sandwich.

Emily stared at the new Per. Last winter Larry had read a book about androids. Emily had got an idea fixed in her mind: perhaps Per was a robot. She had watched him for signs. Was he real? How could you tell? In France Per had grown his hair and beard long. Now, with his wild hair and missing tooth, he looked like a pirate. Perhaps he was a criminal, with a band of men.

Madame Olivier was scandalised — a missing tooth, *tiens*. For her, the beard and long hair were shocking enough.

Emily fed a piece of salami to the elder sausage dog, Agnes. She said to Madame Olivier, 'My father has a gun.'

'A gun?'

'A pistol,' Emily said. 'This long.' She held out two hands.

'Get away,' Madame Olivier said calmly.

There was a football field below the olive grove where local games were held. When there was an important match a line of policemen was stationed in the olive grove to stop people watching the match for free.

On a hot, still day Emily listened to the crowd singing: *Allez Menton, Allez Menton, A-Allez.* Hunting alone for lizards, she came to the line of police. She spied on them from behind a tree until one of them saw her and nudged the others. They glanced, shrugged and turned away. They were watching the match. The one who had seen her beckoned. Emily held her hands cupped in front of her. The policeman ambled through the grass and asked what she had in her hands. He was young, with a smooth brown face and black hair. He had a tiny chip out of his front tooth. His cap was shiny, his uniform exact and neat. Slowly she opened her fingers and showed him the grey lizard, motionless in her palm, its throat throbbing. In a quick convulsion of its whole body it rushed up Emily's arm, fell off her elbow and disappeared into the long grass.

The policeman turned his mouth down in a sad face, like a clown. He parted the grass with a stick, trying to find it.

'No, it's gone,' she said. Then she saw it. She pounced, and picked it up, but the tail dropped off and lay, wiggling horribly, near Emily's foot. The policeman made an expression of disgust. Together they leaned down, peering. Emily got it between her finger and thumb and the young man made such a face they both laughed.

On the bank the policemen raised their arms and shouted. Goal! His superior called roughly, telling him get back. The young policeman clicked his tongue, threw the stick into the brush and jogged away, turning once to smile over his shoulder. She could hear him being lazily told off.

She roamed through the sun-striped grass, savagely thinking. She liked the policeman a lot. The grass was dry and brown, the paths were dusty. Everything was still in the midday heat. The sky was blue patterns through the lattice of branches, and the leaves had that graceful, grey, feathery sheen that made the light in the olive grove so dreamy and soft. A wizened grandfather and grandmother took turns to wheel a pram up and down under the trees. The baby thinly wailing under its cover. They leaned close and made cooing, clucking sounds.

Po po po, said the old man.

Emily drifted near to the wire fence. Madame Olivier's dogs set up a yapping in the basement. The old woman cursed them and banged her shutters. A train rumbled by.

And in the garden, Beth was calling, 'Marie, Marie.'

Javine wandered out onto the balcony and stood running her hands through her yellow hair. Her breasts bulged over the front of her tight top. Her neck had three little bulges of fat, like rings, on which her gold jewellery rested.

Marie pointed up at her. Javine waved her pretty coloured scarf. 'Hello down there.'

Javine had brought wine for lunch. It was too hot to eat on the terrace. They sat at the wooden table inside, in the shade. Javine leaned back and put a cigarette to her red lips; Per started forward and lit it. She blew out a long grey stream of smoke.

'I am working in London. These last four months all alone. No friends, no family. But that is the way to work. I am working on a new idea. Something crazy, something to *catch* you by the breath.'

Per stared out the window. A blush had spread over Javine's throat. 'This light,' she said fiercely, pointing to the terrace, where the spiky cacti stood in their pots, cutting green shapes out of the sky. 'This Mediterranean glow. It is incomparable. These blues and greens. These oranges. These reds and blues and . . . ' She shook her head and smiled simply. No, it was impossible. Words failed her.

'Yellows?' Beth frowned.

A flash of laughter across Per's face.

Javine tossed her head. 'These turquoises. Especially so. I know that *you*,' she leaned towards Per, 'are sensitive yourself to these *sub*-tleties, these storms and changes of light. You bring them to your work in a way that is . . . ' She crinkled her eyes as if she were tasting something delicious. 'It is genius,' she whispered.

Per cleared his throat. 'No no,' he said with a laugh — he felt suddenly clogged, drowsy. He traced a pattern on the table with his forefinger.

Beth smiled strangely. Javine looked at her without expression. She tapped her fingers on the table and breathed in through her nose. 'I must see where you work, Per Svensson,' she demanded. 'Your lair, away from the noise and bustle. Your *fictory* of ideas.'

'Sure,' Per said, glancing at Beth. 'It's not far away,' he said. He started to clear the table. Below the window the gardener cleared his throat and hoiked. Madame Olivier shouted at him. The dogs yipped and yapped.

Emily, on her best behaviour, went to get her colouring-in book. She had been working on a page of geometric shapes, making a complicated pattern. It had taken her hours; her felt pens were nearly dry.

Javine leaned over. 'Ah, what are you doing with these little shapes?'

'Colouring in.'

'But why do you not draw your own pictures? Why do you colour these little diamonds and triangles? You could make your own pictures, express yourself, see?' She turned to Beth, 'All children are natural artists. But we force them into these little boxes, into other people's *black lines*. To stifle the creativity.' She crushed her hands together, mangling something between them. Beth and Emily saw creativity slide out like a squashed beetle and fall to the floor.

'We're not very good at drawing in this family,' Beth said.

'But this is the mistake. Everyone can draw; true expression, it is the thing we must find.'

Beth half-closed her eyes. Her shoulders drooped. But she rallied, 'Shall we go for a swim?' and left the room to gather up the bathing suits and towels, and to check on Larry. She peeped in and saw him reading a book on geology, the windows open and the palm tree waving against the bright sky. 'Should we make him get up?' Per had wondered, but Beth was against it. She understood him. She might have done the same if she could. To read in the sunny quiet — what luxury. To escape from this ravening Javine.

In the sitting room — bright silence. Javine smiled at Per, her head on one side, as if they could both hear, but only just, some beautiful, distant music . . .

Emily stolidly coloured in: a diamond, a triangle.

On the table in front of her, the solid metal petanque ball Per used as a paperweight was struck by the sun, making a little dazzle of silver light. Emily put her hand on top of it. The curve of cold steel. She rolled it, until it was at the edge of the table. It was heavy.

Javine swished close, trailing her scarves. Resting her hand on the table she crooned, 'Give me your pen. I will show you how to draw a cat. A pretty little pussycat.'

Emily handed her a pencil. Javine began to draw in quick, clever strokes. 'We make our own picture, see. Not other people's lines.'

Silence. The scratch of the pencil. Emily gave the ball a tiny push. Down plunged the heavy object — *thud*.

Javine gasped. She screamed. Emily shrank down quick-small in her chair, clenching her fists. Javine crumpled, making a strange sound: grrrrnnnnnn.

Beth rushed in. She and Per knelt over Javine, who was hunched on the floor, gripping the damaged foot in both hands.

'What happened? The boulle ball? Do you think she's broken? I mean . . .'

And Per, hovering, trying to be helpful: 'Could you hop to the couch?'

''Op?' Javine almost shouted. 'Oooooh.'

They pulled off her pretty sandal. Emily looked over the edge of the table at the damaged foot. It was a weird shape. The square, blunt toes had little hairs on the knuckles. It was a fascinatingly ugly sight. Already it was swelling, the circular bruise growing dark.

Per helped Javine over to the couch. Beth hurried to find some ice.

Emily looked at the cat Javine had drawn. He was walking along a fence, the line of his body just right as he balanced himself, placing one careful paw in front of the other. It was clever, Emily thought, to get the sense of him just keeping himself from falling. But there was a hole gouged in his head and at the tip of his nose lay a broken pencil lead. The pencil line veered away from the hole, across the page. The cat had been shot in the head; the pencil lead was the tiny bullet.

Emily drifted near to the couch, holding the drawing. 'I'll colour him in,' she offered, far too casually.

But no one was listening.

'Right,' Per said, 'It's time you got up.' And he banged the shutters.

Larry poked his legs over the side of the bed. He was so thin. But Per had been skinny all his life. In fact, when he'd reached twelve stone, he'd joked to Beth that he'd finally Achieved Fatness.

Larry peered up at his father through round spectacles. He had buck teeth, tiny vulnerable shins, small tentative hands.

Per hardened his heart. 'Fresh air. That's what you need.'

Larry drooped about, languidly picking up clothes. 'Use both hands,' Per said. And as the shirt slipped out of Larry's grasp, 'Get a hold of it. Hang onto it, can't you. Use your *fingers*.' Per hustled him into his sandals and marched him out. 'Right. Where's Milly? Milly.'

Javine lay on the couch, her foot wrapped in a flannel and resting high on a cushion. She shot a plume of grey smoke into the air and tapped the cigarette on the side of the ashtray. Per saw himself wheeling the couch to the edge of the terrace and tipping her off into the rock garden. But she'd been very good about the accident, very forgiving. And she was rather fetching, lying there; she looked — he searched for the right word — rather beautifully *palpable*.

Larry had slipped away from him. But not back to bed — he emerged from his room with a notebook and pen. He looked fresher already, resolute. Per cheered up. 'Go out and play,' he said. He looked at Larry's thin shoulders and felt a rush of love for his poor, sensitive boy.

He watched from the terrace. The children opened the gate and went out onto the path. Larry was explaining something. He paused, showing Emily his notebook. She looked up at Per. Her face was a mask.

It was the hottest time of the day. All was still. Down the side of the building a tap was dripping; water plinking onto cool stone, in the trench of shade. The sky had a sheen over it, a mesh of light. Insects zoomed and hovered over the bright flowers. In his mind Per sought out cool places, the ivy-covered wall by the pedestrian tunnel, the path up to the graveyard, smell of waxy flowers, cold concrete, the path between the cypresses; the long grass at the top of the olive grove where the road ran under high banks, through striped, tawny light.

Beth came out and stood beside him.

'Are you going to show her your little *fictory*?'

'I don't think she can walk,' he whispered. He moved close to her. He could feel her laughing.

Emily and Larry sat on a wall watching for cars. Larry took notes. When a Ferrari or a Maserati throbbed past he recorded the make and model and the number of exhaust pipes. The record for exhaust pipes was six: three on each side.

Emily stared up at the grey mountains. The sky above them was intensely dark blue. She wanted to go to the beach. She liked climbing on the breakwater, looking down into the deep water. There was a whole landscape down there in the green swirl — mountains and valleys in rippling strands of light, schools of tiny fish flying through them, their silver sides flickering as they turned and turned.

Larry saw a sports car pulling in to the kerb along the road. A handsome couple got out and walked away.

It was a Lamborghini Mura. A beautiful specimen. Larry lingered over its shining flanks. It was green — no blue — a bright iridescent blue, the colour of a scarab's wing. He sketched it, showing Emily, pointing out the dashboard, the chrome racing steering wheel, the plush interior.

But soon the handsome man returned and shooed them away, and stood polishing a speck on the door with his sleeve as his companion swayed along the pavement on her heels. They got in and sped off in a series of jerking, throaty blasts.

'They're the Rich,' Larry said solemnly, and Emily saw the Rich careering through a red landscape in mad, bright cars with fantastic shapes, a crowd waving tiny flags.

'Watch out,' Larry shouted, too late. She had ploughed into a stack of dog shit. They wandered along to the marina, Emily scraping her sandal along the pavement.

She pointed into the water, 'Look a that.'

Swimming just below the surface was a strange, tubular creature with a red head and white frills undulating out of its body.

'What is it?'

He didn't know. They crouched down. She said, 'It looks like those things you play that game with. Babmington.'

It did look just like a shuttlecock. But it was alive, the white frills pulsating in little feathery bursts as it propelled itself along. They couldn't catch it or poke it with a stick; the boardwalk was too high above the water. Larry fetched some small chips of stone from the beach. He dropped one down, right on top of the creature.

There was a rapid swirl and the feathers of the shuttlecock splayed out and then closed, drawing the stone inside.

'It's sucked it in,' Emily shouted. 'Look, the stone's inside it.' The creature was see-through. They could see the dark shape inside the body.

'Let me do one.' Emily dropped another stone, but missed. Larry let fall a twig and again the creature swirled its tentacles and drew the stick inside itself, and they could see the shape inside the body, next to the stone. Emily tried again. With a little twist and flurry the creature absorbed her stone. It slowed, the dark shapes jumbled inside it. The little feathery quills flickered. They dropped a few more pebbles. The creature began to sink, the quills trailing after the body as it drifted down. Larry thought of a drowned swimmer, arms and hair waving in the swirl as the bubbles rose . . .

'We sunk it,' Emily breathed. She looked at Larry.

The creature was a white blur under the water. Then it was gone.

'It's hiding.' Troubled, Larry took off his glasses. The world jumped nearer, and the distance was a silvery blur, like water.

'Do you think it's dead?' Emily persisted.

'No, it'll spit the stuff out.'

'We've killed it.'

'No. It probably eats stones all the time.'

'Eats stones all the time!'

They crossed the burning road. The light struck off the cars. Below the road, beyond the marina, the beaches were dotted with hundreds of brightly coloured umbrellas. There were boats far out at sea, little black dots on the quivering horizon. A grey heat haze lay over the mountains and the houses on the hillside were bright blobs of colour. In the gardens the flowers hung on juicy creepers and the cactus plants curved their cruel spears against the stonework, shadows like scimitars. Grey lizards, little dragons, lay motionless in the sun, scurrying into cracks as they passed. A woman scolded a cat and put it outside her door, and the cat leapt on to a wall and eyed them. Emily reached up and stroked its hot back and it rolled over and flexed its claws and looked at her upside down with one evil green eye. Orange and lemon trees in the gardens, a line of tablecloths drying on a line. Scent of dust and cypress and dog shit. Leaning against a wall, out of sight of the sun, a thin woman rifling in her bag, track marks on her arms, glanced at them, gave a blank shrug and shambled on. They climbed the steps, studying the cracks in the walls. Once, on this path, they had seen a pink and red snake, curling away through the stones.

It was a hot night. They sat at a table in the square. The cafés were full of people eating the evening meal, children and passers-by milling around the tree in the centre where a singer was performing. The singer had a nervous tic and a high, pure voice. The waitresses pouted and rolled their eyes and scurried around the tables. From her glassed-in niche in the wall above them the Virgin Mary coldly surveyed the scene.

'I'm absolutely full, and drunk as a skunk,' Beth said.

'She doesn't approve,' Per said, pointing to the Virgin.

And the Holy Mother gazed back, small and chilly behind her glass. No, not at all, she confirmed, in a tiny voice of steel. Emily looked up at the little statue, stiff in her rigid blue robes. There was a wire connecting her light to the wall. The light flickered, neon white. The Virgin had no face, only a rosy pink blob of painted plaster. The rest was worn away.

The children had ice cream. Marie banged her spoon on the table and a creamy splash shot across the surface. Javine rested her bandaged foot on a chair. She smoked cigarettes and drank a thimble of green liquid, like poison. She rubbed her damaged foot.

'I hope you'll be all right to walk back?' Beth asked warmly.

'One must walk. One must exercise,' Javine said. 'As the Zen master says, one must roam around and drop down 'ole.'

'Drop down a hole?' Beth concentrating, polite.

Emily saw that flash of laughter across Per's face, so quick it was like a bird passing the window, a streak of movement then gone, the pane open and blank again.

'*Whole.* You must "Roam around, and at the end of the day drop down, whole." It is Zen,' Javine explained.

The Virgin Mary's neon tube gave a little pulse of light. It buzzed. A moth landed flapping on the glass, showing Her its furry underskirts. The singer under the tree struck a last, high note, so sweet that the crowd burst out clapping.

Per paid the bill and they made their way through the crowds. Lights were strung between the buildings. Emily and Larry dawdled, gazing at the sugary bright sweets laid out in wooden barrels. But Emily was watching for her enemy.

He was a street performer who painted his whole body in glittering gold paint. Every evening, as soon as it was dark, Golden Guy appeared in the street and struck a pose, as rigid as a statue. He would only move when a tourist gave him a coin. His antics made the crowd laugh, but Emily knew there was something menacing, a kernel of anger, hidden in every move he made. Emily never laughed at his performance, she only watched, waiting for the dark note.

There he was, a small crowd around him. A tourist tossed a coin. Golden Guy broke into a wild jig. The crowd laughed and clapped. And when the tourist turned away, laughing, Golden Guy made his fingers into a pistol and shot the man in the back of the head.

Emily went close. Golden Guy turned his head a fraction and looked at her. His eyes cold in the glittering face. The eyes moved, watching her. He knew her. She was the one who stared and never laughed.

She felt that he was very dangerous. She lingered on this thought: you would not know him without his paint. He could be anyone. She might pass him every day in the street and not know.

This was secret knowledge. It was the kind of thing she kept from Larry: The more often Golden Guy saw her watching — the more often their eyes met and something — her knowledge — passed between them, the greater the danger that he would seek her out. He would be disguised as an ordinary man. She would not know him until he came close, and she recognised his eyes. And she couldn't explain it, but she had to stand at the front of the crowd every time, had to wait until she was absolutely sure he *had* seen her.

But they were calling, 'Milly, Milly.'

They crossed through the deserted market, leaving the crowds behind. The moon had risen and there was a glittering trail of light across the water. In the dark near a wall a light flared and a group of faces crowded round. Teenage voices, laughter. Girls and boys kissed cheeks and rode off on noisy bikes. Above them the flats were lighted islands of lamp shades and striped sofas and fringed drapes. The salty scent of the sea, the rustle of the wind in the palms. Javine smoked as she limped, moving her wrist in languid swirls.

Round the corner, by the tunnel, the streetlight made a long oval of light. Two police cars were parked up on the pavement, and four policemen had a teenager against the wall.

The boy was tall and thin, his face angular and dark. What everyone called a Nord-Afrique. His jacket was short in the arms and his wrists were curled against his stomach. He wore cheap cotton trousers with holes in the knees. They were kicking him. He pulled his knee up and curved his hands over his face, trying to protect himself. His movements were gentle, almost tentative.

One policeman wedged his forearm under the boy's chin, holding his head up. Another punched the boy in the face. He punched again and turned. Emily stood still. It was her friend from the olive grove. She had shown him the lizard. He shook his fingers. Was that blood on them?

Beth clutched Per's arm, 'They can't do that. They're hitting him. Stop them, it's terrible.'

And Per, starting forward, 'Oh no.'

But Javine was hobbling towards them. She lurched, limped, launched herself furiously at the four policemen. They paused, uncertain, holding the boy.

She let them have it: Unspeakable . . . Monstrous . . . Close friend of the Mayor . . . Beating up a child . . . Official complaint . . .

Slow and sullen, they loosened their grip. The boy sank down. He flattened himself against the wall and then, delicately, like a cat, extracted himself, edged along the pavement and fled into the darkness.

The policemen faced Javine. For one uncertain moment they were poised, like animals. She drew herself up and glared. Per and Beth hurried up beside her, dragging the children by the hands.

Emily's friend came sauntering, prowling, towards them.

She knew him so well. She had thought about him very often. There was his smooth face, his freckled nose, his one chipped tooth. But strange, how strange — the eyes were not his. He looked directly at her. He did not see her. He looked longest at Per, turned and said something to the other men. They came nearer. They were going to do something to Per.

But a noise — the crackle of the car radio — broke the moment. The men relaxed, shrugged and slouched back to their cars. They revved their engines and talked into their radios. Emily looked through the window as they drove away. One elbow crooked, his chin tilted, he was adjusting the rear view mirror, smoothing his shining hair.

Beth and Per surged around Javine. 'Phew. You were great. I thought they were going to kill us.' Per lit her a cigarette, Beth kissed her on both cheeks. Even little Marie clapped and laughed.

Suavely, Javine took Emily and Larry by the hands. Her fuming cigarette poked out the corner of her red mouth. ''Obble on,' she said.

The adults talked. 'Those monsters,' said Javine. 'Fucking pigs.'

'*Cochons*,' Emily piped up, and the adults laughed. She giggled. But something happened. A different self in her got up and stood apart and knew a secret: that the policeman, too, had a different self. And if everyone had different selves, how could she know which was real?

Beyond the breakwater someone was swimming in the dark. The moonlight caught the shining drops as they flew off the surface. The sea surged, hissing, on the stones. They walked through the courtyard, their footsteps crunching the gravel. The cactus plants made fantastic, contorted shapes against the sky, and the moon touched the tops of the olive trees with a silvery glow.

From her lair in the basement Madame Olivier silenced her dogs with chocolate and watched them pass by.

Dark night. Moonlight through the curtains. When Emily closed her eyes her head whirled. When she opened them she saw marbles running slowly from one side of the ceiling to the other, as if the flat was a ship tossing on a rough sea.

'You've got a temperature, Milly.' Beth's hand on Emily's forehead felt like ice.

Emily shivered and shivered and couldn't get warm.

'Another one down,' Beth sighed, and went to get a cool flannel. She sponged Emily's head and tucked her in. She sat on the bed until Emily had gone to sleep, then she went out onto the terrace. Per and Javine were smoking. The sky was full of stars. Per handed Beth a glass. They sat together, talking, watching the clouds draping soft black shapes across the moon.

Emily woke and looked about her. The adults had gone to bed. All was silent. The chair was a black tombstone, hung with coiled snakes. The curtains moved in the breeze and shadows shifted on the walls. Standing in the wardrobe was a witch.

Emily froze. Terror stopped her breath. She blinked hard. The witch was looking straight at her, moving — just minutely. She was smiling. There was something so insinuating, so evil, so confident in the smile that Emily screamed.

Beth burst in. 'What is it? What's happened?' Her voice was frightened.

Emily sat up, clutching at her mother. 'There. In the cupboard. There.'

Beth looked all around the room. Then, relieved, 'There's nothing. You gave me a fright.'

Behind Beth the witch moved, smiled. She was round and solid, her body was heavy.

'There, in the cupboard,' Emily cried. 'A witch.'

Beth crossed the room. 'There's nothing in the cupboard.' She put her hand into the dark space and waved it.

But the witch smiled, delighted at the joke. 'She can't see me,' the witch said to Emily. 'She doesn't know I'm here. But I am. And there's nothing *she* can do about it.'

'I'll tuck you in,' Beth said. 'It's only a dream.'

'No no,' Emily shouted. 'Don't leave me with her.'

'Look, I'll turn on the light.'

But the light only made the witch laugh, and then she showed her teeth. They were jagged spikes. And the smile, so sly and intimate, said, 'How funny. They can't help you. Only we know I'm here. You and I are all alone.'

Emily threw back the bedclothes and ran out of the room. Beth went after her. Lights came on. There were muffled voices, Larry said sleepily, 'What's going on?' From the spare room Javine called, '*Tiens*. Who is screaming?'

Beth turned off the lights and tucked Emily into the big bed next to Per. She got in beside her. The child was hot and feverish. She lay on her back staring at the ceiling, her eyes moving as though she was following something up there.

'The ceiling is full of marbles,' Emily said faintly.

'But no witches,' whispered Beth.

They lay awake. Outside, the night was alive. A cat jumped up onto the balcony and walked neatly along the rail. He stopped to wash his paw in the moonlight. Something rustled through the long grass in the olive grove — the cat's ear revolved to catch the sound. Footsteps sounded on the road, and from the mountains came a faint pulse of light and a fainter answering *boom*.

On the ceiling the marbles rolled in streams, and turned into cold glass eyes. The Holy Mother flew past the window, laughing in a voice like birds. Over a red plain, past flag-waving crowds, Golden Guy sped in a glittering car. Where had he gone? Without gold he was nothing but eyes. What colour was he really? But she would know him when he came. She would know his eyes. Wouldn't she?

The cat touched the surface of the bird bath with his paw. He shook the water off and strolled across the moonlit terrace. But Agnes, the old sausage dog, dreamed she was chasing a rabbit. From the basement came a long, low growl. The cat stiffened. His feet splayed out and his tail stood out like a brush. He ran over the rail, lurched sideways, landed in the grass and lay still. Then he got up and sauntered away, as though nothing had happened.

OPPORTUNITY

When Reid Harris was working undercover for the police he had no steady relationships. He slept around.

A case took him first to Whangarei, then further up the country. He moved from place to place. At one stage he was living alone in a little house in the Far North. His undercover name was Brad Richards. There was a girl called Charlene Heka who lived across the paddock, and she used to come over and have a drink with Reid on Friday afternoons. These afternoons were strange; he was always waiting. He used to go into town late on Friday night and deal drugs with the crew he was in with, and from about four in the afternoon he would be waiting for a call. He never knew when it was going to come. He had an old deckchair set up outside, in a spot sheltered from the wind. You could see the sea, the misty islands and the currents spreading over the water, and the only sound was the wind in the grass and the popping sound of a ball cock in a water trough over the fence. Reid sat out there in the stillness and he could feel the energy mounting in him, knowing that Friday was the big night. The tension ran up and down his arms like little rivers of poison. The door would bang across the paddock — Charlene never closed doors, only slammed them — and there she'd be, in her mint-green T-shirt and shorts, wobbling her way over the uneven ground.

The first time she came she brought half a bottle of rum. Reid had his eyes closed and she came around the side of the house. In a second he was up out of the deckchair; she was lucky he didn't grab her by the neck. He didn't know how old she was. Late teens, maybe. She had a funny face. He could never decide whether she was beautiful or ugly: big shining brown eyes, a snub nose, a curved, overfull mouth. She was thin, with shapely legs and her hair was wild, growing in an afro. No, she was beautiful, he thinks. She said she'd seen him in town, and did he want a drink, and soon he'd brought her out a chair and they were sipping the sharp sticky booze mixed with some coke he had. He remembers how beautifully the rum burned down into his stomach, and how good it was to have all the tension inside him met with something, given something to fix on. He was lonely, he needed company, and there she was.

She lived with her uncle, a monstrous looking man with a raddled and twisted face; he had a scar that hiked his nose up, making his left nostril too big. Reid told her he looked like Quasimodo and she shrieked with laughter, but she said he was a nice, kind guy, that he'd looked after her since her mother died, even paid for her to board at Queen Victoria School in Auckland. She'd come back up North and started working in a clerical job in town. She said she wanted to be a manager. She said when the wind blew over the paddock it looked like a big invisible comb straightening out the grass. She said all sorts of things, chattering on while Reid listened, or while he thought out what to do that evening. She asked questions about him, and he told her he was on the dole and working out what to do next. She smoked menthol cigarettes, one leg hitched up on the side of the old armchair he'd got out for her.

That first time she came to visit they'd got through a lot of rum before the phone rang. It was Teina, as usual, with Reid's instructions.

Reid sometimes dreams about Teina, about what happened to them. He hasn't seen him for years. Teina worked for a man the police were interested in, a large-scale dealer called Huru Wright. In order to gather evidence against Wright, Reid had had to befriend Teina. He realised, after a while, that the friendship he'd invented had become real.

Teina said Reid was to go to a house on the other side of town, an address he didn't recognise. Reid turned to find Charlene looking around the room, picking things up and making cheeky comments. After the phone call he was on edge as well as slightly drunk. He grabbed hold of her hips and pulled her towards the bed. He pulled her clothes off, and he had the impression she was laughing. Afterwards he lay there with a huge feeling of relief. He started hugging and kissing her but she jumped off the bed, got dressed and ran off. He went back to worrying about Teina. As he got in his car and left for town Reid wondered why she'd rushed off. He asked her the next time she came over, but she just shrugged and stared off over the paddock.

They became a ritual, those Friday afternoons. For Reid it became a kind of need. He started to think he couldn't face the evening if he hadn't had a few drinks and a roll in bed with Charlene.

One day she sat up next to him and said, 'You don't care about me.' He stared at her. It was true; she was like something he'd made up in his head, something he needed. The next time she visited she kept stalling about getting into bed, and Reid got anxious, thinking he wouldn't be able to get going until she came across. He started rushing her; Teina had rung late and he only had about half an hour.

'Say please,' she said.

'Please.' He was getting wound up.

'I'm not in the mood. You'll have to force me,' she said, with a sly, stubborn smile, hooking her leg up on the seat and lighting another menthol.

Did he force her? Well, Christ, he only had half an hour. Teina was so sharp and vigilant that Reid was getting paranoid. He had a mountain of evidence against the people Teina worked for. He was yearning to be pulled out so Huru Wright could be arrested and he could move on.

Did he force her? She told him to, so maybe he did. The truth is he can't remember now. He remembers that he liked her, but that sometimes he had trouble separating her from his own pressingly serious needs. That she bounced around him and talked at him, and that he screened out most of it, not bothering with the idea that she had her own inner life, her own desires.

She started to suggest that she move in with him. She was sick of Uncle Quasi; he was nice but always nagging her to get home on time and not drink and smoke.

'Not a good idea,' Reid said. 'I'll be moving on.'

'I could come with you.'

'Not where I'm going.'

Did she ever cry? No, he's sure she didn't. Maybe when he said that. He doesn't know. She came at him out of the heat and silence of those Friday afternoons; she was always coming at him, and when he didn't see her any more he was left with fragments of memory: her wild hair, her stubborn expression, her walk as she teetered over the clumpy paddock in her high-heeled sandals.

One night, outside the McDonald's in town, Reid was talking to Teina and a man from Melbourne, Andre Moran. They were arguing and Reid was staying out of it. Someone slapped him hard on the back and he turned to see Charlene and two other girls done up in elaborate clothes and make-up, Charlene tipsy and laughing and the other girls nudging and giggling.

Reid gripped Charlene's arm hard, bent over her and said, 'Not now.'

'Why not?' she said loudly. Her friends looked askance at Teina.

'I'll see you on Friday,' he said.

She stood her ground. Her friends, half-laughing, tried to pull her away.

'Just Fridays is it, Brad?' she said in a high voice.

'Please, Charlene,' he said.

'Please, Charlene,' Andre imitated. 'You want to come in the car with us?' he said.

'Yes,' Charlene said boldly. Her friends backed away.

'Come on then.' He opened the car door. She hesitated, then, with a challenging look at Reid, went to get in.

'No, you don't,' Reid said, grabbing her arm.

'Why not?' Andre said. He went to push her in the car.

'Forget it. She's a head case.' Reid dug his fingers into the soft flesh of her arm, deliberately hurting her.

Teina inclined his head at Charlene. 'Sounds like he loves you,' he said.

She was staring at Reid. She raised her free hand. He caught her wrist, wrenched her apart from Andre, marched her along the street and shoved her away. She stumbled, going over on one ankle. Her friends caught up and stood about, shocked. Her eyes filled with tears of humiliation and rage.

They walked away from him, arms round one another's shoulders, turning to give him the finger. 'Fuck you! Bastard!' They weren't much more than schoolgirls.

Did she ever realise what he spared her that night? He could imagine what Andre Moran would have done to her. She was so young and naive. How old is she now? Time hasn't changed her much, only she's broader in the hips and her face has lost its open eagerness. She's smartened up; she became a manager as she said she would. She has three children, boys. She lives in Melbourne. Married a builder, a tall Australian guy, arms all knotted with lean muscle, pinheaded and thick as a plank. He glares with fixed intensity, convincing himself, whipping himself up. Oh, if he could get his big hands on Reid. She looks five times more intelligent than her husband, but she's nervy, unstable, damaged somehow. Her forehead is lined. Her husband stays as close to her as he can, moves around her; he's always got his face up close, whispering in her ear.

Reid stares across the courtroom but she won't meet his eye. Her performance is smooth; she always had a pleasing way about her. But he remembers her when she was thin and raw and yearning, and she was an actress back then, as she is now. She was lonely and intense, she tried to change the shape of the world, and it wouldn't bend. She was always coming at him, out of the heat and silence of those stalled afternoons, and she's coming at him now, crossing time just as she used to cross her uncle's paddock, coming back through the years, to get him.

Shame. Fear. Rage. Reid feels them all. Charlene points at him across the courtroom, identifying him. She paints a picture of that time, all subtlety and nuance removed, a picture in black and white, no, not black and white, in primary colours, in cartoons. She talks baby talk. I young and soft. He big and savage. He force me when I say — I scream — no! She twists a hanky in her hands. The prosecutor questions her in a voice throbbing with compassion. 'You had no mother in whom you could confide?' The jury is motionless. It's her finest hour.

Reid has plenty of time to wonder about her. Why is she doing this to him? He knows the official part of it: that a group of police in the undercover programme and in other sections have been investigated; that an inquiry was set up to look at historical complaints after two women complained they'd been assaulted; that Charlene was visiting New Zealand and heard about it and came forward to make allegations against Reid, after how many years? He has a theory about her motive. She remembers that he hurt her feelings — that he was the one who hurt her *first*. She was the kind of girl, sensitive, lonely, vulnerable, who was always going to get hurt. She tried to bend the world and it snapped back in her face. And she thinks that Reid, among others, deserves to pay. It doesn't matter how. If her purpose is served by telling lies, then so be it. Bad things must have happened to her after Reid; perhaps he made her vulnerable, and the vultures started to circle. Men are predatory, that's what the Crown Prosecutor says. And women? Women are big on revenge.

Reid said to his lawyer, 'Look at her eyes. Her expression. She's mentally ill.' The lawyer doesn't answer. He knows this doesn't help.

The hearing drones on and then, in a lull just after the morning adjournment, while the lawyers are arguing a minor point, Reid hears the door creak open and turns and sees . . . a pale, intense woman with blonde hair. At the shock of recognition something comes loose in him, sends him spinning. She stands for a moment by the door. He can't close his mouth but sits staring, twisted around in his seat. Their eyes meet. She edges quietly along the rows and sits down, never taking her eyes from his face.

Since then she — Lisa Green — has attended the trial every day. Silent, watching, clear-eyed, she expresses it to Reid by her stillness: the perfect weight of information, of all that she knows.

That day. Years ago. He remembers how hot it was. On the beach the waves broke evenly, sending sparkles of light across the water. Teina lay in the shade under the pines and smoked a joint. Reid watched the seagulls shifting about gingerly on their red feet. A hawk flew in spirals over the trees, sailing on the still air. There was a group a long way down the beach, a man and two women and a young kid. The beach was remote, it took an hour of off-road driving to get there and it was all Maori land, so there wasn't usually anyone around. Reid wondered who they were. The man swam out through the breakers and the women stood in the shallows and watched, taking turns to hold the kid.

Teina complained about his love life. He had a nice wife but he was a terror for taking on other girlfriends. It wasn't surprising, the success he had; he was tall and good-looking, in a sharp, slightly scary way. He had presence, force. He was good at making people laugh. He liked to be the DJ at parties, and he could sing. Reid had done a lot of partying with Teina; some nights they ended up in his car, still buzzing after everyone else had run out of steam, smoking joints and laughing. Often, too often, Reid forgot about what he was doing, what he was supposed to be doing to Teina. They talked about everything, even about their childhoods. Teina said his father used to beat him with the electric jug cord until he passed out. He said because of that he never hit his five children. He was teaching his oldest son Pawhau to play the guitar. His wife had had meningitis and nearly died, and sometimes he had to drive her all the way down to Auckland to see specialists.

Teina was clever. He'd been good at staying out of trouble, had never done any jail time in his life. He was making a living working for Huru Wright, none of it lawful or legitimate. Big trouble was waiting for Wright and his people — that was what Reid was there for. Reid liked Teina. He was happy about what he was doing, but not about how it was going to affect Teina. He didn't want to see him arrested. The more time he spent with Teina and the closer they got, the worse Reid felt.

They waited. Andre Moran had a hangover and had gone off into the trees. Teina didn't like him. Andre was a pasty-faced, cold-eyed guy with a habit of getting too close. He always seemed to be inching around Reid, sizing him up, breathing in his face. He made Reid nervous, and he was already on edge all the time.

Teina drew on his joint, one eye squeezed shut against the smoke.

'Hey. Brad. You all right, bro?' he said in a breathless squeak, holding the smoke in.

'Yeah.' Reid had a bad headache.

'You look a bit . . . peaky.'

Reid laughed. He looked nervously at the wall of trees. 'What's Andre doing?'

Teina flopped over on his back. 'He's a nasty fucker,' he said idly. 'I caught him talking to my Parekawhia; she was sitting up high on the fence and he was sort of standing between her legs. I wanted to smash him.'

'He's coming back,' Reid said.

Andre gave them both a sour glance and stood a way off, wiping his hands on his pants.

The group on the beach were loading their gear. The younger woman stood at a distance, shading her eyes, looking at them.

'Who's this?' Teina said.

The woman was walking towards them, the glittering sea behind her. The shadows of the pines were lengthening; a sudden squall of wind blew a little tornado of sand up at their feet.

She came up close, out of the dazzle of light. Reid's body gave an involuntary jerk as he saw who it was. He couldn't believe it. Lisa Green. She was from his past. He knew her. She knew him. The real Reid.

'Reid,' she said.

'Who?' he said.

'Reid.'

He looked at Andre and Teina. 'Who's this?'

She said to him, in her familiar, soft voice, 'You were in Dunedin, remember? Just before I left the flat. When you were in the *police*.'

Andre and Teina looked at Reid. They didn't move.

'Are you still in the police?' she asked.

'I don't know who this chick is,' Reid said. He started to back away.

She said, 'Weren't you going to be a *detective*?'

They were all very still. She smiled at Andre. 'I was sure it was him. He used to have a little star tattooed on his shoulder.' She shrugged and walked away.

Reid saw her face through the car window as they drove off. Intent, watching, clear-eyed. Now, in the courtroom, she looks just the same as she did, all those years ago. She's heard about his trial and she's come to watch. What does she want, what does she have in mind?

Lisa Green might deny it but Reid knows it was revenge when she outed him that day in front of Andre and Teina. It must have been four years since he'd seen her last, but she remembered he was heading for detective back then, and she remembered her grudge. She was clever and sharp, she could see those two were criminal types; she would have guessed Reid might be acting undercover. He remembers the way she spoke, the things she made sure to say, to ID him. Telling them about his tattoo. No, she knew what she was doing. She was throwing Reid to them. She had an old score to settle; she came across him by sheer chance. She went to a beach one day and there he was, right up the other end of the country from where he used to know her, pretending to be someone else. Here was an opportunity and she took it.

He hadn't done anything bad to her. All he'd done, four years before, was help the landlord kick her out of the Dunedin flat they were living in. Here was another woman with *hurt feelings*. How could she take such revenge? Is she mad? Or is there something else, did she have some feeling for Reid back then, before he booted her out in the street? He can't tell his lawyer about her, can't even tell his wife Angela that Lisa Green's sitting in the public gallery, her eyes boring into his back. She wears a gold cross around her neck. He needs to know what she wants with him, what more she knows.

Someone is made vulnerable, and the vultures start to circle. Silence. Lisa Green's car disappearing over the dunes. The beach was deserted. The late afternoon wind blew the marram grass, shaking the dry branches of the lupins. Andre reached inside the truck and pulled the rifle out through the open window. He breathed heavily through his mouth. His eyes glittered. Officiously, he ripped Reid's T-shirt sleeve up and found the star tattooed on his shoulder. Teina looked at it wordlessly. Everything seemed very near. Details stood out sharply. The edge of the pine shadows. The delicate traces of pink in the western sky. Gulls turning on the bright air.

Teina held his face between his big hands. Reid forced himself to meet his eyes. He looked sick.

Andre pointed the gun at Reid and made him walk over the low dunes towards the pines. The sand was white, rippled, the grasses waving. The air was clear and glassy, the light dancing and dappled. It was like walking along the bottom of an aquarium. Everything was beautiful.

They crossed into the pine forest, into the cool shadows under the trees. Sunlight angled down through the dusty air, the light was honey-coloured.

Andre hit Reid with the butt of the gun. He staggered sideways, astonished by the pain. His eyes filled with tears. Andre recovered his balance, aimed and cocked the gun. No one said anything. The pain in Reid's head and neck filled him; it was overwhelming.

There was a dull crack. Reid turned. Teina was standing over Andre with a rock. Andre lay on his side, blood oozing from his head. His foot twitched in its brown boot. The rifle had fallen on the ground. Reid leaned against a tree and he and Teina stared at each other. Then in a spasm of movement Andre was up and staggering for the gun. Reid shouted with fright and rushed him, pushing him down, forcing his face into the pine needles while Teina raised the rock. Andre had his hand clamped on the gun; Reid couldn't make him let it go. His legs thrashed, he got hold of

Reid's neck with his free hand. His boot caught Teina full on. Teina hit him. The sound was sickening. He went limp, fell back, but started fighting again.

When they'd got him to stop, each sitting on one of his arms, Reid checked his pulse. He was dead. There was a bad wound on his scalp. One of his eyes was slightly open, a bit of light glittering in the slit between the lids. Blood ran out of his nose. Reid checked his pulse again. They were both terrified he would jerk back to life.

Teina hung onto Reid's arm. His face was streaked with blood and his eyes and nose were swollen where Andre had kicked him.

'Bro, what are we going to do?' he said.

They sank down in the pine needles. Teina's expression changed. He let go of Reid's arm. 'You're a detective.' He started shaking his head, muttering.

'Thanks,' Reid said.

He shook his head.

'For stopping him,' Reid added.

'We killed him, bro.' Teina groaned and held his head in his hands. 'What are we going to do?'

Reid caught the fear in Teina's voice and the enormity of it struck him. They'd killed someone. He felt panic rising.

He said, 'It was self-defence. You were defending me. He was going to shoot me.'

'I can't plead self-defence. He wasn't going to kill *me*.' He moaned again.

'You can, we'll say exactly what happened.'

'Oh my head.' He lay back, grunting with the pain.

Reid looked around. 'It's going to get dark.' They looked at the dead body. They both had the horrified feeling that it might jump up and attack them. It was that fear and Teina's groans of pain that made the panic swell in Reid, until all he could think was that he had to get Teina out of there; that they had to get away. The clearest thing to him was that they were together in this, that Teina had saved him, even after Lisa Green had revealed the truth.

They got Andre into the truck and drove deep into the forest. Teina knew all the most remote tracks and trails. They had spades and picks in the truck for working on the dope plantations. They buried the body on a lonely point above a cliff, near a gannet colony. The gannets watched and clacked their beaks and shat down onto the rocks below.

They were both hobbling with pain. Teina's nose looked as if it was broken, and Reid had a ferocious ache in his head and neck that made digging agony. The ground was tough. No doubt they didn't do a very good job.

Reid practically had to carry Teina to the truck. They drove back to his house. They cleaned themselves up and sat at the picnic table outside. They were both shaking.

Reid remembers he was starting to doubt then, to regret having buried Andre, and to wish that he could report the whole thing. But the fact of having buried him seemed to seal their course — it was too hard to explain away. And maybe, thinking back, the shock of having killed someone, the horror of it, made everything that was coming loose in him finally break free. He and Teina had done it together, and they would have to get through it together. Teina was certain he wouldn't survive a police inquiry, that he would be jailed. Reid couldn't convince him otherwise. Keeping quiet, Reid was making amends for betraying Teina's trust, and paying him back for saving him from Andre. Which makes Reid a bent policeman — about as bent as you can get. But he cared about Teina. The most important thing, he decided in the end, was that Teina should get out of the situation unscathed.

Reid said, 'It's true, I'm police.'

Teina shook his head. 'I can't believe it.'

Reid said, 'Let me think this out. Please mate. Get me a beer.'

They sat drinking, facing one another.

'We're in this together,' Reid said. Teina shrugged, wincing, his fingers playing over his bruised face.

'If you don't warn Wright about me, I'll make sure you get away. You'll have to go far away, to Australia maybe. If you tell anyone about me, it's all off, and you'll be pulled in too.'

Teina laughed. 'Fuck you,' he said.

Reid said, 'I'm police, but I'm your friend, bro. I'm still your friend.'

Teina didn't warn Huru Wright about Reid. He got away to Australia with his family and worked as a linesman, stringing power lines all over the Outback. He did well. He lives in Sydney now; there's a pub where he sings some nights for his rugby club. His daughter Parekawhia is married to a famous league player. His son Pawhau plays in a Sydney band.

A DOC survey team stumbled across Andre's body. Over time, wild pigs had uprooted and partly eaten it. There was a small amount of publicity. They couldn't identify the body, or the exact cause of death. Andre Moran wasn't even his real name.

Teina got away and Reid stayed. Huru Wright was arrested and convicted of drug dealing. Reid came out of undercover and started working his way up through the ranks. He was high up in the force when the sex inquiry started. A woman complained she'd been assaulted in a police car by a Whangarei detective. Other women came forward and the inquiry widened. There was publicity. Charlene surfaced and made her allegations against him, and he was charged and suspended from the force. Here he is, Reid Harris, facing two counts: rape and indecent assault. And behind him sits the other, Lisa Green. Only she could know the joke: he is falsely accused of rape, actually guilty of something else. It wasn't murder. It was self-defence. But he covered it up, for Teina.

When Lisa heard of a corpse being discovered in the pine forest, did she think at first that the body might be Reid? What a shock then, to discover that Reid Harris is still alive and making the papers as a senior policeman charged with rape.

Reid never went looking for Ms Green after that day in the forest, to pay her back for the trouble she caused him. He couldn't. She's the only person who could find out what he and Teina did. It keeps him awake at nights. He thinks she knows. She's guessed. He turns it over in his mind. She deliberately put him in danger that day. Some time later, but not far away from the same spot, a murdered man was found. The body has remained unidentified and no one has been charged with the crime. But the date of death has been estimated, publicly, as around the time she exposed him to Andre and Teina. Lisa Green is clever; she must speculate that if the body is not Reid, then it's someone else connected to her bit of mischief that day. Because how could violence not have resulted from it?

Lisa Green. She was shy and quiet. She was a Christian. They were living as flatmates in Dunedin. Reid had gone down there to escape his parents. They are what you call 'dysfunctional'. His father, Aaron Harris, is a long term alcoholic. His mother, Rima Richards, eighteen years Aaron's junior, was a Fort Street 'masseuse' before she found God. She's all right now, but she and Reid have very little in common. Reid's father had other children from a previous marriage — one is a doctor, one is a university lecturer. Reid supposes he is the low side of the family. It was made plain when he entered the police that his background had been noted, that he would have to show himself different from his parents.

Their other flatmate Sean tried to go out with Lisa Green but she wasn't interested. Reid used to wander into her room and chat to her and watch her TV. She liked him; they were friendly with one another. Reid was absorbed in police work, and Sean was studying law. She was doing a diploma in tourism. Reid thought everything was going fine, but she started getting on Sean's nerves for various reasons, and then one night she had an argument with some of his friends that ended with her picking up an ashtray, throwing the contents in a girl's face, and slapping the girl hard. Then she threw the ashtray against the wall. When Reid got home Sean told him that was it. The ashtray had 'sentimental value'. He wasn't going to have 'serious violence' against his friends. He was the leaseholder and he was going to kick Lisa Green out. He tacked a little notice to her door. It was pretty tough, Reid thought, but she accepted that she had to go, and she lay low and didn't make a fuss.

One day Reid came home and found her packing up. He was in low shape from doing nightshifts, and he was irritated to find her there. He remembers her hugging her box of crockery to her chest and staring at him childishly — appealing to him, he supposes. Something bad kicked off in him. They had an argument. She threw his keys out the window. That annoyed him so much he manhandled her out. Her box of plates and cups ended up on the landing outside. She sat there on the floor, looking up at him. She was absolutely still. Her face was white. They had a further exchange. He can't recall what was said, but he remembers feeling shocked, and bad about what he'd done. The way she looked at him, he should have known she'd come back. There was something so strange. Four years later, by sheer chance, she found a way to take revenge. And now, when he's in trouble again, she sits behind him in the courtroom, pale and still . . .

He looks into her face and thinks he can read his secrets there.

According to Charlene, Reid threatened to hurt Uncle Quasi if she told anyone about his 'attacks'. She only ever visited him twice she says (Twice! Week after week.) — first when her uncle had sent her to ask to borrow a hedge trimmer (inventive little bitch) and the other time to ask Reid to sign a local petition (ditto). It turns out there was a petition going around at that time, about some highway bypass, although, Reid's lawyer notes, no record of him signing it. It was on the second occasion, she alleges, that he whipped the clipboard off his diligent little neighbour, dragged her into his lair and raped her. She was 'too traumatised' to tell. Uncle Quasi is dead now. Her friends have no memory of that meeting outside McDonald's, when Andre tried to get her into the car. They're on their own, Charlene and Reid, in fantasyland.

He thinks back to those dreamy, boozy afternoons. Her leg hooked up over the leg of the armchair, the smell of her menthol cigarette. Her hair blowing in the wind. He remembers how he used to feel, not quite rescued, but relieved when he heard the old screen door clang shut and saw her wobbling across the paddock. Memories. Things he hasn't remembered for years. Charlene horsing about, Charlene nagging at him to let her move in. Charlene poking though his belongings, wanting to 'get to know him'. Always asking where he was going, who were his friends, trying to wriggle her way into his private life. She thought she could write poems — there was all that girly talk about the wind being a giant comb untangling the grass, and sunsets and falling leaves and patterns on the sea. She sulked and then came out unexpectedly with a joke, she talked too quietly, she was kind-hearted, she was sweetly vain. When it got dark she turned on the radio and watched herself dancing in the light reflected in his windows. She drew childish cartoons: smiley faces, cats, puppies. She wanted them to have a picnic up at the creek. His days were saturated with secrets and lies and violent crime, and she wanted him to go on a picnic.

Is this what she wants, that he will finally *think* about her? All the data he absorbed and didn't pay attention to comes back to him now. He realises he liked her very much. He cared about her, as much as he cared about Teina. He never hurt her. His nemesis, his avenging angel: as much as he was able to love anyone back then, he loved Charlene.

Reid gave evidence, denying everything. He outlined their relationship in detail. Cross-examining him, the prosecutor launched into a question with a name: 'Now. Mr Wright ...' The judge jumped in, prissy-polite. 'Mr Harris, you mean.' The prosecutor explained he was going to ask *about* Mr Wright — the man Reid had been gathering evidence against. Judge, prosecutor, jury, gallery, all chuckled cosily at the misunderstanding, and Reid on his stand grinned like a sheepish schoolboy. Afterwards, he was pissed off about that grin. He swears he will never smile in this courtroom again.

Reid is on bail, but each day he has to go into custody. He spends adjournments in the cells. His jailers are two security guards, Ted and Anson. Ted is a raspy little Englishman with an open, innocent face. He often looks dimly surprised. Anson is about six foot four, blond and ugly. They are polite, neutral, even after Charlene had everyone craning in thrilled silence as she whispered Reid's terrible crimes. When she gave evidence that day Reid had a strange sense that it was not he who was on trial. Charlene was talking about somebody else, some violent bastard. Who? Uncle Quasi? Her husband?

He reviews her performance. She's good in the witness box. Doesn't overdo it. Makes concessions, agrees she could be wrong sometimes. Not histrionic; her voice is low, pleasing, full of feeling. More in sorrow than in anger is her line. She's a mother now. Doesn't want other young girls to go through the same. She's still an attractive woman: beautiful is more convincing than ugly. She's up there on the stand, fucking him. Fucking him. You lying little bitch, I should have let you get in the car with Andre that day, let him rip you to pieces, the way you've ripped my life to shreds.

He wakes from a dream in which he punches her until he can't hit her any more.

The last day. Reid wakes up in the morning and Angela's sitting on the edge of the bed. He reaches up to touch her shoulder. She doesn't turn around. Today's the day he could be going away for seven years, eight, nine. They move quietly, getting ready. The air feels like glass; as if sudden movements will shatter the silence into screams. From the back of the taxi he looks out at the city and feels that he's already far away. There's an easterly storm, the harbour is whipped into grey waves and the trees in the park are tossing in the wind. A sign blows over and over across the road. Rain splatters on the windows. Outside, the media are gathering. There's a lot of interest in the case.

Lisa Green is in court. She sits with her eyes lowered, holding her gold cross in her fingers. The place is packed with journalists. Reid can't listen any more; he feels as if something has carried him far away. There is a film between him and the world. People move and talk soundlessly behind cold glass. He catches sight of Charlene and her Australian husband. He hovers around her, stands over her, keeps his face close to hers. Reid wonders where, in his strange, broken life, he has seen that man before.

The judge finishes summing up. The jury files out to consider a verdict. The waiting starts. Reid's guards dream the hours away. His lawyer ducks nervously in and out. Reid can't eat.

The jury's still out, the hours creep by. In the afternoon Reid is in the men's room when the guard Anson bangs on the cubicle to say the jury has reached a verdict. Out in the courtroom there's a great crush, people are squeezing in, standing between seats, everybody craning to see. The registrar is over-excited, and marches about ordering people to make room, to switch off phones. Reid feels little rivers of poison moving up and down his arms. The jury is not looking at him; this is supposed to be a bad sign. His heart is beating so fast he can feel the pulse in his throat. He has never felt so exposed.

The judge comes fussing in with his hokey, ingratiating smile. He takes off his glasses, polishes them and puts them on. With excessive politeness he asks the jury if they have reached a decision. The foreman replies that they have. The registrar stands and asks for the verdict on each charge, and the foreman delivers it each time in a strong, clear voice.

And the glass silence shatters with a howl of sound, Angela leaps out of her chair, the crowd is surging forward. Reid steadies himself, his head so full of white noise that he can barely stand. He looks up through stinging tears and there is Lisa Green; she's on her feet, holding the gold cross in her right hand. With the noise and movement of the milling crowd it's hard to be sure, but she's looking intently his way, and the expression on her face looks like relief to Reid.

PARARAHA

Emily came out of the bedroom and saw Per out on the balcony. He was peeling an orange with a knife and throwing the curly rinds into the bush. She joined him and they looked over the valley, at the kauri and manuka trees standing still in the bright morning air, the greeny-blue hills on the horizon, sharp against the cloudless sky. The cicadas had started up with their sawing that by the hot afternoon would be a shimmering wall of sound; in the distance they heard the warbles and clicks of a tui. A car passed by on the gravel road and the dust rose and hung in the air, shot through with tiny sparkles of light. Far way, two kilometres down Lone Kauri Road, the surf was crashing onto the beach, sending its distant, sighing roar up the valley.

On clear mornings like this she felt so alive. Two days ago she had been invited to stay at the Brights' bach with her friend Amy, up on the Piha Road. They'd crept out in the early morning and Emily had climbed high into a huge pine tree at the back of the section. She could see the whole valley spread below her, the beams of sun breaking over the hill and the dark trees slowly colouring. Watching the sun rise over the bush Emily's eyes had prickled and she got goosebumps with happiness. But Amy had made her get down. She was eight — six months older than Emily. She was good at maths and hardly ever smiled and was often irritable and shitty. She had stood waiting at the foot of the tree, grumbling.

Emily had climbed down after a while, because Amy was getting pissed off, and she liked Amy's bach and wanted to be invited back; there was the pine forest — a whole acre of it — and the house that looked like a log cabin, and the series of stone fishponds where you could find, among the weed and lily pads, shiny green and brown native frogs.

'Look,' Per said quietly. There was the tui, landed in the manuka, swivelling its tail, letting out bright warbles of sound. They could see its pompous shiver as it puffed out its feathers, the green sheen in the black breast, and the white cravat under the neck. The bird opened its beak and they heard the shiny drops of sound, plonk, click, with a sound echo, like water dripping into the rain-water tank.

Emily turned; her mother was standing in the doorway. Beth gave Per a steady, significant stare. Then she turned away and disappeared around the side of the bach, heading for the outside toilet.

Per looked after her, scratching his chin. He glanced at Emily, and she knew, because she knew Per better than anyone, that he was checking to see whether she'd noticed the look — the kind of glare Beth gave Per when there'd been angry voices in the night, sudden eruptions of rage that were followed by cold silences, words heavy with hidden meaning.

Emily looked up at Per with an open, innocent face, pretending she hadn't noticed. But he knew she had — she could tell. He picked up the peeling knife, weighed it in his hand, and, with an antic flourish, hurled it away into the bush. Emily laughed. He made a comical face, and stuck a piece of orange peel on his nose.

They went inside.

Emily's brother Larry had a map spread out on the table in front of him. He was explaining about tracks, and Beth was half-listening and grappling with their little sister Marie. Beth dumped Marie in Per's lap and leaned over the map.

'You come out at the beach,' Larry was saying.

'Would we meet you down there?' Beth asked distractedly, taking a jar from Marie. She looked at Per, over Marie's head. She was trying to think of a way to punish him. He had a will of iron. And he always thought he was right.

'You can take Sam with you,' she told Larry. Sam was a boy of five who was being dropped off with them that day, while his parents went back to town for supplies.

Per gazed out the window, over the bush. His mouth was slightly open; he had a sudden, vacant look. He was thinking of his studio in town. They hadn't yet run out of supplies, and there was no excuse for him to drive back to the city and spend some hours alone in the silence of the empty house. They had the whole six weeks at the bach, crowded in together with the noisy children. It was luxury to drive the hour back to the hot, musty closed-up house, to enter the quiet rooms where the sunlight shone dim and yellow through the curtains, to get on with some secret project, to drift about, make private phone calls, without some kid roaring in the background or Beth glaring because of last night's argument. And then, after he'd done everything he wanted to do, he would go to the supermarket, and speed back to the bach in the evening. When could he make the next trip? In two days, he decided. But perhaps, today, he might slip away to the phone box at the beach, and put in a call to . . . He caught Beth's eye. There was something bright, almost forensic in her stare.

'Marie, no,' Per said, snatching up the butter knife, and the little girl jumped and began to screech.

Larry was measuring out distances on the map. 'It'll take a few hours,' he said, pushing his glasses up his nose and looking important.

'Don't do that,' Beth sighed to Marie. She took the little girl out of Per's lap and set her down on the floor.

Larry traced the track with his finger. 'It's called the Pararaha Gorge. The track takes you to the sea, then you walk around the rocks back to Karekare. Or over the Zion Ridge if the tide's too far in.'

'Good,' Beth said. 'Will you need lunch?'

Larry was the eldest. He led and Emily followed. It was Larry who'd decided, that summer, that they would look for green geckoes up the Ahu Ahu Track, Larry who'd led the lizard expedition during which, to Beth's surprise, they had actually found two of the bright green native geckoes in the ti-trees just off the track, and brought them triumphantly home in an ice-cream carton. He had designed a habitat and researched the geckoes' diet; he'd shown Emily how to feed them mosquitoes and flies, and they'd thrived and eventually even bred. It was Larry who'd made and stocked the salt water aquarium that had kept him and Emily absorbed for weeks, hauling water up from the bay in buckets to keep the creatures alive. Larry who read geology books and took Emily (and Beth, lugging Marie) fossil hunting, who knew the names of different types of rocks, who made lists and told them the names of insects and birds. Last year, when Per had had a job in London, Larry had got hold of a map of historic ruins and had led them all over Cornwall, finding ancient sites and burial mounds, Emily absorbed, their parents good-naturedly tagging along, enjoying the project themselves.

Larry's ideas usually turned out to be correct. He was only ten but clever and purposeful. And Beth, used to Larry being right, and distracted by vague thoughts of wifely revenge, only said, 'I'll make three lunches. You do your walk, and we'll meet you at the end,' and thought no more about it, but turned to fix her eye on Per, who didn't look away this time but glared, and got up, and began to wash the dishes with terrible vigour, threatening to smash every plate to pieces.

But it was while he was doing the dishes that he got his idea. It seemed so good that he stopped and stared into the soapy water. When Marie began to tug on his trouser leg he whipped around, picked her up, carried her out to Beth and put her down at his wife's feet.

'I've got to write something down. It won't take long.'

He went up the steps that led through the bush to his hut, a hundred metres above the bach. Up here he had his desk and a camp bed and some books. The bush had grown up around the hut, and possum droppings littered the path, and the wind sighed in the trees, sending twigs clattering onto the iron roof. Once when he was standing on the verandah a wild pig had crashed out of the bush and looked at Per with a hot, angry eye before crashing away over the hill.

The room was hot and stuffy. He left the door open, took out the cigarettes hidden behind the copy of *Zen and the Art of Motorcycle Maintenance*, and sat smoking at his desk, writing pages of notes. He had a horror of losing ideas. He had to get them down while they were fresh. Otherwise, with all the noise of the family, he might lose them for ever.

He finished and sat back, relieved. His sudden clarity had to do with last night's argument. Angry, unable to sleep, he had lain awake and the ideas had started whirling around in his mind, seeking their own form. Beside him, Beth was brooding, but he had floated away into his own secret territory. She'd sat up and delivered a fresh harangue and he'd felt as if she was calling to him from a long way off, through a locked gate. He saw a little figure calling in a tiny voice, through iron bars.

He looked at his notes and felt happy. He thought of Beth tidying the bach, alone with Marie. He mustn't let her grapple with that demanding kid on her own. He jumped up, locked the hut and jogged down through the bush to help.

Up on Lone Kauri Road, the trampers reached the first track. Larry solemnly checked the map.

'Hurry up,' Emily said, and kicked him on the ankle.

They entered the bush. The dirt track was narrow and deeply grooved; in winter it would turn into a slippery mudslide, but now it was dry, winding between spindly black trunks of the ti-tree that grew in a tunnel over it. It was downhill all the way and they ran it, hanging onto the trunks when they got up too much speed.

Sam's sandal came off. Emily held onto his tiny shin and fastened the strap. He was a quiet boy with small eyes set deep in a watchful, freckly face. He balanced himself, a hand on her shoulder.

He said, 'I'm hungry.'

'Didn't you have breakfast?'

He shrugged.

She gave him a packet of raisins

When they caught up with Larry he was standing in front of a big green sign. PARARAHA GORGE, it said. WARNING. STEEP BLUFFS. FAST WATER. THIS TRACK IS FOR EXPERIENCED TRAMPERS ONLY.

'Shit,' Emily said.

But Larry only said, 'Right. On we go.'

Emily followed him, anxious, protesting. But he was determined. 'They always put signs like that,' he said loftily. 'It's for fat old tourists.'

The track levelled, the bush opened out, and soon they could hear water flowing. The sun beat down and Emily forgot about the sign as they joined the river and began walking on the grassy track alongside it. The river was broad and slow. She watched the insects zooming over the bush, the swirls and eddies in the clear water. The bush smelled spicy as the sun heated it.

They came to a place where the river ran into a deep, dark pool. Sam shouted, 'I saw an eel.' They tried to find it, and bombed the pool with big rocks. They walked on and the gorge began to deepen, the hills rising high on either side. There were steep bluffs now, and the river was wider and faster, bordered by huge boulders that they had to clamber over, searching for the track on the other side. They came to waterfalls, where torrents of water smashed down into boiling pools and then rushed away over the rocks, the rapids whirling and roaring so that they had to shout to be heard. The spray rose and the drops of water hung sparkling in the bright light.

They stopped on a clear bit of the riverbank and ate some sandwiches. Sam's sandal kept slipping, and they tried to fix it, but he complained that it pinched his foot. Emily lay in the sun and felt it burning through her T-shirt. Her nose had begun to peel. They picked a target and idly threw stones at it, and they lifted up rocks, trying to find freshwater crayfish.

The sun made everything shine. The bush stretched away in all directions, tangled and dense. Emily watched a hawk floating high above the hills. Sam stood in the shallows on his spindly legs, poking in the water with a stick, hunting for creatures.

Larry took up his map again, studying it in the important way that made Emily want to kick him. They packed up their things and went on.

The track led them away from the river sometimes but always joined it again. They were right in the gorge now, the hills rising above them. They came to a place where the track narrowed and became a thin, sodden ledge.

They hesitated. 'Is there any other way?' Emily asked. But there wasn't. They didn't want to leave the track. Soon they were walking beside a steep drop, and the track almost petered out. The river ran down a series of rapids and waterfalls, edged by boulders that progressed down the gorge like a giant staircase. They had to climb down the rocks, sitting down and slipping onto the next huge step, the enormous river rushing beside them, soaking their clothes. They had to guide Sam's legs.

It was slow going. Halfway down Emily looked back and saw the stone pathway rising behind them, the high bluffs looming against the blue sky and the water roaring over the lip of the waterfall, seeming to hang and drift in the air before it plunged down to the next level, exploding against the rocks below. She felt how tiny they were, just ants. She wished she hadn't looked back.

They were helping Sam down the last of the giant boulders when he slipped. He let out a howl of terror as he felt himself falling. Emily and Larry lunged at the same time, pulling him away from the edge. They steadied him and looked down into the foaming cauldron below. Emily closed her eyes and saw two tiny legs disappearing into the green water. Sam sat hunched on the rock, shivering.

Emily grabbed Larry's arm and shouted over the roar of the water, 'It's your fault. The sign. We shouldn't've. He's too small. It's too big.' Jabbing her finger at the river of boulders.

Larry hesitated. He looked at where they'd come from and then looked downstream to where the river raced away around a bend in the gorge. She could see what he was thinking. They couldn't go back. They couldn't pull Sam all the way up that jumble of boulders again; he was too small. It was too dangerous.

But what would they find if they went on?

Beth lay in the warm water of the lagoon. The cliff rose above her and ripples of heat danced along the black sand. From a distance Per and Marie could see her figure in its pink bathing suit, lolling in the dark water that reflected the cliff.

The tide was in and the surf crashed onto the beach in even, rolling breakers. It was a perfect day. The lifeguards' red and yellow flags hung limp in the still air. All over the beach, bodies lay inert on coloured towels.

'There's Mummy,' Per said, pointing. How strange and surreal it looked, the bright, synthetic colour of Beth's bathing suit in the middle of that hot, iron, ancient landscape.

He buried his nose in Marie's hair. A warm, salty, foody smell. She really was cute when you looked at her properly, with her blonde hair and round blue eyes. She tipped a mound of sand onto his knee, moulding it gently with her spade. Per patted her head. He was charmed.

Beth listened to the roar of the surf echoing up the cliff. She lay and dreamed, her hair spreading on the surface of the water. The lagoon was shallow; the sun heated it up like a bath. When she raised her head she could see two little blobs wavering in the heat haze, Marie waving her red plastic spade and Per diligently making sandcastles.

She sighed, patting the water with her hands. It didn't please her when Per was being good. When he tried to make amends by minding Marie, hovering attentively, making impractical suggestions. One part of him was sincere, she thought, but another part, the ungovernable Per, was busy elsewhere, in a secret compartment of his mind. If she accused him, the sincere Per would be affronted, puzzled, hurt; he would hotly defend himself, even though the other, secret Per was hiding somewhere, slyly dreaming — laughing even. He was infuriating.

But it was good to have him on duty with Marie, and the other children off on their walk, and to lie here and think. Her head was full of the dreamy roar of the sea.

Beth looked up and saw a dark space in the cliff, dense black shadow. A gull floating near it turned and turned, bright white against the black.

'We can't go back,' Larry said.

Emily hauled Sam to his feet. He stood before them, small and desolate. Larry took off his glasses and wiped them, squinting at the blurred world. His peering made Emily furious. 'Idiot,' she snapped. He ducked nimbly away.

Ahead of them, the river cut a deep cleft through the rock. There were big branches caught against the boulders, protruding at odd angles where they'd wedged, the water spraying out around them. Careful not to slip, they climbed around an ancient fallen tree, its roots still clinging to the bank. They made their way slowly down towards the bend. There was a haze of spray over the water, catching the light and making rainbows between the bluffs. The roar of the water beat in their heads; the light was painfully bright, the sun struck up off the rocks and burned their faces. They rounded a jutting boulder and now they could see beyond the bend to where the stream widened, the fast water sluicing out in white jets of foam over the surface. Floating, turning in the green water, was a great mass of logs.

The logs were green and mossy and rolled slowly in the water, bumping against one another in the current. Emily imagined running on them, faster and faster as they rolled. If you fell off they would close over your head and you would drown. There was a hollow woody sound as they bumped against one another.

'They used to transport timber on this river,' Larry said flatly. Normally Emily would have asked him who 'they' were and why they put logs in the river, and where the logs had been supposed to be going, but she only looked and said nothing.

The track resumed, flattening out again, shrouded over with ferns. It was like walking in a green tunnel. Emily saw an eel rise from the depths and put its broad nose just out of the water, the tiny horns dimpling the surface. The grey cliffs loomed oppressively close, sometimes so close that they shut out the sun. Sounds reverberated between the bluffs; their voices came back at them, and when they dislodged stones the echoes cracked like gunfire.

They dreaded what they would find around the next bend. Emily tried to bargain: 'If we see the sea round the next turn I promise I'll . . . ' But she couldn't think of what to promise, nor could she think to whom she was making promises. And there was no welcome sight of the sea, only the endless gorge. There were thick puriri and nikau glades, forests of toetoe where the white plumes rained down tiny fibres that made them sneeze and the cutty grass caught their legs and scratched their arms.

They'd been walking for ever. Sam kept up, stumping silently along on his thin legs. The sun had moved right across the sky. They were hungry again, and stopped, but this time they didn't laze in the sun and look for crayfish, they sat quietly, each perched on a grey rock, not saying much. Then Larry picked up his map and they went on.

They had been crossing a long, spongy stretch of tussock when the bank, which had been getting boggier, suddenly heaved. They shouted and grabbed one another for balance. Larry poked the ground with a stick. Brown water welled up and they saw that they were walking on a floating carpet of weeds and grass. The boggy strip seemed to support their weight and they carried on. Then Emily bumped into Larry's back, and behind her, Sam overbalanced and grabbed the back of her shirt. There was no more track.

They were looking at a wall of tangled bush, the kind of terrain where, if you entered it, you could be lost within minutes. They went along the edge, trying to find the way, but there was nothing except the river and the bush, and beyond, the great outcrops of rock rising up to the sky.

It was a bad feeling. The bush seemed to crowd closely around them and they had no idea which way to go. Emily and Sam sat down. Larry ranged away from them, and after a long, leaden silence they heard him shout, 'I've found something.'

They scrambled up. The track was tiny and faint, and it led them away from the river, zigzagging up the side of the bluff.

They set off. Sometimes the track disappeared then resumed again, sometimes it doubled back on itself; it wasn't much more than a sheep trail. They climbed higher and higher, and Emily was glad to get away from the river. They would walk over the crest of the hill, she thought, and the bush would give way to open ground and at last there would be the sea.

But after they'd been climbing steadily for a long time, Emily hauling Sam and Larry leading the way, she heard Larry shout out.

Sam sat down with a bump. Emily went on.

Larry was leaning against a manuka trunk. He held out his arm and wordlessly pushed her back.

The path had brought them right to the edge of a sheer drop. When she looked over Larry's shoulder she saw the sickening wall of rock and the river thirty metres below. She imagined Larry, an upside-down figure plunging, spinning and screaming, down the grey cliff. The nerves jangled in her hands and feet and she had a feeling of betrayal, as if the trees and ferns and flowers were united in secret malice, the insects in the bright air vibrating with tiny, poisonous laughter.

'I nearly just kept walking.' Larry's voice was sick.

She said, 'We'll have to go back.'

Beth and Per lay near each other on the sand. All along the beach the heat haze wavered and danced. The only sound was the roar of the surf.

Marie was digging a hole. Her sunhat kept falling over her eyes. It was a nuisance. She tugged it off and screwed it into a ball. They were always making her wear it, even though it scratched and made her itchy and covered her eyes. And it was hideous. Marie liked to look nice.

Per had his chin on his hands and was staring down at the sand, concentrating. Beth lay face down, her head on her arm. Their calves were lightly touching. Slowly, Per reached across and rested his hand on the small of Beth's back.

Marie rolled the hat into a sausage and poked it down into the hole. She took her spade and filled it in, patting the sand over it. Then she flopped quickly down onto her stomach and lay very still, holding her breath.

Slowly she turned her head. No one had noticed.

A girl sprinted up the beach and leapt onto her towel, reaching down, exclaiming, to hold her sore feet. Marie listened to her shrill complaining — the black sand got so hot that you had to wear shoes. Once they'd met a tourist who'd set off in bare feet and got caught in the heat on a long stretch of beach. He was in a real state, his feet badly blistered and burned.

Three figures were coming across the dunes. Marie watched the mirage splitting the figures apart into silvery bubbles. At first they seemed to be floating above the liquidy blur made by the light, but as they got closer they solidified and shrank and turned into a man and a woman and a girl wearing straw hats and carrying coloured beach towels. The woman leading, the man and the girl trailing along behind.

The Brights, Robyn and John, trailed by their daughter Amy, greeted Beth and Per. They dumped their gear and sat down in the sand.

Beth rolled over and said lazily, 'Nice, eh.'

Robyn took Amy by the arm and smeared suntan lotion over her in swift efficient dabs. Amy smiled at Marie.

Marie hated and feared Amy. She was a big girl — Emily's friend — who never lost a chance to deliver a vicious poke or kick when Emily and her parents weren't looking. Once she forced a big piece of mud into Marie's mouth and then said in a shocked voice, 'Look, Emily, she's eating dirt,' and had rubbed Marie's face extra hard, pretending to clean it. Marie spat into the sand at the memory, and crept closer to Beth.

John Bright solemnly coated his nose with white zinc. He stretched out his skinny legs, dug his long white toes into the sand and started singing in a bass voice:

Home, home on the range
Where the deer and the antelope play

'There,' Robyn said, pushing Amy away. To Marie she said, sugary, 'Would Marie like Amy to take her to the lovely lagoon?'

Marie shook her head. No, thank you very much.

Amy, who had been gazing dopily into space, looked suddenly interested. She eyed Marie's soft little arms, so satisfying to twist and pinch. What fun to poke sticks into a small foot, to see the mouth open in howls of infant distress. Amy got a hot feeling just thinking about it.

She said casually, 'I'll take her if she's not too shy.'

'Would Marie like to go and make lovely sand castles?' Robyn asked Marie.

The little blonde head shook emphatically. No, Marie would not.

'Would Marie like a nice little paddle?'

Marie pushed her face into Beth's shoulder. 'No.'

Robyn said, 'I made sure Amy would never be shy. I exposed her, socially, from a young age.'

But Beth said, 'You go ahead, Amy. I'll bring her along later.'

John's singing rose above the murmur and roar of the sea.

> *Where seldom is heard*
> *A discouraging word*
> *And the skies are not cloudy all day.*

And Amy, thwarted, gave Marie a meaning look and slouched off across the hot sand.

'Where are your other lot?' Robyn asked, arranging herself comfortably on her towel.

Beth said, 'They've gone on a bush walk. We're meeting them down here.'

Per looked up. 'Actually, you'd think they'd be here by now.'

They all scanned the beach.

'They should be coming around the south rocks,' Beth said.

'Where have they been?' Robyn asked.

'It's a track. The Pararaha Gorge. They're meant to come around the shore.'

Robyn said, 'The Pararaha Gorge? That's a tall order. Who's taking them down there?'

'They're by themselves,' Per said.

'By themselves?' Robyn said.

Beth rolled over. Per stared.

John elbowed himself up. He said carefully, 'The Pararaha's a big tramp. It's a long way. It's rough terrain too.'

There was a silence.

Robyn's eyes were bright. 'Didn't you know?' she said.

Beth looked fearfully at Per. 'It was a project of Larry's. He thought it up. He's got a map. And they wanted something to do with Sam.'

'Sam?'

'The Richardson's Sam.'

'But he's only *five*,' Robyn said. 'Do you mean to say that three children aged ten, seven and five are . . . ?'

Per rounded on her. He said in an iron voice, 'You're saying we've made a mistake. You're saying they're too young.'

'It's a marathon. A hugely long way. And there are cliffs and rapids and and . . . John?'

John nodded. 'It's a tough one,' he said.

Beth picked up Marie. She said, 'Oh God. What should we do?'

Per said, 'I'll go round there.'

'Round where?' Beth said.

'Round the rocks. To see if I can meet them. And if I can't find them you'll have to call the ranger.'

Beth rocked Marie back and forth.

Robyn shaded her eyes. 'Here we go,' she said, waving out.

A smiling couple lugging a chilly bin between them came staggering across the sand.

'Over here,' Robyn called. And to Beth and Per she said brightly, 'Well. Here come the Richardsons.'

They were crushed. Sam immediately caught their fear and began to wail. There was nothing for it but to turn around. They walked all the way down the bluff, until they were back at the riverbank.

Emily had started to hate the river. It laughed at them, dashing along over its rocks, it menaced and mocked. She slipped and grazed her foot, and the river babbled and sighed and chuckled to itself.

She and Larry looked for another track. They were wary of entering the really dense bush; they knew how easy it would be to become confused, especially here where the gorge had widened out and there were gullies and dips in the terrain.

The sky was still bright but the colours were changing, the

sunlight growing yellower as the afternoon wore on. Emily thought with fear of the gorge at night.

Larry frowned over his map. Sam bleakly ate the last sandwich and Emily stared down into the shallows, where the water rippled over ochre stones and the weed waved, and the eels curled and slipped between the rocks. She saw a crayfish poke its claws out from under a rock as if to check the underwater weather — the swirls and flurries of sparkling mud, the tiny leaves whirling lazily past its door. It shot back under the rock again, quick as a flash. The feathery river weed was combed and parted by the current, and tiny bubbles of air were caught in its strands and lifted off, and whisked away.

Larry said, 'I've got it. We're so stupid.'

He got up, snapping his fingers. 'We don't *have* to find a track. All we have to do is follow the river. We want to find the sea, that's where the river will take us.'

He was so convinced that Emily and Sam felt a bit of hope. Emily prayed to the Unknown Somebody that Larry was right.

They went on. When the riverbank gave out, they waded and swam. The water was cool and fresh; they sank in brown mud, slipped and slid over stones. They swam in their clothes and shoes. Where the river was flowing too fast they clambered along the bank, hanging onto the ferns.

Now that they had given up searching for a track they felt they were making progress. Sometimes they could lie in the water and let the river carry them along, sometimes they swam and waded through long slow lagoons, where the nikau palms grew thickly overhead and the water lay brown and sun-striped and sluggish.

There were fewer rapids and waterfalls now. The land had begun to flatten out and they were no longer walled in on both sides of the river by steep hills. The afternoon sun blazed down, the bush was still in the heat, light glinted off every leaf and the cicadas were so loud that the air seemed to shimmer and vibrate with the sound. There was still no sign of a track but they kept faith with Larry's idea: a river must lead to the sea. As long as they stuck with it, they wouldn't get lost.

Emily saw a plane high in the sky, a tiny silver dart. And she saw that shadows were starting to cross the bush. Now they were walking through a kind of grassland; the river was broad and slow and there were little tributaries, marshy pools, banks of toetoe sticking out of the middle of muddy bogs. Larry shouted from up ahead; the track had resumed, winding and overgrown and pitted here and there with the hoof prints of cows.

'Listen,' Larry said. They could hear a distant sighing roar — the sea.

They were in a wide, shallow valley. There were tussocky paddocks, fields of low scrub, and, in the distance, cows grouped under a tree. Water lay everywhere, in brackish pools along the edge of the path, fringed by great banks of native reeds. They passed pools filled with bright green weed, and frogs sitting on lily pads in the shade of the waving stalks. The heat was intense. The sun was lower and burned into their faces. They were so tired they couldn't talk.

They came to a sign. Larry consulted his map and Emily couldn't raise the energy to kick him or to ask him how far they had to go; she only looked at the sign with dull resentment; she thought there was something shameless about the track, the way it had just turned up again, all cheerful and business-like, as if it hadn't abandoned them in the middle of the bush.

And now, finally, the sea was really roaring, and when they crossed a wooden bridge over a marsh and followed a narrow path under a row of cabbage trees, they came to the foot of a vast black sand dune. Emily looked up the glittering iron slope to the intense blue sky. She had never seen such a dune, its spine curving like the back of a giant lizard, its rippling flank so black that it had a sheen of blue.

They began to climb, their feet sinking into the hot sand. Sam started to cry as the sand got into his sandals, burning his feet. They reached the top and there before them was the huge curve of the coast, stretching many kilometres south, all the way to Whatipu, and to the north towards Karekare, a desert of black sand and dunes and scrub rippling with heat waves, and, far across it, fringed with surf, the wild sea. Emily turned and turned; it seemed to her that the whole landscape was full of bright, violent motion. The fluffy toetoe waved in the wind like spears borne by a marching army, the surf ceaselessly tumbled and roared, the light played on the sand, casting a powerful, shimmering glare. Where the black desert met the land there were enormous, grey cliffs that sent the sound booming off them. Behind them lay the green valley they had come through, with its marshland and cabbage trees and the river that had spread into many waterways, spilling out towards the sea.

They walked along the backbone of the great dune, and across a boiling expanse of beach. Then they came down into a trench of scrub under the cliffs, where cabbage trees grew along the edge of a stream, and pohutukawas hung off the cliffs. Here they were screened from the roar of the sea by the dunes, and there was a path of hard, matted grass that was easy to walk on.

But Sam sat down on the grass. He couldn't go on.

Larry climbed up onto a dune.

'I can see people,' he shouted.

Far away, near the sea, there were figures walking in a line. Little shapes against the dancing, glittering water. Fishermen or trampers, heading for Whatipu. She saw that the light was changing. Soon the sky would turn orange and the sun would go down; there would be no twilight, only the sudden, absolute dark.

'Look what I got,' Larry said. His hand was full of blackberries. There were clumps of bushes, laden with fruit. They picked more and carried them back to Sam. The little boy dragged himself up with a persecuted look and consented to trudge on, his mouth stained with red juice.

Emily saw a circle of light against the headland. It was a tunnel, cut out of the rock, made a hundred years ago, Larry said, when there was a small railway line around the coast. He stopped and looked hurt. Emily had thrown a stone at him.

They walked through the tunnel, running their hands over the cold stone. 'Now we're nearly there,' Larry said.

But Sam sat down again, and this time he wouldn't move.

'Christ, Svensson,' Hugh Richardson kept saying. 'Christ.'

He was lucky, Per thought, that Hugh was too civilised, too repressed, to give him the tongue-lashing he deserved. All he could do was explode every now and then with a little wounded exclamation. '*Christ.*'

They had crossed around the rocks and now faced the immense wasteland of sand, stretching away in the polished light towards Whatipu.

There had been a scene on the beach. The Richardsons' mounting alarm, Beth's anxiety and remorse. Per had felt utterly sorry for Beth and furious with himself. He couldn't even remember the discussion that morning about what the children were doing; he had assumed that Beth was handling all that, and of course she had been distracted, and hadn't understood what they were meaning to do, and now they were somewhere in this huge landscape or worse, lost in the bush or drowned.

'Bloody hell, Svensson.' Hugh loped along next to him. 'It's going to get dark.'

Per looked along the line of coast and felt a part of himself crumbling with misery and panic. Should they go back now, summon more help? Now they'd come this far it would take a long time to get back, and meanwhile the dark would come on. He couldn't go back; he couldn't turn away and leave them, even if it was the rational thing to do.

Images floated in his mind. The smiles fading from the Richardsons' faces. Marilyn Richardson bursting into tears. The children in sunlight, waving as they walked away.

They joined the track. Four fishermen appeared near the cliffs and Hugh scrambled towards them, holding up his hand. 'Have you seen three kids?' he called. 'Three lost kids.' The fishermen conferred rapidly in their language, shook their heads and marched past. Per stared after them uneasily, wondering why they were so taciturn. Was there something shifty about them? The fronds of the cabbage trees rustled over their heads, as sharp as knives.

Per looked up at the wall of rock, at the deep black spaces. He felt as if the cliffs were ringing with a terrible sound. The iron echo rang in his head. The whole landscape was reverberating, crying out to him. The crash of the waves on the shore, the cliff-echo. The black rock, the black sand, the seagull shifting on its red feet, its shiny black eye with no light no depth in it.

There was an orange tinge to the sky now. They passed through a manuka glade and came out on a long stretch of scrub and marram grass. Ahead of them they saw three small figures, sprawled in the grass at the edge of the track. They rushed forward.

But the children's faces were covered with blood.

Hugh's shout, the surge of his own blood, the horror and fear. Per ran and ran. He reached them first and they held up their little smeared hands. Blackberry juice.

'Christ,' Hugh exploded for the hundredth time, swinging his boy up into his arms.

Per would never forget it. It would stay with him. He would make sure of this, by writing it down. The ringing of the cliff, the wild sound, the iron song the land had sung.

He took his children by their red hands and thanked the God he didn't believe in, thanked Him anyway.

THE OTHER

Ford was in his study at home, writing a lecture. There was scrabbling on the iron roof; it broke into his thoughts. He looked across the garden to the hill in the distance, saw its green shoulder, the clouds black behind it, felt a prickling in his neck and back, looked at the words on his computer screen. He pressed his feet against the legs of the desk, stretched, and heard the back of the chair give a series of protesting cracks, like small bones bending and snapping. Thoughts of violence filled him. What was happening?

There was rain, now the garden was drying, the leaves dripping, the grass lifting itself vertical again. Many tiny sounds. Rustling. Water in the pipes. Making a cup of coffee he looked out at the drenched green square of land: lawn, fruit trees, a white fence, the street. The suburbs on a Sunday. Birds on the roof, far away, the cries of children on the playing field. A girl, straight-backed, erect, face forward, sailed the length of his fence, the handles of her scooter just visible above the palings. She did not turn to see his face behind the glass. The kettle steamed up the window. He allowed himself a piece of cake. He was getting heavy. These days, when he looked down, he saw more and less of himself.

He finished the cake, the coffee, another piece of cake. He shaped his lecture: it needed little work. He was known as an entertaining, as well as a rigorous, teacher. In the faculty he was approachable, friendly, reliable, utterly scrupulous in all matters — professional, social, intellectual. He was prolific: the author of three books, over a decade's worth of articles. His work was known internationally. Professor Ford Lampton. He had worked hard and made a good life for himself. The girl on the scooter, had she turned her head, would have seen an ordinary sandy-haired guy with a benign, slightly dopey expression on his broad face, plucking at the collar of his rumpled shirt. (She would not have seen the Other: a shambling, cake-devouring ogre.)

For Ford there was something oppressive about Sundays. In the sleepy silence and peace his mind did its own equivalent of spitting on the pew. It had always been like this. But Sundays *now*, the new Sundays, were something far more like torture.

He sat down. The chair creaked and cracked. He read four pages, wondered, should he move away from here, find a new house? Somewhere near the sea. Or perhaps a year's sabbatical at an overseas university . . . These thoughts gave him a feeling of excitement that was like another kind of emptiness.

The birds' claws scratched and scraped on the roof iron. They swooped down onto the lawn, looking for the old crusts he'd thrown out. It was summer. That morning when he walked (staggered) up the path in his robe to collect the newspaper at 7am the cat from next door came slinking towards him, its belly low, head down, growling melodramatically, a live bird clamped in its jaws. The bird flapped one mangled wing. He ran at the cat, cursing. If he'd caught it he would have kicked it in the head. What sense was there in this? He lived alone. At other times the cat was his friend.

In the middle of the previous year Ford's widowed mother-in-law, Mrs J Bandaranaike, had slipped on the mossy deck of her Te Atatu Peninsula bungalow, and broken her hip. Her cries for help were eventually answered by a neighbour, and she was carried off to hospital. When she was released Ford's wife May, her third and favourite daughter, began spending the weekends with her, helping out. Often he joined them on Sunday afternoons, dutifully raking leaves, emptying bins, sitting on the deck with the little bright-eyed old invalid, sipping tea and watching the tide coming in over the silvery inlet. Mrs Bandaranaike had a strong line in wry, acid jokes — she and May spent their afternoons laughing in a sly, in-joke way, while Ford dreamed like a big, awkward bear on his deckchair, only surfacing when the old lady poked him humorously with her walking stick and asked for some small favour, more tea, or to adjust the awning to keep the sun off, services he was eager and grateful to provide.

The late Mr Bandaranaike, an eye surgeon, had been a secretive, repressed person; it was from her mother that May inherited her radiance and humour, her easy-going love of the comical and quirky. She had married Ford in a spirit of, what could he call it, hilarity? That was almost not too strong a word. Not that he was a *very* bad catch. But he was big and lumbering and not Sri Lankan. The senior Bandaranaikes were not opposed, luckily for him. They were tolerant, neutral. Being fiercely patrician Sinhalese, the only thing they would have regarded as a disaster would've been if their beautiful May had come home with a Tamil.

He enjoyed his Sunday trips to the Peninsula. Mrs Bandaranaike's house was a long, single-storeyed wooden structure built directly above the water, with a view across the gulf to the city and a stretch of tangled garden in front, through which a track wound down to the shore. May and Ford would walk down to the edge of the big shallow bay, skim stones onto the mudflat, watch the sun go down over the city buildings in the distance. Together they threw off Sunday's dreary grip. They always returned in good spirits and, if they felt like it, May and Mrs J would disappear into the kitchen and prepare something good — May cooking and Mrs J directing from the kitchen table, and they would eat out on the deck, the old lady's legs swathed in green cloth to ward off mosquitoes.

On the last evening they spent there together, Mrs J described a severe storm in Galle, where her family lived.

'It was terrible,' she told Ford, laying her hand on his arm. 'The whole family had gone out just before the floods came. They returned to a horror.'

'Oh God,' he said, making the appropriate face. 'What?'

'All the servants had been washed away!'

May, coming in with a teapot, laughed out loud. The light shone on her face. A moth rocketed off the lamp, fluttered wildly, and landed in her hair. She put her smooth brown hand up to her forehead, looked down at them with her startling, intelligent eyes.

Ford drank moderately at Mrs J's, enough to be legal but exhilarated by the dash down the motorway, weaving among the tail lights of cars hurrying in from the west. He noted how wild and unrestrained the driving was on that section of the motorway. The western suburbs are famously the home of boy racers, petrolheads, white motorcycle gangs. It was on this road one heavily raining Sunday, without Ford to drive her, to *look after her*, that May, returning from an evening with Mrs J (Ford was at home, working on a journal article) was passed by a car full of stoned skinhead youths who cut her off, causing her to skid and lose control and to crash head-on into the base of an overhead bridge.

May was a qualified anaesthetist. She had passed the exams to become a consultant just before she died. Ford thought about this. As she passed from consciousness to unconsciousness to dying, did she know, with forensic accuracy, what was going on?

The night she died. It was around eleven when he heard the knock on the door. Out in the street a car alarm beeped and whooped. He had been reading, stretched out on the bed. May had told him she would be visiting her mother after a late shift at the hospital. When he opened the door, expecting her with her arms full of books and papers or having dropped her keys down a grating or some such thing, he saw two cops, one old, one young, and in the face of the younger he saw a tremor of excitement, a suppressed thrill.

They made Ford sit in a chair.

'She's died,' he said, thinking of Mrs J. A rich sadness. He saw May at the scene, kneeling and gazing upwards, two professional fingers pressed to her mother's neck. Mrs J's body — sprawled in the garden where she'd tumbled off the deck stairs, or crumpled in the bathroom: electrocuted/slipped on soap/drowned. Perhaps she'd fallen asleep over a book while oil burned in the forgotten frying pan . . .

The elder policeman was talking. Ford was confused by the habit police are trained into, of describing incidents in the regulation tense. 'She's been cut off by another driver. Every effort has been made. Unfortunately she's been seriously injured and . . . '

'She doesn't drive,' Ford said, antagonistic, scornful as a teenager. It was the first sign of what he was to become in the weeks and months that followed: a person stupider, more bewildered and ashamed than the competent adult he had been.

There was a pause. The younger cop dipped his head and made a small sound.

'We're talking about Dr May Bandaranaike? Your wife?'

Ford stood up, looked at the younger cop. His face burned.

'Just what is this about?' he asked reedily.

The elder cop launched in again. 'She's been in a serious car accident. She's been cut off by another car.'

Ford walked away from him into the kitchen, picked up his keys and returned. 'I'm ready. What do we need to do?' May needed him. Action must be taken at once.

But there was nothing to be done. Nothing anyone could do. They held up their hands, urging him to sit, at least to stand still.

'She's dead,' the younger policeman blurted, as if he couldn't stand this any longer. The elder frowned at him and he shifted on his big feet and looked down.

Fragments of what followed (Ford winces, thinking back, poor Simon): they extracted his brother's name from him, rang him and asked him to come.

Simon and his wife got out of bed and drove over. They arrived to a fraught scene: some ancient memory had led Ford to an ancient packet of cigarettes on top of the high bookcase; he was working his way through it at a dizzying rate while pacing and talking non-stop and drinking wine from a bottle he'd found in the kitchen. He remembers the elder cop chasing him round the couch with a mug of hot sweet tea, the younger flapping his hands and surreptitiously opening a window as the room filled with foul smoke. Some small amount of wrestling with the wine bottle: '*It's not the best way, mate*.' He felt like a monstrosity, like Frankenstein's monster, as if he should burst out of the house and run baying through the foggy streets, pursued with revulsion and fear by normal, decent folk. Panic, horror, a sense that he had become grotesque, all this rose in him as he confronted his younger brother in his designer clothes, his shoes without socks. (Simon is a rich and successful doctor; these days he's a sort of obstetrician and gynaecologist to the stars.) Ford leered at him, raised his bottle and said, 'So they've brought you along for the show.'

Simon said nothing. A feeling of pure woe struck Ford; he had a sense of his old self whirling away. He would never get it back, not properly.

Simon's wife Karen took the bottle from Ford's hands.

The policemen began tiptoeing gratefully to the front door. Ford heard Karen seeing them off: 'Under control now. The shock. Of course.'

And then a hushed conference at the door. Would Simon accompany them? Would only take half an hour. To spare the grieving husband (and to save having to deal with him). Simon was summoned into the hall. 'No problem,' Ford heard him say.

Karen made cups of tea while Ford's brother rode into town in the back of the police car and laid formal eyes, for the last time, on May's face. He signed the papers. Ford let it happen, but he regrets it now. It should have been him. He could have stood it. If he wasn't there to hold her hand as she died, he should have been there soon after. These details added up: somewhere, behind one of the doors in his mind, is a festering compost heap of shame.

That morning, the morning after, Ford lurched from his room, where he had slept for two hours, fully clothed and face down on top of the bed, and found Karen asleep on the couch under a mound of blankets. Sunlight shafted through the windows and the evidence of his binge was scattered everywhere — ash, cigarette butts, red wine stains on the carpet, the empty bottle rolling on the deck. (And an old liqueur bottle — where had he dug that up from?) A wine glass, broken at the stem, lay in two pieces in a patch of light on the dining table. There was a peaceful, exhausted air in the house, like the morning after a wild student party.

Simon was sitting at the table out in the garden, a sleeping bag wrapped around his shoulders. Ford opened the French door. It had been a cold night. There was frost on the lawn.

A weird numbness had invaded Ford's brain. The only thing he felt, every now and then, was horror that he felt nothing. He also had the sense that the 'horror' was a small, badly stitched seam that would burst into a vast and unmanageable hole if he inspected it too closely.

Ford told Simon he was sorry if he had been 'difficult'.

Simon said, 'We just watched you until you ran out of steam.'

Ford looked sharply at his brother, but there was nothing in his face except weariness and sorrow.

'Fuck you,' Ford said.

Simon looked up, startled. 'What do you mean?'

Siblings. They were bickering already. 'Sorry I ruined your evening,' Ford went on, mechanically.

'For Christ's sake.'

'Sorry you had to go to the . . . ' he couldn't finish. 'To identify . . . Because I was "indisposed".'

'Don't mention it,' Simon said.

Ford spent the day sinking through several more layers of madness. At noon he went to sleep, after which he rocketed off the couch with a single idea in his mind.

'I have to see her,' he announced, staggering into the kitchen. Simon and Karen were eating sandwiches. They looked up warily. He snatched the phone and rang the police station. Put through to one department and then another, he glared at Simon, glassy-eyed. 'If you don't see them it doesn't sink in,' he said, cupping his hand over the receiver.

A stern-voiced woman came on the line. It was not possible to see the deceased at this time, she explained. There were procedures. Investigations. The serious crash unit, and so on.

'My brother's seen her. Why can't I?' Ford demanded, as though the policewoman was his mother and he was six years old, and deprived of a treat. He caught Karen glancing at Simon, and treated her to the foulest look. The woman transferred him to an authoritative male voice that took a different, more disconcerting tack. 'May I ask exactly why you wish to see the body at this particular time?' (Is there something you'd like to tell us, sir?)

'I'm having trouble understanding that what has happened is real,' Ford said.

Needless to say, this did not get him what he wanted.

'Better to see her tomorrow, once she's been looked after.'

'Looked after?' Ford shouted. 'What does that mean, looked after? She's dead.'

God knows what the policeman thought, what notes he was taking down. (Ford felt guilty of something all the time, but what? Everything.) Or, perhaps more likely, he thought very little of it. Ford supposed he was nothing the policeman hadn't encountered before. In his lowest moments, when he caught a whiff of that dung heap of humiliation he carried around inside, he found it hard not to believe that the world wasn't sniggering at him during those days, rolling its eyes, looking on in suspicion and disgust while he, the mad widower, flailed and flapped like a dying bird.

Karen was near the end of her tether, and needing to get back to her children, left with her mother on the midnight dash to Ford's house. She stood up, rolled her neck and said, 'I think you should go and lie down.'

Ford took a step towards her. '*You* go and lie down.'

Simon tried to get him to eat something, at the same time managing to signal to Karen, with repeated frowns, that she should shut up.

Ford looked at them, nearly crazed with contempt and then, quite suddenly, all the rage went out of him. There was a metallic taste in his mouth. He sat down and accepted a sandwich.

He tried to make things right. 'I'm sorry, Karen. You go and get the kids. Thank you for coming.'

Karen gathered up her things. At the door he apologised some more.

'You're in shock,' she said dryly. She combed her short blonde hair with her fingers. She couldn't wait to get away, understandably enough. She hadn't got on very well with May, who used to make uncharitable jokes about her, and once, although Ford wasn't sure on what evidence, told him Karen was 'a nasty little redneck'.

Simon stayed with Ford for nearly a week. He took time off work and simply followed Ford around. Together they drove out to Mrs J's. (Sitting with May's grieving mother and sisters, Ford came close to unpicking the fragile little seam in his mind — horror came close and he reeled with the nearness of it and had to walk away with Simon down to the bay.)

He went with Ford to the funeral parlour where they stood over the alien waxwork of May. Her forehead had been damaged and patched over. There were matt areas of pastel-coloured paste. Her newly lopsided face glistened with make-up and her hair was curled in an unfamiliar style. This was what the police had meant by her being 'looked after'. Ford pressed his lips to her forehead. She smelled of chemicals. He felt nothing.

Out in the street a line of blackbirds on the telephone wires, cottony cirrus in the sky. Suburban stillness. He held onto Simon's arm. Some terrible damage was being done to him. He couldn't feel it, but he knew the weapon was there, gouging his heart to shreds. He followed his brother like a sleepwalker, like one of May's patients, unconscious under the surgeon's scalpel. When I wake, he thought, it will be too late. I will be in pieces, too near death to feel.

After the funeral he stayed with Simon and Karen out at Whangamata, and tried to behave himself in front of their children. Little Marcus, Claire and Elke took him walking along the beach and he held their hands and inspected rock pools and made them laugh by hopping with his trousers rolled up through the freezing stream. They ate Karen's organic meals and took short walks around the coast. Late at night he watched reruns of old TV shows with Simon. Throughout he felt, how could he describe it? Outside himself. He lived through those 'recuperative' days as an automaton, while another self howled outside the window, beating his fists against his face.

May used to be fond of Simon. She flirted with him. He is a

handsomer version of Ford, not as big, not as loud and (Ford asserts, sibling-competitive) not as forceful. He has a big medical practice in town.

May flirted with him in her wicked, playful way, but he has 'boundaries' and 'standards'. You wouldn't get very far trying to draw him into a life of crime. Not like . . .

Ford and Simon's father. When Ford first met May, he'd been entertaining the idea of re-establishing a connection. (What was he thinking?) He had not seen his father, Aaron Harris, for a long time. Aaron had left off menacing their mother with late-night phone threats, and was reputed to be holding down a steady job. He must have got control of his drinking, was Ford's optimistic conclusion. Perhaps now was the time to mend old rifts, start afresh.

Ford rang him. He should have been put off by the cacophony in the background — someone tuning up a trumpet, over which a woman's voice rose in wailing, anguished protest.

'You try living in a boarding house,' Aaron said morosely, drawing on his cigarette and blowing out in a series of rich hacks and gasps. Ford heard the low moan of a saxophone, someone shouting. 'Fuck off, cunt!'

'Friends of mine. Practice,' he said.

'Putting the band back together?' Ford said, in high spirits, buoyed by the presence of beautiful young Dr Bandaranaike, who was lounging on the end of his bed and watching with an encouraging smile. Ford had been seeing her for three months. He had briefed her on his childhood, his father's violent drunkenness, his mother's suffering. Their escape into the arms of an aunt, and his mother's eventual remarriage to Warren Lampton, a good man.

'It sounds like a Dickens novel,' May purred, although Ford doubted she'd ever got through one of those — she was strictly a science and maths boffin. She had fastened on the idea of Ford's father, was 'dying to meet him'. He sounded 'so picturesque'. All her incitements lulled him, spurred him on. (He was in love with her; he was off his head.) Her robust sense of comedy, he thought, would see them through any difficult bits.

'Wha'?' his father snarled.

Ford felt a tremor of doubt, but pressed on.

'Would you like to meet for a coffee?' he asked. May hadn't taken her eyes from his face.

'Coffee? Fuck!' There was a blaring noise, as if he'd actually blown his nose into the receiver.

Ford named a café.

'The what and what? What? Fuck!'

On the appointed day, as they made their way down through Albert Park, May squeezed his hand and said, 'This'll be interesting.'

Ford said nothing. It was a warm, bright morning. Around the fountain the gulls shifted watchfully on their red feet. They passed the statue of Queen Victoria; some joker had put an empty beer bottle in the crook of her arm. Doubt was wafting through him like a cold little breeze. He didn't want it to be too interesting; neither did he want May to be too 'interested'. He wondered why he hadn't thought to have a preliminary meeting.

Forty-five minutes later, walking back up the hill, May was silent and grim-faced and no longer holding Ford's hand. He escorted her to her car, looking on hopelessly as she wrenched on her seatbelt and slammed the door. She wound down the window and said in a high voice, 'How could a person (he could tell she wanted to say creature) like that have produced you and Simon? How is it *possible*?'

A pain concentrated itself in his stomach. All thought of making light of the debacle, of salvaging it with a joke, drained away. He turned and walked off, his eyes stinging. He couldn't tell her anything then, let alone the things that hurt him most. Simon looks like their mother. So do their sisters. Ford, of all the siblings, is the only one who physically resembles Aaron Harris. The bad one. The Other.

After May drove off that day he thought it was the end of everything. He had lost her. He could hardly blame her if she never wanted to see him again. He locked himself away, threw himself into his work. He felt tainted, utterly depressed. About Aaron

Harris he had a dull feeling of hopelessness, beyond anger. He dreamed he was entering a room to see May leaving with Simon, waving goodbye, her smooth brown arm jingling with bracelets. 'Simon's just like you,' she trilled, 'only he's good.' (Though even in that dream he felt nothing but love for his brother. No jealousy, only sadness.)

He was in a bad state, delivering his lectures in a monotone, drooping about the common room, poisoning himself with instant coffee. At the end of that week he had an appointment with a student who'd sidled up to him after a lecture and confessed her difficulty with the area they were covering. He faced up to her, warily, because there was something unusual about her manner, a wrong note. Ms Smith was her name. Her mouth quivered with nerves when she talked and he'd noticed a habit she had of pulling her jersey off the shoulder, wiggling her flesh, and staring at him during lectures with an insanely fixed expression. When he got out his diary and offered her half an hour to go over the subject she let out a shocked little laugh, as if he'd suggested something terribly risqué. He looked at her sourly.

Ms Smith was late. He poked his head out and saw her at the end of the corridor, apparently picking up some Xeroxes. She looked up, made a big thing of hurrying along. He got her seated across the desk, as far away from him as possible, and asked her what she didn't understand. They went over the topic, but it was hopeless; all she did was stare and laugh and twist her fingers in her hands, until, irritated beyond belief, he felt like asking her, 'Would you prefer it if I just unzipped my fly?'

There was a silence. The phone rang. He lunged for it, grateful for a break from her twitching gaze.

'Hello,' May said, and he slid back in his seat and felt something in his body woozily rearranging itself.

'Hello,' he said huskily, 'I didn't expect *you* to call.'

'Why not?' she said. Oh happiness. Why not?

'I've missed you,' he said. He glanced up. Ms Smith had fixed her eyes on the glass paperweight on his desk, within which the yellow light from the window burned.

'Mmm,' May said. 'My nephew made me take him to the

Observatory yesterday. He told me about supermassive black holes. Did you know there's a giant black hole at the centre of our galaxy? In three billion years we're going to collide with the next-door galaxy, Andromeda. He tells me this will throw us into the black hole. The end of Earth. So I thought I'd ring you.'

Ford laughed.

She was suddenly brisk. He heard the jingle of her bracelets. 'Shall I pick you up after work? About six?' (Yes. Anything.)

'I'll be here.'

He hung up, rubbed his hands, smiled dewy-eyed at Ms Smith. He could have hugged her.

'Where were we?' he said, grinning like a wolf.

But she stood up, clutching her books to her chest.

'I get it now,' she said, blushing desperately. A piece of paper slid out of her bundle and swooped across the floor.

'Oh? Really? I'd be perfectly happy to . . . '

'I understand,' she said, clutching at her papers, crashing against the chair. A mad, rigid smile spread across her face. She rushed away.

May came to collect Ford in her little car. They went to a restaurant. He wasn't going to mention Aaron Harris, but after a few wines May did and laughed, shrieked about it in fact. She was tough; you couldn't deny it. (Or was there something slightly hysterical in her tone?) Ford told her he admired her, that she was brilliant. He held her hand. Happy times. They went back to his house. They fell into a routine after that: nights, whole weekends together. A few months later she moved out of her flat and into his house. Later, they got married. He asked her; she said yes. Then she rolled onto her back (they were lying on the bed) stuck her elegant, pointy-toed leg in the air and said, 'I think you'll make an excellent first husband.'

It's lucky and *rare*, isn't it, to find a person who makes you laugh. He was lucky. Had been lucky. Was.

These nights. The cat climbed in the window and disturbed his sleep, purring and kneading the sheet with its claws. He heard the car alarm yowling. Loneliness. Nightmares. He dreamed the cat was at the end of the bed, an arm dangling from its mouth. Something moved in the ceiling (a rat?). The sound of jingling. There were policemen knocking on his door. Then he was back in the café years ago, introducing his father to May . . .

'A black lady!' Aaron Harris says. He looks as if he can't believe his luck. He gives a gruesome wink, pulls a bottle out of his pocket and tips cheap sherry into the coffee Ford puts in front of him. May, seated across from him, goes still. Ford should take her by the arm and leave but something makes him freeze, his stomach thrilling with little shocks, as though he were standing at the edge of a cliff.

'Queen of spades,' Aaron goes on happily. 'You know what they say about the black ones. Where'd you pick her up? Good fuck? Looks handy. Nice tits. You've got nice ones, dear. Where do you work? K Road? Sauna and massage? Curry special, on the house?'

He has yellow skin. Shaking hands. Finishing the coffee, he goes on swigging from the bottle he keeps in his pocket. His glasses hang around his neck on a plastic chain. His teeth, when he laughs, are flecked with black. His voice is rising, lines of foam form on the sides of his mouth. Two waitresses are whispering; the man behind the counter is coming to ask them to leave.

'What colour your kids going to be? But you won't want kids. Won't want to spoil her. Keep her fuckable every night. Don't want some *saggy* old black *bitch* on your hands.'

The inside of his mouth is dark purple. His laugh is high, crazy. Ford can't speak. May is motionless, she simply can't believe. There is something Ford wants to explain to her, to everyone in the café: my father is not really like this. This (this performance) is an act of will, something he is doing to me. He knows you can't use these words, say these things. He is saying them to hurt me. Violence.

The old fist clenched, shaking. The café in a small uproar, other customers thrilled by the drama, the owner hovering over them with his cordless phone, 'I'm sorry I'm going to have to ask you to leave.'

He shouts, with a spray of spit. 'Get away from me. I'll go when I like. Fucker.' His eyes are grey slits. It's May who gets up, takes Ford's arm and pulls him away.

'Little cunt,' he shouts after them, as they leave.

Perhaps Ford was wrong about it being a performance. Perhaps that *was* the real Aaron Harris. The thing that was left, now that he'd burnt the life out of himself, and everything good was gone.

He woke at dawn. Grey light, iron thoughts. *This world.* May who was good was dead. Aaron Harris, who was bad, was alive, and spinning round the city like a black hole. Ford had seen Aaron not long ago, when he was driving home. The old skeleton bent against the wind on Symonds Street, his coat flapping around his knees. He was toiling through the dusk towards whatever flophouse or pub he had in his sights. Cold misery. Ford thought of back alleys, grimy windows, dead-eyed girls. Aaron's 'boarding house' was four rooms above a brothel. The Land of Opportunity was the establishment's jaunty name. Mornings he took tea and sherry downstairs with the girls. What did May have in mind when she said 'Dickensian'? A cheerful old gent — down on his luck but a heart of gold. The puppy he dotes on, the urchins he befriends . . . Aaron Harris was addicted to prescription drugs. In the brothel he sometimes participated in drug deals. (No doubt breakfast degenerated quickly into vicious transacting, all-out brawls.) How did Ford know this? Aaron had told him, in one of many abusive late-night phone calls. Ford gave up changing his number when Aaron took to ringing the department secretary. He spoke to her politely but the threat was there. He knew he was Ford's secret. That Ford could not let it be known he was the son of a person so crazy, so debased. He used to daydream that Warren Lampton was his father. But he does not look like Warren. He does not look like his mother. He has the height, the build, of Aaron Harris.

May stood between Ford and all this — between Ford and who he is.

Once, when he and his mother were mulling over some crime of Aaron Harris — after they left he'd rocketed around them like a suburban terrorist, never having accepted their flight — Ford lost his temper and shouted at her, 'What were you thinking?' Strange question to throw at one's mother, like an exasperated parent. How could you have been so stupid as to have conceived *me*?

'I was very young,' she said. (Eighteen.) 'I got pregnant. What you did then was get married. Of course it was a mistake.'

Then she added hastily, 'A mistake to marry him. But not a mistake having you. You take after my father, not him.'

She has always loved Ford. No small feat, when you consider how she could have been put off him by his resemblance to Aaron. She is like Simon, good-natured, straight. She and Warren Lampton are a happy couple, both overweight and freckly and wholesome. He is literal-minded, somewhat solemn, whereas she, through natural intelligence and early harsh experience, has a cynical, humorous edge. Once she'd realised her mistake, she set out to make things right. It was a shrewd move marrying Warren. He was a town-planning expert back then; now he deals in property, and owns houses and commercial buildings in Tauranga where they moved to get away from Auckland. They live in a big house on the sea front at Mount Maunganui. A tough, rich, benign old couple. Survivors.

'Aaron wasn't always mad,' she told Ford, biting her lip and staring defensively at the backs of her hands. 'He was clever. He was older, knew a lot; he had flair. I admired him. The drink destroyed him, that's all.'

Ford preferred to believe her. *The drink destroyed him.* Better that than his having been insane from the day he was born.

At dawn the cat jumped silently off the bed and went out the window. It spent most nights with Ford, but still he did not know where it lived.

After a bad night of dreams, the cat coming and going, the birds seeming to start up indecently early, Ford felt unexpectedly good. It was a hot bright day, the sky cloudless, the light glancing off cars and the wind turning the leaves and making them shine. He stood in the garden, holding the newspaper. The cat, the bird murderer, wound itself round his legs. Its name was Ticket — this he knew because it had a tiny collar round its neck with the name in scrolly lettering surrounded by quotation marks, and a phone number. Someone fed Ticket, yet they must lock him out at night. Ford didn't have the heart to do so himself. Something wound tight in him welcomed the cat's nightly disturbances — he feared going into too deep a sleep, relaxing too much and being caught unawares. By what? He did not know.

The recycling truck came rumbling along the street. The shirtless brigands who collected the bottles jumped off the back of it, scooping up the bins and hurling the contents into the skip. A lot of glass was being dropped and smashed on the road. When this happened they laughed. Gap-tooth brown faces. Terrific legs and torsos — all that running. Ford looked down at himself and thought he might try going for a run, at night when no one could see him. This, like ideas of travel, gave him a fluttery, weightless feeling of excitement. Getting in shape. The new Ford. On good days the world seemed full of possibility, new beginnings. On bad days he feared that without May he was sinking, and that he would turn into the thing she had shielded him from. Otherness.

He decided to walk to work. It was already hot at 8.30 am. Summer was here, after the terrible winter. A relief. He had developed a hatred of the cold, having spent the lonely months after May's death shivering in his badly insulated villa, lacking the will to get its cracks seen to. In the evenings he'd simply put on extra layers of clothes, until he must have looked like a tramp, crouched under the lamp with his books. Beady-eyed, snappish. The soiled coffee mug on the table, the grimy spoon sticking out of the tin of beans. (Oh God.) His bed was piled with rugs and quilts. He wore two pairs of socks, and cranked up the gas fire; it got less effective as the winter wore on, until there was only a small radius in which he could move without being frozen.

May and Ford had bought the house, a picturesque villa, during the previous summer. The gas fire looked nice, with its fake pile of rustic logs, but it gave off little heat, and gusts of cold air blew down the chimney. May would never have stood for such discomfort, but would have sprung into efficient action at the first sign of winter, summoning builders, plumbers, insulating experts. She had consulted her mother (Mrs J was a seasoned drover of tradesmen and domestic help) and had intended to install underfloor heating, ceiling and wall insulation. But after she died, left to himself, Ford had simply weathered it.

The lowest point was a rainy weekend when he couldn't get up. Simon found him on Saturday afternoon, wearing a ski hat, the covers drawn up to his neck. He'd ignored the thumps on the door, until eventually Simon climbed in Ticket's window, landing on the end of Ford's bed. Ford said nothing. He had turned his face to the wall.

'Christ. The state of this place.'

Ford wouldn't look at him.

'I'm going to get Karen. She's waiting in the car.' Things were serious, his tone implied: something had to be done.

He brought her in and Ford heard them muttering in the hall, then their children thumping through the place, and Karen telling them to go out in the yard. Simon appeared with a cup of tea and said, unhappily, 'Come on, mate.'

He sat up, letting out an evil waft from the covers, and reached for the cup. And then, horror, he felt a hot wetness start at the corners of his eyes.

'Nice hat,' Simon said. Ford ducked his head, let out a snicker of laughter.

Simon smiled briefly and pulled up the blind, letting in the cold grey light. Karen appeared at the door, surveying the bedroom with nodding, tight-lipped resolve. Ford sat marooned in his foul nest — it would have been more embarrassing to get up and reveal what he was wearing — and stared at them, marvelled at them really. What good people they were. (How could they stand to be near him?) Simon was picking up cups and dirty plates; Karen was rolling up her sleeves and muttering about 'popping up to the shops for what we'll need'. They kept glancing at each other, little wordless communications. With a jerk of her head — her hands were full of empty tin cans — she indicated a soiled pizza box; he nodded, looked over at Ford, then at the door, suggesting they give him a bit of space. This was how they communicated over the heads of their children.

When they'd tactfully withdrawn, Ford rose from the stinking scratcher and pulled on some clothes. He tottered out to the kitchen. It was, he had to admit, a pretty bad scene.

'I suppose I've let myself go, slightly,' he said to Karen.

She straightened up, holding a bulging rubbish bag in one hand, and laughed. Actually laughed. And then she put her hand on his shoulder — she'd never touched him before — and said, 'How about you take the children somewhere. They'll just get in the way.'

Marcus, Claire, Elke and Ford, dismissed, made their way to the park, where he stood about dreamily and watched them play in the light rain. He felt pale and trembly, like an invalid allowed out after weeks of illness. The children took his hands and pulled him along to the shops, where they persuaded him to buy the drinks and sweeties that Karen had banned from their diet; then they wandered along the shop fronts looking at the junk in The Treasure Chest and Sanjay's Antiques. The rain got heavy and thundered on the shop verandahs.

He took them to a café and bought meat pies, and sat dreaming in the warm fug. Elke, the middle child, was adopted. Nice, prosaic Marcus looked like his mother: those clear, unimaginative eyes. Claire — he wasn't sure. She was darker and more angular than her pretty blond brother. She had long fingers, coarse, wiry hair and an intense, narrow face, all sensitive nose and pointy chin. Ford had hoped she would turn out to look like his mother, but there was something in her harsh, mocking laugh — she cracked up at the slightest opportunity — that reminded him of . . .

Sudden lightness of the head. If May and he had had a child. He'd wanted to, she'd said she did too, but she'd put her career first, and didn't want to hurry things. He remembered her telling him how her father, Mr Bandaranaike, had pierced her ears in his surgery when she was two years old. Ford saw a tiny bejewelled May, arms full of bracelets, earrings flashing. A flower in her hair. No use thinking such thoughts. No use. Hail clattered on the window. He watched a seagull turning, bright white against the black sky.

When they got back there were stacks of rubbish bags at the front door, the dull, lavatorial scent of cleaning fluids. Karen was shouting to Simon over the roar of the vacuum cleaner. They sat on the front verandah so as not to track mud onto the clean wet floorboards.

Simon emerged with a cardboard box of empty bottles and set it down. He said lightly, gazing off, running his finger along the verandah rail, 'I hope you're not drinking too much, mate?'

He was thinking of Aaron Harris. Ford gave him a hard glance, but his expression was guileless and open. As Simon had got older he looked more like their mother — short and heavy, with a thatch of hair, a round, honest face. When he was a toddler their mother used to get Ford to follow him about, pulling him down from fences, heading him away from roads. Ford remembered the way his brother's hair grew in a sandy spiral on the back of his head.

Karen declared her work finished. Ford insisted on ringing for takeaways. Bustling around his gleaming kitchen he produced the dishes and cutlery they'd cleaned, set the table with a bright cloth, made everything nice. He poured out wine, drank moderately, helped fill the children's plates. He was reeling with gratitude and shame. After dinner Karen sighed, rose from the table, gave her thighs a little slap with both hands and looked meaningly at Simon.

He saw them to the door. She gave a theatrical little shiver and drew her jacket over her shoulders.

'Brr. You take care of yourself, now.' Her expression was rich with virtue, with 'good old-fashioned commonsense'. Ford had the urge to snarl, to say something atrocious, which he buried by shaking his head, compressing his lips and kissing her on the cheek, as if to say, 'words fail me'.

'Karen,' he murmured.

Satisfied by this hammy show she laid her hands on her children's heads. She and Simon gazed at the children in silent respect for something — innocence, family values. Then she clapped her hands, sending the little mites skipping out to the car: 'Hurry, hurry, you'll freeze to death!'

Claire pressed her white little face against the car window, making fish lips at Ford. Bloodless flesh under glass. Uncanny child.

Simon looked at Ford from under his pale lashes. 'Thanks,' Ford said. And then the sudden rush, all the blood concentrating in his face. He gripped Simon's arm, pressed his forehead into his shoulder. 'This cold . . . ' he said. It was all he could get out.

Simon went off down the steps, whistling. Ford thought of summers long ago. The bridge of brown freckles on Simon's nose. That whorl of sandy hair.

The day after that, Sunday, Ford drove out to the Peninsula. Mrs J gave him tea at the dining table, in front of the streaming panes. Her hair was fastened on top of her head with a comb. She had a sharp nose, round cheeks and a pronounced gap between her teeth that made her look like a benign witch. Outside the sea gleamed silver and there was an unnaturally high tide. Rain drummed on the tin roof. Mrs J lighted her magic lantern and gazed out over the inlet. Her second daughter glided in and out carrying bundles of linen. Some effect of the light made the view framed by the window glow softly, a watery tableau of rain and silvery sea and luminous cloud. Ford wondered at Mrs J's capacity for peace — admirable, unobtainable — he was not, could not be calm.

'How are your parents?' she asked in formal tones. She looked at her reflection in the back of a teaspoon and pursed her lips.

'My mother and stepfather are fine. My real father is not well, he's an alcoholic.' Ford startled himself by saying this. He could not have told her while he was married to her daughter. They had always let it be known to the Bandaranaikes that his father was 'overseas'.

She raised an eyebrow.

'Not just a drunk, he's mad, insane.' (What was he doing? Why the reckless hyperbole? She would ask him to leave the house.)

'How interesting,' she said coolly. 'Tell me about him.'

He shifted in his seat; awkwardness making him fidget. The wicker cackled beneath him. 'He was mathematically gifted, also musical. He became an alcoholic and was never able to manage a proper career.' He sat back and looked at her, feeling helpless. This hardly covered the lurid creature his father had become. Ford himself found him hard to believe. His gaunt face, with its prominent cheekbones and Roman nose, the ravaged contours, the mouth set in a line of thwarted ambition, bitterness, spoiled hope. Ford saw him jerking along the street, pulling his coat around his emaciated body.

Mrs J looked out at the rain. 'I know all this,' she said absently. 'May told me.' She stood up. 'Shall we walk down to the shore?'

They made their way through the garden. Ford went ahead, lifting wet branches for her, kicking aside bits of fallen brush, while she followed under a hot pink umbrella, sniffing the air and looking round alertly. The rain twanged on his umbrella and the long grass soaked his trousers. On the shore the water was swollen and still, the drops spiking into it. The high tide had covered the path, and a green soup of sticks and weed lapped against the sea wall. The city buildings were just visible through the watery mist. They walked on the grass above the path, around to the headland then turned back. He was absorbing what she'd told her: May had spilled the beans about Aaron Harris, 'ages ago', and Mrs J hadn't demanded an immediate divorce or banned him from the house. A beam of light broke through the cloud and shone on a patch of sea. Gulls wheeled over it. How desperately one clutches at straws. It hardly mattered *now* what Mrs J thought of him, yet still he felt a stirring of hope, a lifting of the spirits. With a little show of courteousness and care he escorted her across a point where the bank had eroded. She lurched and gripped his forearm and something stirred in him; it was the sight of her small brown hand — May's hand — on his freckly wrist. Oh, the ache in his eyes.

Later, he left the peninsula and joined the queue hurtling onto the northwestern motorway, the red tail lights shining malevolently ahead, the overhead bridges rising up and falling away behind. There was a tailback; soon he was crawling and as he passed the spot where May had died he saw that someone had put up a small white cross. He peered out at it, wondering who had put it there, but the flow speeded up and he drove on, the wipers swishing, the rain whirling round the orange lights. One of the skinhead youths had died in the crash too, a week after May. Perhaps the little monument was for him. Ford had received a letter from the boy's family, a mixture of apology and justification that he had merely skimmed, before shoving the cheap pages of notepaper away in a drawer.

Driving, he was thinking about his niece, Claire. The previous day in the café she'd looked up from some pinching game with her brother to find Uncle Ford staring intently at her, brooding over her bony features, her wiry hair. She'd faltered, given him a quick, apprehensive glance, before turning back to the Chinese burn she was administering with her broad hands — Marcus, eyes watering, holding out but slowly disappearing under the table.

Something occurred to Ford then. He'd been studying the children for traces of Aaron Harris. Grimly, he'd identified them in her. That crazy laugh. Those raw cheekbones and expressive hands. The poor child.

He must stop this obsessing, must leave the phantom of Aaron Harris behind.

He had a piece of paper folded in his top pocket. When they'd returned from their walk he'd told Mrs J about the problem of the uninsulated house. She'd sat down and written him a list of tradesmen she regarded as suitable.

'Because you don't want to be dealing with any old crook,' she said.

Using Mrs J's list he acquired builders: Jayden, Curtis and Shane. Shane was an enormous, silent Viking with pale blue eyes and a mullet haircut. Jayden and Curtis were his pimply, tattooed boys. Their associate, Vince, skulking, cadaverous and with a rattling cough, installed the underfloor heating. Whenever Ford walked in on them, pale Jayden and Curtis would start and exchange stony, significant looks, as if he'd interrupted the plotting of a drug deal or bank robbery. Vince, too, had a prison whiff about him. When they huddled out in the barbecue area for smoko he paced, as though used to taking the air between high walls. Shane was their leader, and spent most of his breaks with a cigarette clamped in his teeth and a cell phone wedged between his ear and his burly shoulder. Ford dubbed them the Nazi bikers, and became almost irrationally fond of them. They tolerated him following them about, rubbing his hands and asking impractical questions. He got quite inventive, and asked them to do all sorts of extras. It cost a fortune, but the house was transformed. No longer the faint acrid tang of damp, the delicate tracery of mould on the sills. As a masterstroke Ford had Mrs J recommend him a weekly cleaner, and was sent two elderly Russian ladies, Galina and Galina, who turned up swathed like twin Russian dolls in cardies and shawls and fur-lined booties. They smiled and apologised frequently, spoke rudimentary, comical English and polished everything until it shone.

On the afternoon when they'd finished the renovations, Ford treated the Nazi bikers to a beer, which turned into an extended session at the kitchen table. At a late stage Curtis and Jayden were sent for more booze and Shane, who had grown melancholy, told Ford that his wife had joined a cult that worshipped a deity called Ramtha. She wanted to leave Shane and their teenage daughter Shanae, and to travel to a commune in Colorado, there to await Ramtha, who would arrive in a spaceship to rescue his chosen ones.

'Good God,' Ford said, thinking of his own departed wife. There was a sudden howl of wind across the roof. They were in the middle of an easterly storm. Rain splattered against the window-panes and there was a smell of ozone in the air. Space. The ether. Like her mother, May had had round eyes, cherubic cheeks, a full mouth and a little gap between her teeth. Ford saw her among gold-rimmed clouds, eyelashes lowered, diligently blowing a puff of wind across a ceramic blue sky. Shane rubbed his great fists over his eyes and sighed, 'Women, eh. Can't live with them . . . pass the beer nuts.'

Ford laughed. It came to him how lonely he'd been. Then the boys came crashing back and the session carried on until they reeled away and he fell into bed and dreamed uneasily — spaceships, May flying, a great void of black space, vibrating with sound.

That morning he came out to the warm kitchen and panicked. Something had been wrenched loose and was spinning inside him, throwing him off balance. There was a moment of reeling fright, as if, after weeks of preparation, he was about to set out on the most difficult venture he'd ever faced, and had realised, with sudden dreadful certainty, that his groundwork was incomplete. He walked to work (legs like rubber, disconcerting twitch under his eye) through streets strewn with the detritus of the storm.

Sticks and leaves littered the pavements, cars threaded through a slalom of plastic cones where lines were down and sections of roads were flooded. He spent the day in an agitated state, not helped by some tricky issues (a feud between secretaries, a student accused of plagiarism).

He walked home, cooked a meal and ate it at the table, trying to still whatever it was that had come apart in his mind. He felt somehow weightless. He got through the evening, and the next. Strange days went by. He found himself jumping up to straighten curtains and polish surfaces — setting things in order kept him calm. He'd become, not so much houseproud, as fanatically superstitious. The house represented the state of things. He must not let things slide. He took to thinking aloud. Don't panic, he told himself (and Ticket the cat). One day at a time. Let's just get through this. That kind of thing.

He'd been so busy battling the cold that he hadn't had time to think of much else. Now he faced other things. Days. Nights. Life.

Ford holds on to the memory of those early days. The first year without May. How he fought his way back. The panic. The fear.

The days and nights continue. He has no choice but to go on.

THE NIGHT BOOK

Karen wanted to have another baby but she didn't get pregnant. She thought about trying IVF but then she changed her mind. She talked to her friend Jenny Francis, whose family ran the Francis Foundation for underprivileged kids. She decided she wanted to foster a girl.

Simon said, 'Why don't you go back to nursing.'

Karen said she could do that any time. They had money and plenty of space. She wanted to give something back to the community.

Simon mentioned her idea to Ford.

Ford was dubious. 'I don't know. Someone else's kid in the house. It's bound to be difficult. High maintenance. But Karen'd do it well. She's got all that energy.'

The way he said it suggested something negative about Karen's energy.

Simon told Karen he hoped it wouldn't upset their own kids, Marcus and Claire. But he went along with it. He signed forms and sat through interviews with social workers. He and Karen were vetted and subjected to police checks. They had to take a special course that went on for days at a very slow pace. Simon thought he could have taken the material home and swotted it up in a couple of nights.

He suppressed the fact that he wasn't all that keen. Karen was seized with the idea. There was no stopping her. He thought, it's not a permanent thing. If we can't handle it, we can opt out.

They brought Elke home. She was eight years old, thin, undersized, with freckles and a sharp face. The information on her was straightforward: her mother had been a teenage alcoholic and her father's whereabouts were unknown. Before she'd been taken into care she'd had an itinerant life with her mother, for some periods in a garage, and then in a car. She'd been to four different schools. She'd been malnourished but was developmentally normal. They were spared contact with her mother, who was working as a prostitute and didn't want to see the child.

She was a quiet and placid girl, not a horror to deal with, but she couldn't stick to normal sleep patterns. She got up almost every night and prowled around the house. Karen tried to get her to stay in bed even if she was awake, but it was hard to get her to break the habit. If she woke, she couldn't stop herself getting up. Karen worried she would go outside, and once they did find her out on the deck. She said she was looking for the cat.

When Simon came back late from the hospital he often sat at the table and wrote journal notes. One night he became aware there was someone standing right behind him. He turned quickly. It was Elke.

'What are you doing? You should be in bed.'

She edged along the table. 'What are *you* doing?'

'I'm writing in my journal.'

'What you writing?'

'Notes. Go to bed. Here, I'll take you.'

'I can't sleep.'

He hesitated. With the other kids, he would have insisted. He wouldn't have allowed them to defy him, and he would have made them get a good night's sleep.

'Why do you get up all the time? Aren't you tired the next day?'

'Nah.'

He sighed. She'd obviously never had a regular bedtime. No routine laid down. Not habituated.

He made himself a cup of tea and her a hot chocolate. 'You have to clean your teeth after.'

'What's in your notes?'

'I had a woman patient; she'd had four babies over the years. Big ones.'

'And what?'

'She had some damage from the births. So I fixed it. I was there when the last baby was born and as it was being born I saw the damage. Whereas when I'd examined her before, I couldn't see the problem. I'd thought she didn't have really have one. It was only when she was giving birth that I saw . . . You don't need to know all this.'

She looked at him steadily.

'Anyway, it was a kind of lesson. That's the kind of thing I write up in my journal.'

'I seen someone having a baby.'

'Have you? When?'

'I dunno. We went there.'

'In a hospital? Did you see the whole thing?'

'From the side.'

'The side of the bed?'

'Yeah. It was gross.'

'Was it your auntie or something?'

'I don't know.'

He got used to her silent entrances.

She looked at him levelly, boldly, as though there was an agreement between them. She sat down and watched him write. He was aware of differences. If it had been Marcus or Claire, he couldn't have tolerated the sitting and watching. Parental irritation and dutifulness would have had him shooing them into their bedrooms, tucking them in. He didn't love this kid. He hadn't spent years setting the best possible routine for her. He hadn't watched her growing up, every step of the way. Karen would have sent her to bed, but Karen was deeply, exhaustedly asleep, as were Marcus and Claire. Elke sat and watched him and he let her.

Sometimes they talked, quietly, so as not to wake anyone.

She said, 'If you make me go to bed I won't sleep.' She said, 'I always wake up in the night. My night's two halves. First and last and there's a waking bit in the middle.'

All through the winter she sat next to him while he wrote in his journal. When he'd finished he saw her to her room and assumed she slept after that. She never seemed tired. (Not that he saw much of the kids during the day. He worked long hours.) He felt guilty that he didn't try harder to get her to sleep. He knew it was because he didn't care enough. He had so much to worry about already — he worried about all the things that were really his.

She was less childlike than Marcus and Claire. She didn't climb on him or touch him, except sometimes to lean lightly on his arm. With these nights, he was spending more time with her than he did with his own kids. Because of not loving her, he'd allowed her into his night hours and now they shared something. He felt faintly disturbed by this, and worried about his own children. But they didn't seem bothered.

Simon was offered a place at University College Hospital in London. They made enquiries with the agency and were told they couldn't take Elke overseas. If they went they would have to give her back. She would be placed with another foster family.

They faced up to the prospect. There was no question of not going to London. The agency suggested they hold a small farewell celebration to soften the blow, giving the child a present of a memory book and photographs. Simon and Karen whispered about this after the kids were in bed at night. They wondered what present they should give her. Karen decided she would bake a chocolate cake.

Simon said, 'Last requests. Like the last meal on death row.'

Elke wrote down something she wanted for Christmas. She mentioned how much she liked her new class. She invited friends home. She'd put up pictures in her room, and she'd brought home a swan plant from school, planted it in the garden and stocked it with yellow and black caterpillars, in the hope that they would turn into monarch butterflies.

They gathered photographs and souvenirs into a file for her to keep. They geared themselves up to tell her that she would be moving on. It started to seem obscene.

It was Simon who suggested that they apply to legally adopt her.

They arrived in London in the middle of a very cold winter. They rented a flat that looked out over an old graveyard. It was a silent place between the buildings, surrounded by brick walls, with wooden seats set among the oak trees and a path winding through the plots. The gravestones were a jumble of crooked and cracked slabs, blurred statues fallen over sideways, rusted railings. It was a peaceful place. During the day people used it as a short cut between the streets. Squirrels ran up and down the trees and sometimes a couple of drunks bickered on the seats in the winter sunshine.

Simon woke up one night at 3am. There was something different about the atmosphere; he couldn't think what. He went to the sitting room, looked out and saw that snow was falling thickly. The graveyard was covered with white, and the hum of the city was muffled by the thick whirling flakes.

Elke came in and they stood together looking out at the silent snow falling and the old gravestones sticking up, black against the icy ground.

'You ever seen snow before?' he whispered.

She shook her head.

'It's not often this thick in London. It doesn't usually settle.'

She clutched his arm and pointed. There was a man walking along the path beside the graves, wrapped in a heavy coat and carrying a suitcase. He stopped and looked about him. He seemed to search for something; finally he leaned down and stashed the suitcase behind a grave. He got up, wiped his hands on his coat, looked around furtively and hurried on. They watched him disappear through the gate, into the street.

'What's he hidden. Let's go and see,' Elke said.

'Not now. In the morning.'

'Now, now,' she pleaded. 'It might be gone in the morning.'

'We can't go down there. It's freezing. What if he comes back.'

'Please. I've got my boots and my coat in the hall.'

'Shhh,' he said. He glanced at the closed bedroom doors.

'I'll go down really quick. You watch from up here.'

He was alarmed. 'No. Absolutely not. Don't you think of going out in the night by yourself. Ever. You wouldn't, would you?'

She shrugged.

He held her shoulders. 'Tell me you wouldn't. You don't know what's out there.'

She didn't say anything. He wondered whether she was capable of sneaking out by herself. He wouldn't be able to sleep now, listening out for her.

He said, 'Oh, all right. We'll have a look. I'll leave the outside door open so we can run back in.'

They put on coats and boots and went downstairs, to the door that opened into the graveyard. Simon looked for something to prop it open. If it shut on them they'd have to walk through the streets, all the way round to the front of the building. He jammed it open with the door mat.

He took Elke's arm and they crunched through the snow.

She said, 'You can write about this in your night book.'

'It's not stories in there, it's real.'

'This is real.'

The streetlights cast an orange glow across the white ground. Simon looked around carefully, reassuring himself that no one would be lurking out here on such a cold night. They found the gravestone and Simon reached behind it. He brought out the suitcase and laid it on top of the grave.

'Open it,' she said.

But there could be anything in there. Something grisly. He put it back, straightened up and said, 'This is ridiculous. We're going back inside.'

Her voice rose. 'No, no. We've come all the way.'

'Shut up,' he hissed. He looked up at the dark windows, expecting to see the curtains twitch aside. He looked at his watch. It was 3.30am.

'I'll look first. You stand there.'

She stepped back obediently. He pulled the case out again, laid it on the grave and unzipped it. There was a metallic jumble inside. He peered in. It was full of cameras, video equipment, CDs still wrapped in their cellophane. There was a stack of magazines. He checked: porno, mostly naked women on the covers, some men.

Rapidly he zipped up the bag. What did he think he was doing, out here in the middle of the night with the little girl, the bag full of someone's illegitimate stash. An icy trickle ran down his neck.

'It's bad stuff, it'll be stolen stuff, we'll just leave it.'

He threw the case back behind the grave. She argued, but he was beyond all that now. He hustled her towards the door, shutting her up. Now all the windows in the block seemed to lean towards him; he felt eyes staring down from every one.

They passed a man in the hall; a doctor who lived on the next floor up. Simon knew him slightly. He saw the man glance down at them curiously as he went on up the stairs.

Inside the flat he helped Elke out of her coat and boots, and hurried her to the bedroom. Marcus and Claire were asleep. He tucked her in. He wanted to say, 'Let's not tell about this,' but that seemed wrong. He eased himself into bed next to Karen, and lay awake, anxious. Once he heard a noise and got up, worried that Elke was prowling again. But all was quiet in the children's room. She was asleep. Marcus and Claire were silent in their bunks. He looked at their soft little faces. He wanted to kiss them but didn't, in case they woke. He stood looking down at Elke. He felt exhausted and troubled. Outside, in the dreamy silence, the snow fell.

He slept and dreamed that Elke had grown to adult size. They were in the graveyard and the snow was falling around them. She pointed to the cover of one of the porno magazines and said, 'That's my mother.' There was a picture of a woman posed naked except for a white scarf draped around her.

Elke said, 'You can't make things real if they're not.'

Simon said, 'But what is real?'

There was snow all around but the dream was full of heat. She had breasts, long hair, a full mouth. She was pulling him towards her. They were lying together on the stone slab. He woke in heat and confusion and thought no. No.

It was Saturday. He didn't have to work. He put on his robe and walked through the empty flat. He heard voices from below. Karen and the three children were out in the graveyard. The kids were wearing woollen hats and mittens. Elke was directing and pointing, and Karen was reaching down into the space behind the stones. Marcus and Claire capered about throwing snow at each other.

Then the four of them gathered round the case as Karen unzipped it. She stepped back quickly, zipped it up and shooed the children away. She looked up at the window and saw him standing there. He turned away and went to the shower.

Karen and the kids played in the snow for an hour, and then came inside, the children flushed and complaining that their hands and feet were numb. Karen's manner was deliberate. She was set-faced. There was an air of suppressed drama in her tone that he reacted against. She gave the kids breakfast, and then sent them to play table tennis in the communal games room downstairs.

She stood over him, hands on hips. 'I get up this morning and Elke tells me about this midnight jaunt. What were you doing?'

'She was up in the middle of the night. As usual. We were looking out at the snow. We saw the guy put the case there. She wanted to see what it was. I told her no, but she went on and on. I was worried she'd try and go down by herself. It was the only way to make sure she didn't go sneaking out there.'

'But to take her out in the dark. In the *snow*. Anyone could have been down there. The man could have come back.'

'It was what I decided to do. I wasn't sure, I don't know. I didn't want to go.'

He threw the newspaper aside. He paced across the room. He said, 'I have to deal with her in the night. You're always asleep.'

'Well, you're usually up writing in your journal. If you don't want to deal with her then wake me up.'

'Sure. I could set off a bomb and you wouldn't wake.'

She said steadily, 'I look after her all day. If she bothers you in the night, call me and I'll take care of her.'

'She doesn't bother me. But I had to work out what to do. Anyway, what's the harm.'

'Well, it's a bit weird isn't it, running around in a graveyard in the snow with an eight-year-old girl in the middle of the night. What if someone saw?'

Simon stared at her. He was furious. 'You wanted her. If she creates weirdness it's not my fault. I just have to deal with it — with your charity case, your whim . . . '

'My *whim*?'

He raised his voice. 'She's a little girl. She's real. What did you think she'd be, a doll? Something you could just play with? You think it's all so simple. Just go out and shop for a kid.'

'What are you talking about?'

'You want to be the charity worker, and then when there's a problem you call me weird. I am not fucking weird. I am just *dealing* with her. While you *sleep*.'

They blazed at each other. They lost track of the argument, said hurtful things. They hadn't argued so savagely since the first years of their marriage, when they used to fight, jealous after parties, or irritated after a boring encounter with in-laws, yelling in bed, tearing strips off each other, before making up in the morning with blistering sexual energy.

She put her hand over her mouth. Tears welled up. 'You don't want her. You never did.'

'That is just bullshit.' For a moment he hated her. There were some things you could never make her understand. Then he was sorry. He put his arms around her.

She said into his chest, 'I'm going to call the police.'

'What?' He pushed her away.

'About the suitcase. It's obviously stolen stuff, and there are all those dirty magazines. We should tell the police.'

'All right. Do that.' He released her. 'Tell them to pick up the bag. And then let's forget it. We'll work on getting her to stay in her bed. That's the only real problem.'

He called her Elkie. LK. Little Kid. She was tough. The children went to an inner-city school that was full of rough kids from the local housing estate. At first, all three children were teased for their accents and their unstylish provincial clothes. Claire especially was mocked for her haircut and her boyish shoes. Elke took action. She got Karen and Simon to take them to Oxford Street one weekend and fit them out with shoes with heels and the right style of jeans. Claire was reluctant and miserable. Elke breezed out of the changing room looking like a local. She got Karen to take her to the hairdresser, and had her hair layered and flicked. She started to round out her Kiwi vowels.

Claire came home in tears. She had worn her new London shoes with thick striped socks, and had been mercilessly teased, the kids surrounding her in the playground, chanting and laughing.

Elke said, 'Well why did you wear those socks?'

Claire turned on her, furious and miserable. She shouted, 'Adopted bitch.'

'Claire!'

Elke leaned against the door, trim and pretty in her outfit, with her layered hair. She had bought herself a cheap silver chain with a little strawberry on it. The strawberry had a smiley face. She looked expressionlessly at Simon.

He went to the bedroom. Claire was crying angrily. The provincial socks were lying on the bed. Her face was round and red and hot. She had put on weight and her legs were shaped like his — not slim like Karen's, but heavy and ungainly. Her hair stood up in dowdy spirals.

He sat beside her and crushed her in his arms. He wanted to protect her from everything. The fact that she was plain and awkward and unhappy made him burn with love for her. She had set out with high hopes that morning, wearing the new shoes and the gaudy, naively coloured socks. Even he could have told her they looked wrong. His poor, clever, innocent girl.

Elke sidled in. She said, 'I'll tell you what to wear. Then they'll leave you alone.'

Claire's face blazed with hatred. Simon frowned over Claire's head, silently telling Elke to leave it for now.

Elke shrugged and went off to the games room with Marcus.

Karen came in and sat down on the bed. She said, 'Claire. That thing you said to Elke. You mustn't.'

Claire made a growling sound, her head in the pillow. She said, 'You love Elke because she's cute and pretty. Everyone likes her more because she looks nice.'

Karen said, 'That's not true. We love all three of you equally. Don't we, Simon.'

'Don't lie. Fuck off,' Claire shouted.

Karen's voice rose. 'Don't swear. This jealousy, Claire. It's something you have to conquer. It's something bad *in yourself.*'

Simon reacted against Karen's tone. It was the hectoring note she struck when she was 'dealing with a problem'. It was the strict voice a little girl would use when telling off her teddy. He saw how it left Claire bereft, hearing that her feelings were something bad *in herself.*

He said to Karen, 'You go and check on the others.'

He soothed her out of the room and then he sat with Claire and told her how much he loved her. It seemed wrong, indecent, to go against all the rules of good behaviour, but he couldn't stop himself.

He told her, 'I love you more, I love you most. You're my little darling. Ever since you were born I've loved you with all my heart. And Marcus too.'

She knew what he was saying, that he loved her more than Elke. She knew it wrong to say it. She was shocked, soothed, gratified.

'Okay?' he said. He hugged her.

She sighed, turned over on her back, picked up one of the striped socks and hit him with it languidly. He went out of the room, troubled. He felt as if he'd done the right thing by his girl and at the same time he had a faintly cloying, disgusted feeling, as though he'd committed a crime.

Before they went back to Auckland, they flew to Australia. Simon did a short stint as a locum at Bundeberg Hospital, where they were short of obstetricians. At the end of the month they went up to Port Douglas for a holiday. They stayed in a hotel in the town, and Simon spent a lot of time on the phone making arrangements for returning to his practice in Auckland.

There was a connecting door between Simon and Karen's room and the children's. Both rooms had balconies that opened straight onto the pool. You could walk out of your bedroom and plunge straight in. Karen worried that Elke would get up in the night and go in the pool. Simon got hold of some wire and tied the kids' gate shut at night, and Karen piled things around it after the kids were in bed, so it couldn't be opened without a lot of noise.

After being cooped up in London for months the children were wild about the pool and the white sand beach that stretched mile after mile, fringed with coconut palms. It was winter, which meant the days were hot and clear, and you could swim in the sea without having to wear a full lycra body suit to ward off marine stingers. In Port Douglas, summer brought rain and extreme heat and the stingers, tiny jellyfish that could kill you if you were stung badly enough.

They took a tourist boat out to the Great Barrier Reef. They were given body suits, since there were marine stingers on the reef, and they all went snorkelling.

Simon swam away from the group and dived in water so clear that the colourful fish seemed to hang in the brightness. He dived down and lay on the bottom. Above him tiny fish veered in bright schools and the sky wavered, chrome blue above the skin of the water. He felt the cold London months washing away from him. He swam up a rope, a buoy bobbing at the top of it like a balloon. The fish swirled around him and the light danced in rings and spirals on the white sand. He came up and saw Karen surrounded by the children. She was spitting on her mask and laughing. He swam towards them.

Karen took holiday photos. Elke was svelte in her lycra suit, Claire was dumpy and brave.

Claire stood on Marcus's foot and he shoved her hard. She slipped and fell over.

Claire got up and hit Elke.

'Why hit her. Hey.'

'She laughed,' Claire said.

Simon grabbed her wrist. 'Just get over it,' he hissed.

She pulled away from him. All the way back on the boat she sulked, and he felt bad, but he was too exhilarated by the sea and the sun to care all that much.

One morning they set out to walk to the end of the beach. The sand was strewn with coconuts. The palms waved and the surf crashed, sparkling onto the shore. Simon walked with Marcus, drawn to the boy's silent, uncomplicated presence, a relief from the undercurrents, the feminine warfare.

He and Marcus walked fast and soon they were a long way ahead. When they looked back the others were three bright blobs in the wavering heat. Marcus bowled coconuts into the sea. The bush along the shoreline made a shimmering green wall against the sky. After an hour they came to the last stretch of beach where a reef ran out into the sea. The water was shallow and bronze in the sun, shirred by the wind. There was a group of windsurfers on the beach, and the sails skimmed over the water, shooting delicately over the waves.

Around a curve of the coast the sand was dimpled with bleached driftwood and the bush near the shore was thick and tangled. The beach ended in an estuary, green water running out through stands of bright mangroves. They looked across the estuarine flats, to where the steamy channels ran through the swamp. There was a sign warning them not to go further, because of the crocodiles. The salties could be three metres long, and they were aggressive. They would even jump up at you when you were in a boat. Marcus wanted to go to the edge of the mangroves, but Simon pulled him back. They lay in the shade of a dead tree stump, bleached white by sun and salt, its branches reaching up like arms.

Marcus poked the sand with a stick.

He said, 'Elke went in the pool last night.'

Simon sat up. 'She's not allowed to do that. How'd she get through the gate.'

'She went out into the corridor and round that way.'

'Why didn't you tell us.'

'Claire said not to.'

'But she could drown.'

Marcus looked at him. His mouth twitched. 'Claire said don't get her in trouble.'

Simon started to speak and gave up. He stared along the shoreline. The three of them were coming along the edge of the water.

They lazed in the shade. When Karen and the girls got there, he could tell immediately that something was up. Karen's answers were clipped. She shrugged away and didn't look at him.

He took her aside. 'What's wrong.'

'Why didn't you wait for us. You went ahead and left us. I had no way of catching up. We couldn't call, you were too far away.'

He was exasperated. 'Look around you. Look at the beach. The sky. It's beautiful and all you can do is throw a sulk?'

'You wouldn't wait. I wanted to stop. I'm tired. I didn't want to go all the way to the end.'

'So why didn't you stop.'

He jammed his cap on his head. His lips were cracked with sunburn. Jesus. Family life.

All the way back Karen acted hurt that he'd left her behind, and she didn't thaw out until that evening, when they were sitting at a café in the main street having dinner. She sipped her wine and her mood started to break. She put her hand on his arm: making peace. He squeezed her hand but didn't say anything. She made a tsking sound and drew away from him.

Claire said, 'Stop it.'

'Stop what.'

'Elke kicked me.'

Karen said, 'Claire.'

Claire went red. 'It's not me. You always think it's me.' She nudged Elke hard, Elke flung out her arm and a drink spilled across the table. Simon got up fast as the cold, sugary liquid cascaded into his lap.

Karen took Claire by the arm. She dragged her out into the street and told her off in savage whispers. Elke licked her sticky fingers and watched.

'Stop looking,' Simon told her roughly. He mopped the table with napkins.

He thought how it would be to live alone, without all the fights and bitching and tears. He'd had the thought before, but it had always served as a way of confirming how much he did want it: family life. He watched the young waitress swinging through the tables, tossing her hair out of her eyes. He thought about leaving. Living alone. Breaking free of it all.

That night Simon and Karen drank a lot of wine. They went back to the hotel, put the kids to bed and watched the TV news channel. He reached out for Karen, wanting her, but she pushed him away. 'I hate it when you've been drinking.'

'I'm not drunk.'

But he was, so drunk in fact that he forgot to wire the pool fence shut.

Karen slept restlessly beside him. He was hot and uncomfortable, scratchy with sunburn and dry-mouthed from the wine. He dozed. Everything was out of alignment, jagged, spoiled. Something was breaking up inside him. He had lost faith or conviction; a force had been unleashed that would break up everything they had. Karen believed passionately in the family. She thought everything was fine; she couldn't see it coming, but it was coming, whatever it was. The falling apart, the breaking down. The fearful, disjointed thoughts ran through his head until he slept.

He woke later and heard the gate creak open next door. He went through to the connecting room and found Elke in her togs, about to get into the pool. She looked up at him with a blank, hard stare, as though they had discussed this already and agreed. He couldn't be bothered speaking.

She slid into the water, and he followed her, swimming in his boxer shorts. They swam without talking, in the cool silence. The spiky plants hung over the water, making shadows like spears. There were strong scents of tropical flowers and damp earth. The water danced and shimmered in the dim lights from the hotel corridor. The cool streams swirled around his body. He thought of all the night hours he'd spent with the strange little girl; her silence that seemed to hold in it understanding, her self-contained, unchildlike ways.

She swam close and put her hands on his shoulders. She moved her thighs slowly. He felt her breath on his face. He closed his eyes and they floated in the silence. He lifted up her hard little body and set her down with a bump on the edge of the pool. He got out and pushed her ahead of him into the room. He put a towel on her and dried her off, then turned away while she put her pyjamas on. He tucked her into bed.

'Don't tell Karen we did this.'

She looked up at him.

'I mean . . . ' He sighed and rubbed his hands over his face. The water was cold on his shoulders, trickling down his back. He was suddenly chilled. 'Don't tell Karen I let you swim in the pool.'

They flew back to Auckland, landing in an afternoon filled with blinding rain. It rained every day for two weeks. The house had been rented out while they were away. It smelled damp and looked shabby. Karen went into overdrive fixing it up.

Simon liked the rain. He drove through the streets in his big car, between his private practice and the public hospital. Late at night he wrote in his journal. Elke's waking was worse after they got back. She came and sat with him regularly.

One night he delivered a baby for a woman whose partner was drunk. The drunk man insulted a midwife. Security was called. Simon came out of the hospital at dawn. The sky was streaked with pink cloud; in the car park the drunk man was getting in a taxi. The grass in the park was all sparkling with dew and the first birds were starting up.

Simon drove home and let himself in to the quiet house. He walked through the rooms. It was getting on for six o'clock in the morning. He stood in the kitchen looking out at the garden. Elke came in and sat down at the kitchen table.

He thought about the baby he'd just delivered, the drunken father, the mother pleading with the security guard to let him stay. He thought about a paper he'd read recently. Research showed that girls who lived with their biological fathers had their periods later than girls who didn't. The presence of the natural father suppressed development in girls. He thought, what does that show but that we are animals. Creatures. Regulated by hormones, by forces we can't control. You can't trick the body.

He sighed. He was suddenly so tired he could barely stand. He leaned over Elke and put his arms around her. He put his face in her hair.

'It's always you and me, getting no sleep. Why don't you go back to bed, LK.'

She looked up at him, her gaze wide and blank. 'Yes, Dad,' she said.

Simon was on call during a weekend when a lot of the staff were down with flu. There was an air of crisis, of heroic making do. Everyone was tired; everyone had been rostered on for too long.

At nine in the evening a woman was wheeled in. She was ten days overdue, and the labour wasn't progressing.

He walked into the room and picked up the chart. He read it and then looked at her. She was twenty-one. She had a round, handsome face, glossy black hair and green eyes. The eyes were striking — too pale for the dark face. She grimaced with pain, showing a couple of missing teeth.

'Hi,' he said. 'Mereana.'

There was a hefty woman in a beige uniform at the side of the bed.

The patient needed her blood pressure taken. He went to do it himself, since they were short-staffed. He said, 'Oh for Christ's sake.'

He pointed. 'Take it off,' he said.

The woman in the uniform looked where he was pointing. She said, 'Oh yeah. Sorry. I forgot. I had to go out for a minute . . . '

Anger and tiredness made him shaky. He said, 'Look at her. Look at her.'

His pager went. He looked at it and swore. He said, 'She's in labour. How far do you think she's going to get if she tries to run away. Even *you* could catch her.'

The woman smirked. 'Sorry. My mistake.'

Simon and the patient stared at each other. She panted and suddenly screwed up her eyes.

'It's a contraction,' he said, feeling her stomach. 'You're doing fine.'

The big woman picked up the plastic handcuff that attached the patient's wrist to the metal edge of the bed. She took it off, giving Simon a hard, ironic smile.

Simon said, 'Mereana. Your baby's in the posterior position. That means it's going to take a bit longer to push out. I'm going to give you something to bring it on. I think you should have an epidural. For pain relief.

She agreed to all this, rubbing her wrist. He saw the mark from the plastic cuff.

'You'll be fine,' he told her, and squeezed her foot through the sheet.

He left her to the midwife and went to get hold of the anaesthetist. He got the patient set up and went to another woman down the hall. He went between the two for a while, then drove home. The drive took him less than five minutes. Later in the night, when he was writing in his journal with Elke beside him, they called him back.

The patient, Mereana was sweating, crying and distressed. She had progressed quickly, and they had allowed the anaesthetic to wear off so she could push. The drugs were making her shake, and she was vomiting.

The prison guard was standing by the bed holding a stack of paper cups. The midwife was peering between the patient's legs.

'Mereana?'

The patient cried and moaned. The midwife looked sideways at Simon, communicating silently. He bent down beside her.

'Is she all right?' the guard asked.

The midwife handed her a cup full of vomit.

'Oh shit,' the guard said. She passed another cup off her stack and carried the full one to the bin, averting her face.

Mereana shrieked. She clutched the sheet and writhed, throwing the monitor off her stomach.

'Careful.' The midwife connected her up again. Simon read the scroll of paper the monitor had turned out.

He said, 'Mereana.'

She was hissing between her teeth. 'Oh god help me.'

'I'm going to turn the baby round.'

The prison guard made a moaning sound. She put her hand to her forehead.

They got her ready, and Simon took up the rotation forceps. He didn't do this very often. It was difficult, but he was confident about it.

The guard did a little skip of tension and knocked into the drip stand. 'You sit down over there,' the midwife snapped, and the guard sat down like she'd been slapped.

There was a silence, just Mereana's sobbing. He angled the

forceps and tried to get a grip. Sweat ran into his eyes. The midwife blotted his face.

He got the grip right and began to turn the baby to the anterior position. Mereana cried out. You needed to be strong. It felt brutal. The grind of metal against flesh, the resistance of flesh, the strange textures of skin and cartilage and bone. It seemed to take a hell of a long time. The patient was swearing and pleading. The guard had her face in her hands. He stopped, steadied himself, carried on.

Finally he got the position right and reached for the next set of forceps. He found the head and began to draw the baby out. The woman was frantic now, crying, flailing her legs, reaching down and trying to push him away. He slapped her hands off, and signalled to the midwife to control her. The head began to emerge properly. The shoulders came free, and then there was the rubbery slither as the rounded belly squeezed out.

He pulled the baby clear and held it up. One look and you could tell it was going to be fine. It let out a cry. In a sudden comic release of tension he thought of getting the guard to cut the cord.

He cut the cord himself, and the baby was placed on the woman's chest. It was a girl.

He looked into the mother's blasted, bloodshot, tear-stained face and said, 'Well done.'

They tidied up. The woman clutched the child fiercely, whispering to it. She looked up at him. Her green eyes were wild.

The guard stood up. She swayed slightly with exhaustion. He heard the jingle of keys at her belt. He pulled her aside. 'You're not going to cuff her. She has to feed the baby.'

The guard just shook her head and sank down in the chair, watching.

He walked out of the room. He went to the nurses' station and wrote in a file. He smelled a sharp waft of sweat. The guard was standing beside him.

'What's going to happen to that baby?' he asked.

The guard leaned on the counter. 'She's got a long sentence. They let her keep it with her for six months and then they take it away.'

'Take it away,' he repeated.

She nodded.

He slapped the file down on the counter and walked out.

He drove home. The kids were in their school uniforms and Karen was rushing around getting them ready. He hugged each of them in turn and said goodbye. Karen hustled them out the door.

He called Elke back. He put his arms around her. His voice was slurred with tiredness. 'LK. We got to change things.'

Claire called from the front path. Elke wriggled free.

He grabbed her arm. 'No more night book,' he said. 'It's all over with that. I'm not putting up with it any more. You gotta sleep.'

She went down the steps. 'Sleep,' he called after her.

She looked back at him and rolled her eyes.

He walked through the quiet house. He looked into the rooms, at the brightness and order. He lay down and the walls whirled dizzily around. He thought about the patient. She would look after the baby for six months and then they would take it away. She would see it only when it was brought to visit.

He slept without waking until the afternoon, and when he surfaced he had a feeling of ease. A beam of light came through the window and made a dancing pattern on the floor. The cat sauntered along the hall and sat in the doorway, its ear revolving to catch sounds. Birds squabbled in the branches outside. Down the street, someone was trimming hedges; there was the whine of a saw. The wind made the trees swell and shiver, flipping the silvery leaves.

The children were playing in the garden. He lay in the sunny room, listening.

THE BODY

They were crammed in the car: Bennie who'd had to be dragged because he didn't want to look at a dead body, the other three children bouncing and chattering, Emily driving and her mother, Beth, reading the map.

'You've gone wrong,' Beth announced.

Emily turned the car around. They drove slowly, peering at signs.

'There,' said Beth in triumph.

They parked. There was a languid silence. They were in Mount Wellington, on a street of shabby wooden houses. Number one, on the corner, was a tiny bungalow with a porch and a scruffy lawn in front. It was hard up against the concrete warehouse that had its entrance on the main road.

Emily looked behind. Bennie, her nephew, was grimacing behind his hands, shaking his head. He was a big boy, nearly ten. She tried a wry, ironic tone: 'It's meant to be good to see the body. It assists in "closure".' She scratched quotation marks in the air.

And Beth, who felt strongly on the subject, having been denied a look at her father when he'd died, and having dreamed he was alive for years afterwards, chimed in: 'It's crucial.'

But Bennie said, 'I didn't know her.'

'You met her,' Beth said good-naturedly.

He sighed. Deep gloom was Bennie's natural state.

They coaxed him from the car, watched by Antonia and Paul, his younger sister and brother, and Caro, Emily's daughter. He stood jigging, his hands in front of his mouth. There was a wide, strained smile on his face.

On the porch were two empty beer crates and an old couch. There was a big pile of shoes.

'I'm not taking mine off,' Emily said.

The door opened. The Reverend Matiu stood at the door in his socks. 'Aah, kia ora.' He stretched out his hands, kissed, made sounds of welcome and professional sorrow.

The children took off their shoes. Beth, looking guilty and vague, took hold of Bennie and yanked him into the hall, keeping hers on.

Emily followed. The Reverend looked pointedly at her shoes, then stepped back, allowing her to pass into the sitting room. The room was dim and very small. Net curtains covered the windows. A floral couch against one wall, a three-bar heater and a small TV mounted on a bracket high in a corner. In the middle of the room was the open coffin, in which Emily's aunt Jenny lay tucked up in a white lacy nightie. She'd been brought here, to her son Don's house, from the rest home where she'd died. Her hair was snowy white; her face was swollen and faintly shone, as though glazed.

Bennie took one look and retreated, covering his down-turned mouth.

'Ugh,' he said.

Chrissie greeted them. She was Emily's first cousin, and the Reverend Matiu's wife.

'Come and see Mum. You can talk to her, see.' She patted her mother's still forehead. 'We're glad you came, aren't we, Mum?' she said to the corpse.

Beth went close to the body, her fists clenched, eyeing it beadily as she might have looked at a piece of beef at the Remuera delicatessen: 'She looks very nice, Chrissie.'

'She's never left alone,' Matiu said. 'We talk to her, keep her company until she goes. In the Maori way.'

'That's right eh, Mum,' Chrissie said. 'Never leave you alone.' She stroked the dead white face. 'I'll make some coffee, eh?'

She took the children into the kitchen. The Reverend withdrew with a discreet cough, leaving them with the body.

Beth sank down, sighing, on the couch.

Emily said, 'The Reverend's taken over.'

'I don't suppose she minds.'

They looked guiltily at the coffin.

'We're not Maori, Jenny's not. Why do we have to do things the Maori way, just because Chrissie married one?'

'How about that coffee,' Beth said.

Emily bent to look at a photo on the wall. 'What about not leaving her alone?'

'Oh ... ' Beth waved her hand. 'We're going for coffee. All right?' she said to the body.

Emily followed her from the room.

Jenny's son, Don, was in the kitchen. He wore his peaked cap pulled low over his eyes. Two young Maori women came forward. Don gestured, awkward, looking away: 'Aunt Beth, my cousin Emily — this is my girlfriend Hine and her sister, May Rangi.'

Hine was thin and pretty; May Rangi was heavy, puffy-faced, her hands and arms marked with crude tattoos.

Hine went to the sink. 'I'll make coffees for youse. Chrissie's feeding the dogs.'

Through the door to the backyard Emily could see Caro standing near a slavering Rottweiler. The Reverend appeared.

'We're having coffee,' Beth said. 'Jenny doesn't mind.'

Matiu smiled in a forgiving way.

'She can hear us from here,' Don said from under his hat. He looked sideways at Beth and let out a giggle. Beth grinned.

Matiu pursed his lips. 'Ah, times of strife, eh,' he said into the air.

'It's very sad,' Beth said. 'We did have some nice times at the end.' She wiped away a tear.

'Kia ora,' Matiu said softly.

The dog barked. Caro shrieked.

'Is that dog all right with kids?' Emily asked.

'Get away you bugger,' Chrissie growled from outside. She crossed the yard wielding a big bone. The dog swiftly followed. There was another shriek.

'No, good as gold, mate,' Hine said comfortably. 'It's the other one you've got to watch, but he's got a muzzle on. Take no chances with him.'

May Rangi laughed. 'He's a bad one.'

Emily went out to the small concrete yard, bordered on one side by the warehouse wall and on the other by a corrugated-iron fence. On a wooden picnic table were three institution-sized cooking pots, one of which contained cuts of raw meat and bones. There was a barbecue and beside it a cactus grew in a concrete pot. The sun came into the yard and a gust of wind blew the fly strips on the door. Caro poked one of the dogs with a stick. It whipped its head around and stared at her, then turned back to its bone with a groan.

'Better not do that.' Chrissie took the stick. Bored, the children trailed inside. She wiped her hands on a stained towel. 'Is Uncle Per . . . ?'

Emily's father, Per Svensson, had been at his sister's bedside when she died — a prolonged, horrible dying: he'd described it to Emily, tonelessly, over the phone. Then he'd gone, not home, but to the studio where he worked. Emily had driven there after the phone call, wondering whether there was something she should do. She'd said, experimentally, 'You must feel very strange.' He didn't reply. She said, 'Should one . . . ?' They were at the door. He didn't invite her in. He was holding the cordless phone, pointing the aerial in front of him like a weapon. He looked fierce. She left. Whether he cared or not, she wasn't sure. But he wanted to be alone.

And now Emily's brother Larry and his wife Raine arrived. They were Bennie, Paul and Antonia's parents. Raine had been to an expensive school down south; her vowels had never recovered. 'Gorgeous shirt, Beth,' she said, reaching over to finger the breast pocket. 'I'm making a dress in that colour. It's going to have paua-pattern shoulder pads.' She smiled and smiled, widening her blue eyes.

'Lovely,' said Beth.

Larry stared and tensely grinned, as though he thought something was going to lunge at him and bite.

'How are you Larry?' The Reverend's tone was caressing.

Larry cleared his throat. He said faintly, 'Good, Matiu. Working seven days a week. It's a fairly big job I do. A lot of responsibility.' He stared at the Reverend, defiant, cornered, managing to sound pompous despite the thing that waited and watched.

'Poor Jenny,' Raine said. 'The children are with her. But Bennie's hiding in the car. He doesn't like bodies.' She let out an abrupt cackle.

In the sitting room the other three children were sitting in a row, their feet up on the edge of the coffin, watching *The Simpsons*.

Raine had one of her rushes of energy. She wrenched open the front door.

'Bennie,' she shrieked. The children looked up, startled.

She marched to the car and dragged him out, loudly telling him off. She hopped about on her thin legs. To the children, she sounded like a strange, harsh bird: Caw. Caw. She pulled Bennie into the room. But he shrugged and veered away and wouldn't look.

'It's only Mum,' Chrissie said, coaxing. 'Don't you think she looks lovely?'

'She looks dead,' he said rudely.

Raine yanked him into the hall. The door slammed. 'Locked him out,' she said. She gave her 'simple seamstress' smile.

Emily pulled back the net curtain. Black clouds were gathering over the street. The sun shone, and there was a strange, green-gold light. Colours were sharpened; for a moment the houses and fences gleamed, pearly-white, and then the clouds crossed the sun and the street went dreary and dark. It was hot. A strong gust stirred the rubbish on the grass. She saw her father's car turn slowly off the main road.

Beth and the Reverend got out a photograph album. There were ancient photos of Per and Jenny, little brother and sister, posed with their mother, playing at the beach. Twins, but different: already pulling away from one another, going in opposite directions. Later pictures: Jenny with her husband, the genial Barry, war veteran Mason, lawnmower salesman, who'd taken care of his invalid wife until he'd died. Their children, Emily's cousins: Don, Chrissie and Ray. Things had got tough long ago, when Jenny first fell ill. Don ran away to live with the Maoris at the end of the street. At seventeen Chrissie married a drug dealer who carried a gun (but now she was a vicar's wife). Ray was the solid, dependable one. He lived in America. He was in sales.

Emily went back out to the yard. Don stood looking over the fence, smoking. This was Don at family gatherings: his back to the group, his cap pulled down low, staring out at something, silent, absorbed. Waiting to be released.

The sky had turned dark over the warehouse roof. Emily watched a bird floating on the wind. Beams of sunlight broke through, shining on the twisted, hairy limbs of the cactus. She thought of the death notice she'd read that morning. It had been placed by Chrissie, Don and Ray: '*Mum. You were a breath of fresh air when all else failed.*'

Fresh air. When all else failed? She said it over to herself, frowning.

Don's shoulders twitched. She wondered, with a little thrill, whether he was crying. But he turned and ground his cigarette out on the wall, and in his blue eyes she saw something remote, secret, hard.

Larry burst through the plastic fly strips, brushing them aside, his chest puffed out, like a lifeguard emerging from the surf. He looked side to side and announced carefully, 'Hello.'

'How's work?'

He looked high-minded. 'It's fairly demanding, Emily. I'm handling literally millions of dollars of orders. I'm responsible for the whole city now. It'd be easier if I didn't have to spend so much time fixing other people's . . . ' But his voice trailed off. His eyes grew fixed. He was staring at the cactus. There was a silence.

'That's an interesting plant you've got there, Don. Is it . . . ?' He stood up and fingered the ugly, ridged green stalk.

'Yeah, it's one of those,' Don said. 'Boil it up, drink it, you're stoned out of your tree. Visions. Flying.' He spat over the fence. 'It's not my thing though, eh.'

Larry gave a strained smile. 'Not your thing,' he repeated.

But it was definitely *his*.

The clouds were rolling in, gathering against one another, dense and black. Emily drove along the Onehunga Mall. There were three children in the car now. Bennie, in disgrace, had been squashed into his parents' car with a group of relatives.

'Something stinks,' Caro whined.

'You were a breath of fresh air when all else failed,' Beth said in a faint voice. There was a heightened silence. They didn't dare look at one another.

Per was in the carpark talking to a slim woman in a blue dress. He leaned close and she threw back her head and laughed out loud.

Beth said thoughtfully, 'Per drives like the wind, doesn't he. Like a fiend.'

'This is Ray's wife, Sherry. From America,' Per said, very taken with the tall stranger who tossed her red hair and shook hands and said how nice to meet noo family. She was sorry it was the loss of Ray's mom that . . .

She was all smiles but Per abruptly tired of talking to her and said, 'Why don't we get started?' He glared around the group. Sherry was disconcerted; Beth looked amused. They started to file into the chapel.

Piped music played. At the front, by the closed coffin, stood a woman in a suit. She was the functionary laid on by Griefcare Funeral Services.

Heat from many bodies in a small space spread through the room. Children's heads drooped, the adults stared, open-mouthed, their eyes glazed. More piped music; they rose to sing. A series of prayers, more singing and then a pause. Emily looked up from a daydream. People were stretching and looking around; the woman in the suit waited with an encouraging smile. 'We can all share memories of Jenny's life. Who would like to be the first?'

Movement in the front row. Someone standing. And a sudden ripple — Per half-rising, signalling angrily, 'No.' Beth turned, startled.

It was Bennie, pushing his way along the row, ahead of everyone, about to 'share' something about his great aunt, whom he had met only once on a hospital visit, when he and the other kids had paid brief, unwilling homage before sitting out the boredom in the TV room with a row of tranced old folk. He was determined, frowning, his fists clenched. He turned to face the room.

But Per's ferocious expression made him waver. He paused. The silence seemed to last and last before, slowly, he made his way back to his place and sat down.

Emily craned to see his face. What an odd boy he was. He hadn't known Jenny at all. What on earth could he have been going to say?

The children came bouncing out with Chrissie's sons, who had made a speech about their grandmother in charming, piping voices.

Per said, 'I didn't mean to be *repressive*. But what was he going to tell us about Jenny? And to push in front of her grandchildren . . . ' He looked around. 'I suppose Raine and Larry are annoyed with me now.'

But Larry, striding out of the chapel, had his mind on other things. And Raine, who thought Bennie would at least have been well spoken, unlike some other people, only smiled and jabbed her son lightly and said, 'Zip up your fly.'

'Are you going to the wake?' Emily asked Larry.

'So it seems.' He glanced behind.

Talking to Larry was like interrupting a watchman on a lookout (on a parapet, on a tower of melodrama): he answered but he stared beyond at some dark distant thing, his replies were cursory, secretive, condescending, because you, poor innocent, didn't understand what was out there . . .

Three o'clock. Hot, mid-afternoon gloom. The city waiting for the storm that went on threatening but didn't break. The clouds were so black they looked purple; sometimes they parted for a moment and a ray of sun lit the green slopes of the mountain. Light and dark on the hillside, shifting shadows.

Emily was driving home. There was a gap in her vision, a black hole with glowing outlines. The pain was gathering, waiting to break through in unbearable streams. She was desperate to get home.

At the wake she had glanced up at the crowd and seen, opening up before her, a long shaft of pure blackness, as if her aunt had carelessly left open a doorway to death, and she was staring directly into it. She'd waited a moment, until she was sure the migraine was really coming, then she went looking for her mother.

And Beth had said, 'Bad luck. You go. We'll bring the kids home.'

She drove recklessly, yearning to be upstairs in the empty house, surrendering to it. She was capable of a kind of furious ecstasy during these crises of pain, and of a strange sense of luxury afterwards.

She shouldn't be driving. It was like accelerating into a black tunnel, its edges shimmering with vivid purples, starry greens. The visual distortions came first, the strange light effects, black holes. The pain was the second stage, the full force of the storm. Her eyes throbbed. And the sky, as if in answer, bulged and swelled with its own troubled atmospherics. The clouds hung heavy with rain, sheet lightning flashed, there was a rumble, then a crack of thunder. She thought the weather had brought the migraine on — the stifling sense of energy, pressure building. And the difficulty of talking to cousins she knew but ought to have known better. Per and Jenny had been twins but remarkably different. There hadn't been many occasions when the families had got together. There were the bare outlines: Jenny's husband was dead; her son Don, since running away to live with the Maoris in his teens now spoke, lived, and looked like a Maori, and ran a stall with Hine and May Rangi at the Otara Market. Chrissie, along with the Reverend Matiu, had some line in good works (social work, counselling?) Ray (the boring one) had escaped to the States. They all had children whom Emily didn't know, although Per had mused, after meeting a daughter of Don: 'Funny about the genes. I felt as if I was talking to my *mother*.'

Emily drove with one eye closed. The visual distortion, the agonised hour in the darkened room, then the languid recovery — it was an intense, private battle. As she turned into her street the sky unleashed itself. Rain spotted then blurred the windscreen, and intensified to a roar. The noise on the car roof was tremendous. The last barrier broke inside her head and the pain flooded in.

Lying on her bed upstairs it occurred to her: this is what dying will be like. And she thought of that first warning at the wake, the shaft of absolute blackness splitting the air, as if a door had opened to . . .

Larry was alone. He got out of the car. Everyone was still at the wake and he had slipped away, saying he wanted to buy cigarettes. Don's house, hard up against the warehouse wall, was small, shabby and deserted. He knocked on the door and called, 'Hello.'

There was a garish pulse of light, followed by an abrupt boom. He stepped off the porch and peered down the south side of the house. The gap between the house and the warehouse wall was too narrow — or was it? Could he squeeze his way along to the backyard? He imagined, with a shiver of laughter, getting stuck halfway; his smothered cries, scenes of consternation as they returned from the wake. On the other side of the house, a corrugated-iron fence blocked the way. Larry dithered, looking at his watch.

Next door was a 'duplex' — two state houses stuck together and sharing a front yard. There was a driveway, a dead car on the lawn, and windows patched with hardboard where the glass was broken. There was no sign of life. He walked along the drive, until he was level with Don's back garden. He could see the cactus, up against the barbecue, too far away to reach — he would have to climb the fence. He glanced back at the duplex and thought he saw one of the blinds move. He couldn't wait; they might be calling the police already.

He began to climb the fence. It was rickety and unstable. When he was wobbling on the top of it the iron buckled. He lurched sideways to steady himself, cut his hand, and his jacket snagged. For a second he struggled, teetering, and he chose to fall forwards — no going back. He landed in the yard, his jacket ripped, his hand bleeding.

He peeped over the fence. A window had opened next door. He ducked down. The sky was black and the green cactus rose, no *reared*, against it, looking . . . magnificent. He was struck with such an exquisite sense of comedy that he leaned back against the fence and shook. Here he was, preparing to steal (and for what a bad, immoral purpose) while the family, all ignorant, were solemnly grinding through Aunt Jenny's wake. He felt in his pocket for the knife, and the fact that he'd swiped it off the refreshment table half an hour before struck him as hilarious. It really was true: he had the funniest time when he was alone.

He inspected the plant, gauging how he could cut the most off without it being noticed. He was expert at brewing up this kind of cactus; if you did it properly it would keep you high for days. What visions, what vistas. It was like booking the most exotic and dangerous holiday. Absolute secrecy was required of course. He had a private place where he could brew up — a flat belonging to a friend. He began to saw. Careful. Mustn't be greedy.

A car door slammed. His scalp prickled at the thought of being discovered. Especially if his father . . . He felt cold at the thought of Per. Don't panic. Don't give up now. The stem was tough but he got through it with a last effort. He wrapped it in the torn jacket, climbed the fence, and was up the neighbour's driveway in a flash. He tipped the jacket into the trunk of his car and drove away, stopping at the petrol station for cigarettes and a plaster for his hand.

Raine had been searching for him. He looked strange, pale, almost radiant.

'Larry. Larry.'

The children lifted their heads, startled.

He went obediently towards her.

Beth was in her kitchen, looking out at the storm. The house backed onto a reserve. The trees were tossing in the wind, and the rain lashed down. It was hot and steamy. At the table little Caro was making a potion. She put in detergent, flour, instant coffee, sugar, salt, pepper.

Per had gone to his studio, two doors along. He had been in a rage on the way home. She'd talked about Jenny and it had irritated him. She had felt him wincing and withdrawing. They had all four grandchildren in the back of the car, and only Bennie might have noticed that Per's silence and her talk stood for something. Me banging my head against a brick wall, she thought. Me kicking down his door.

Caro added tea leaves and Ajax to her mixture. She broke a glass.

'Careful,' Beth said calmly.

She picked up the broken pieces. The other grandchildren were downstairs. She had invited all four to stay the night.

It was sad about Jenny. She wanted to talk about it, have the odd luxurious cry. Per knew this, and reacted with cold contempt, as though she were a frivolous tourist traipsing through his private battlefield. What would he say? 'Be sad if you like. I'm not stopping you. You don't need me.'

Now he was alone, locked in his studio. He would never tell her what he really felt. He was hypersensitive, difficult. It was unfair . . . Beth missed her younger daughter Marie. But she was far away, in London.

'I want to cook it,' Caro begged. 'Please.' She wrapped her arms around her grandmother's waist.

Sighing, Beth poured the mixture into a cake tin. She opened the oven.

'We'll turn the heat up really high,' she said, sliding in the tin.

Caro nodded. 'We'll feed it to people,' she whispered. 'Make them go funny.'

They sat together at the table, and soon the mixture began to heat up, sending a pungent, unpleasant stink out into the reserve.

Late in the evening, when the storm was at its height, the lights went out. Per walked through the house, trying switches. He went outside. The power was out all along the street. He remembered he'd left a window open in his studio. He felt for his keys, closed the door behind him and ran two houses along. He worked in the top half of this second house, and rented out the bottom storey, which was converted into a flat. He went to the window and looked out at the reserve. As far as he could see beyond the park the city was in darkness. The wind roared, sighed, howled in the big trees. When Jenny was dying he had sat at the bedside and listened to the terrible, harsh gasps, and he had closed his eyes and silently begged it to stop. Please, please stop suffering, die. He'd wanted to block his ears, to put a pillow over her face, and he'd sat, stony-faced and listened, in agony. At some point he'd stood at the window and seen, far away, a ship sailing out past the islands towards the open sea. He'd walked out of the room. The doctor was by the nurses' station. Per said, 'She tried to commit suicide last year. She was brave, it was her choice. They brought her round. Why?' And the doctor, a young man, looked at him with tired, intelligent eyes and said, 'She hasn't got long.'

Per stood in the dark. He saw her aged thirteen, coming up the street. Vivid, pretty. Slamming the gate, hurrying, angry about something. Sun on the garden, on the dry stone wall. Late summer. The smell of cut grass. Her dress. Her hands. She frowned and shouted over her shoulder at him, and ran off up the path.

He felt a crushing weight, his chest froze, and a sense of horror came over him. He sank down and sat on the floor in the dark, his hands over his face.

Images ran through his mind. The Reverend Matiu, an Anglican vicar, but still cleaving to the Maori way, talking to the body, never leaving it alone. Strange. It's good to have respect. But to stroke the body and converse with it, to pretend that it can hear? I could have pulled its hair, I could have pissed on it, what difference would it make? *The damage is done.* Her grandchildren believed she was in heaven. But there's no God, he thought. Matiu's church, all churches, are an intellectual slum. We come from dust and return to dust. There's nothing — no door — behind the sky. She bored me, irritated me, filled me with guilt. She married a simpleton; I had an intellectual life. But in the dying, emptying face I saw something, felt it, raged against it. The destruction of part of myself.

He walked slowly back to the house. Beth came up from the lower floor carrying a torch. They lit candles and sat in the living room, watching the white flashes lighting up the trees. The candle flames made shadows on the walls.

Per put two candles on the side table so he could read. He

rearranged them, trying to get the best light. She watched him angrily. That's how he is, she thought. He works. He reads. Life goes on. It's as if nothing had happened. It's unbearable.

She threw her book aside. 'How can you read?'

He said stiffly, 'I'll get another candle.'

She turned to him, imploring. 'Say something. Please.' She put her arms around him, squeezing him tight, begging him to understand how she felt.

He sat silent, looking over her head, into the black shapes beyond the glass.

Everything was quiet and still. At 4am the wind had died. The rain had stopped. Per and Beth were asleep, but downstairs the children sat in a circle round a lit candle, dividing a horde of sweets.

Caro didn't like the strange shadows leaping on the walls. She moved closer to Paul. There were three green lollipops, and one yellow. Yellow was much nicer.

'Don't touch,' commanded Antonia, and Caro whipped her hand away.

They listened. Bennie pulled back the curtain. In the reserve the trees were still, and there was a streak of pale light, like a seam, in the black sky. Antonia counted out the sweets, arranging them in piles. Bennie watched her ironically.

'You're such a control freak, Antonia,' he said.

They were silent again. Caro kneeled up on Bennie's bed, looking out the window.

'Let's go out there,' she whispered.

'It's wet,' he said kindly.

But Antonia sat up and snapped her fingers. 'Good idea.'

Caro tried to look solemn, and beamed. 'Really? Shall we?' she said loudly. They shushed her.

Antonia crept upstairs. She took two more candles, Per's biggest umbrella and a box of matches. They put on their clothes.

The lock on the back door was stiff and creaked loudly. They would have to climb out the window. Bennie eased the window open and climbed down the trellis. They got Caro onto the windowsill and dropped her down to him. She landed awkwardly, knocking him over. He put his hand over her mouth.

Antonia threw down the supplies, and she and Paul slid down and dropped onto the grass.

'How are we going to get back in?' Paul asked.

Caro stared at the dark trees, which could have been hiding something unseen and terrible. Everything looked different. She tried to make out shapes and outlines but the trees looked to her like huge figures, their arms outstretched, bending towards her. Above the reserve the sky was dark, streaked here and there with stray gleams of light. All around was the rustling and gurgling of water in the drenched grass, and far away a sighing roar, as if they could hear the last of the storm passing out of the city and whirling away, over the dark countryside and out to sea. There were so many sounds, and yet everything was so still, it seemed that the park was holding itself in check, waiting.

'There might be a homeless person,' Antonia said.

There was a sudden rustling in the trees and a series of harsh, coughing barks. They moved close together. They knew it was a possum, but it was such an eerie sound they felt unnerved, until Paul darted forward and hurled a stick. The possum went quiet. They heard it crashing about in the branches, heavy and ungainly.

Caro looked at the sky and saw that the grey seam had grown wider, that a pearly light was coming from it. Inside that opening was the daytime. It was still dark, but the trees were no longer so black and monstrous, and as she watched, a fine, delicate rim of pink appeared on the edge of the clouds. There was a squall of wind and the trees heaved, sighed, subsided.

They walked through the park, away from the houses. Antonia knelt down and lit the candles, setting them carefully on the path. They sat beside her and she put the umbrella up over them. They huddled in the circle of flickering light. There was a long dreamy silence. They watched the light turning gradually from dark to grey, and soon the colours of the trees and flowers began to show, and there were sparkles of light in the drenched grass. A bright patch gleamed at the edge of a roof and a streak of light came over the corrugated iron and shone on the trees. The clouds had frayed in places and there were pale spots that might soon become blue sky. They listened to a rat scuttling in the bushes, a car starting up in the street, the possum again, further away, making its harsh purr. A bird flew up and wheeled away, cheeping indignantly. Another beam of light crossed the grass, a twig cracked, a second bird started.

Caro looked at the seam in the sky with the daytime inside it. She'd never been outside in the night before. It was beautiful, mysterious, solemn. The darkness changed the shape of things and the dawn changed them back. When I grow up I will go out every night, she thought. And she saw a grey cat sitting on the path, watching her with unblinking eyes. It walked across the park, picking its way delicately through the wet stalks, its fur covered with tiny diamonds of dew.

First thing in the morning, Saturday, Larry went to visit his friend. They boiled up and consumed his stolen prize. Then he went home to work in his garden, a long, steep section that he and Raine had terraced and cultivated. He had made a bird table, and he watched as the sparrows and blackbirds squabbled and hopped and pecked. The garden was full of life. He moved through it, his head pleasantly buzzing. The sun was hot on his back; he was dazzled in the bright light. He had cut down a small dead tree and was chopping it into pieces in order to carry it down the hill and load it on a trailer. He was enormously strong. The dead wood splintered, chips flew around him. Words came into his head and seemed to hang there, glowing, like paintings in a dark room. Yellowhammer. Kingfisher. Blackbird. The leaves shone, the palms were yellow, buttery. The air was full of tiny insects that scattered, regrouped, streamed through the brightness. Chop. Chop. The air flew apart, whirled to the sound of his axe. He worked fast, singing parts of songs.

When the tree was all in pieces he stopped and looked up. At the top of the hill, a few feet away from him, a man was watching him. He stood against the blue sky, moving slightly. He was all in black. His clothes were so black that they seemed to Larry to be an absence of matter, as if the shape of a man had been cut out of the blue sky, revealing a void behind. Larry stared, gripping his axe. He lifted it slightly. The man made a gesture: careless, scornful, as if to say that nothing could touch him. Then he came slowly down the path.

Larry dropped the axe and backed away. He blinked. The man had gone.

He went inside and locked himself in the bathroom. He looked at himself in the mirror. His pupils were large and dark. He sat on the edge of the bath. After a while, he had a shower.

He walked into the sitting room. Raine was talking to his mother on the phone. She clapped down the receiver and said, 'I've got to finish the wedding dress. You pick the children up.'

The wedding dress, commissioned by an old friend from school, was spread over the dining table. The table and floor were cluttered with paper and material and scissors and pins. The material was buttery, slippery, shimmery. It seemed to Larry to have a kind of rippling life in it; if he moved his head it looked like a stream of liquid running over the table and onto the floor of the sunny room. His wife stood with a piece of material over her arm, the sun behind her, lit up like a saint.

He went out and stood in the street and stared at the leaves, the patterns they made, light on dark. He looked at the hard blue sky, the atoms dancing in it. Raine opened the window and shouted from upstairs, 'Take them to the park. And get something for dinner.'

Larry waved vaguely and got in the car. The steering wheel was hot. He enjoyed the acceleration as he shot away from the kerb. After last night's storm the city was fresh and glittering, the sky blue, every outline sharp, with the photographic clarity of a perfect Auckland summer day. Mount Eden was wearing a shimmering halo of paler light. Larry drove and the air parted in front of him, silvery, liquid. He shot through it, as quick as a fish.

Bennie let him into his parents' house. He looked warily around for his father, but Per liked to spend Saturday afternoons in his studio. His mother got up slowly. The children milled around her, Caro with her vivid little face, like a troll. They were a cluster of trolls, gnomes, in a warm cave. Antonia did something with a roll of tin foil; he stared at the trail of silver it left in the air.

They were saying things.

'We went out in the dark. We had to knock on the door to get back in. They got a surprise. We made a cake. Look.'

Cake. A funny word.

His daughter gnome. Snaky blonde hair. His elder son, the light on his spectacles, so you couldn't see his eyes. Silver-eye. Wax-eye. Peeping at him from behind the opaque glasses. And the air, the way it parted as he came forward, the weight of the air, not silvery in here but warm and blurred.

She handed him a cup. Steam curled and slipped through the light. Careful, he thought. It was harder to keep steady in here.

He crossed to the kitchen and looked out at the trees. There was a trench of dark shadow beneath them. He listened to the drops of sound the tuis made, cluck, click, scratch, a pause, then a 'plonk', like a stone falling into water. Rosellas flew from tree to tree, flashing their bright reds and greens and yellows.

The trolls ran in and out, leaving scatterings of disturbed sound. His mother said something. He sipped his coffee, rigged up a smile then struggled to get rid of it. He turned its full beam on Paul, who looked disconcerted and ducked his head.

Larry put the cup down, but it hit the edge of the sink and cracked. He stood over his children, fighting down the smile. 'Off we go.'

At the door he wondered whether anyone had noticed the cracked cup. 'The air can be very . . . heavy,' he observed quietly.

He swooped out to the car, hoping this would cover it.

'Where are we going?' Bennie asked.

'Killing time,' he told them. He thought about this phrase. It chimed in his head.

Killing time.

He drove them to the top of Mount Eden. They got out and looked over the suburbs. 'It's so beautiful,' he said. There were puffy clouds in the west; from them the sun shot down beams of light, what the Maoris called the ropes of Maui. He pointed. The children looked obediently, shading their eyes. They lay in the grass watching the clouds move in. The wind blew in the white flowers. Above them, on the ridge, busloads of tourists chattered, smoked and clicked cameras.

The drive down the winding mountain road was exhilarating. He stopped and bought ice creams. But when they got home he'd forgotten about the supermarket. Raine shouted and complained. He watched her from across the room. She snapped and sparkled. The air flew away from her, sensitive to sound. After a while she went out to buy groceries, taking Paul and Bennie with her. He was left alone with Antonia. She turned on the television.

Six dressmaker's dummies lived in an apartment. Three male, three female. They talked; in answer, from somewhere unseen, came waves of laughter. The dummies tossed manes of blow-dried hair. Their mouths opened and closed. Their voices were nasal: quack quack quack. The laughter came blowing back, first a trickle, then a gust, then a real shriek. He listened to the quacking and laughing, and he became aware that Antonia, sitting on the floor in front of him, was part of the pattern; she leaned back and kicked her feet and squeak squeak, drew her elbows into her sides and giggled into her cupped hands.

He got up. He pointed the remote control and pressed the red button. There was a dry click. The dummies disappeared.

Antonia flew at him, grabbing for the remote, whining, cajoling. She made noises: 'Aw. Aw.' He held her off. Fantail. Silver-eye. Tui. She was as light as a bird.

She stopped trying to grab the remote. She stood up. Her eyes filled. She stared at him with her liquid eyes: a lost look. 'Why are you *smiling*?'

She ran away upstairs. Her bedroom door slammed.

He followed her, light-heartedly tiptoeing up the stairs. He stood outside her door, listening. He knocked softly. Silence. He knocked again. He could sense her in there, frozen, like a little animal. He went on knocking for a while, until he forgot why he was doing it. He laid the TV remote outside her door, went downstairs and outside. He saw there were some weeds. He began pulling them out, kneeling on the concrete path, absorbed.

NYMPH

When Simon Lampton saw Viola Myers in the street for the first time in two years, he couldn't help himself. He gave her such a foul look that his whole face contorted.

Viola, who had been regarding him in a cool and neutral fashion, sharpened up. She looked suddenly interested. Later, he would remember this change in her expression. It was as if he'd dropped his shield and she saw it, and somehow she was engaged. Activated.

Simon got to his office and sat down at his desk. He looked at his hands. A line of yellow sunshine came into the room and played on the photo of Karen. He thought about the incident with Viola and his father. It still gave him pain.

For years the old man, Aaron Harris, had caused so much trouble that Simon had frequently wished him dead. They never spoke except when Aaron rang drunk, and raved until Simon hung up.

Once, on the way to work, he had seen his father's car parked on a patch of waste ground near the city. Later when he was driving home it was still there, and it had come to him that the old man was inside it, dead. He'd stopped the car on the side of the road, surprising himself with the strength of his feeling. Grief and pity, sudden shaming tears. But later still, when he drove slowly back, the car was gone, and his feelings closed over, leaving him cold. He caught glimpses of Aaron every now and then, the old man making his way through the city, conducting his presumably shady affairs. Aaron existed in a parallel universe, and as Simon moved through his own world a connection would open, and he would blink at the sight of the old man cruising along the street in his battered car, cutting across him, the familiar profile set in a leer of mad, scarecrow defiance, shrieking off round a corner with a taunting parp on the horn and a foul blast of phantom exhaust.

Viola Myers had been taken on as a temporary assistant in Simon's medical practice. She was strange, intense, lawless. She had plagued him with her staring. She was unnerving; she seemed to be in some kind of maneating overdrive that made her lamp him wherever he went. The practice manager Clarice said that Viola was absolutely hopeless. She was dreamy, impractical and ungovernable. One afternoon Clarice came back from her break and discovered Viola lounging with her feet on the desk reading a fat medical file. 'As if it was a novel,' Clarice said. When admonished, Viola had seemed amused. Clarice was already campaigning for her removal.

Aaron Harris had been borrowing a taxi from a friend and driving night shifts. He was invariably drunk when he picked people up. Simon and Karen, and Simon's brother Ford, had worried about this. Simon said to Ford, 'Why does he go on inflicting this on us?'

By chance, while driving the cab late one stormy night, Aaron had spotted young Viola toiling home from the pub. He had stopped and picked her up. During the journey they had got to talking. They'd soon established there was a connection between them — Simon — and on the strength of that, had gone back to Aaron's squalid little flat for a drink. Some time after Viola had rung Simon in a panic from Aaron's flat, saying that his father had gone berserk, and asking him to help her.

He had hesitated only a moment before ringing the police. Then he'd rushed over, extracted her and, after a stop at the police station, had taken her back to their house. The old man was banned from driving taxis after that. He had no income and had gone into a serious decline.

Simon had been glad to help Viola, since she'd genuinely seemed to need rescuing. But in some part of his mind he disliked her too. She had linked the worlds he'd tried to keep separate. Through her he had struck the blow against Aaron that he had wanted and not wanted to strike. Aaron took an overdose of pills not long after. A neighbour found him. He was clinically dead for a minute in the ambulance. He recovered, discharging himself from hospital and carrying on just as before. Simon thought it was rage that kept Aaron going. Rage and malice. You all want me dead, don't you. That would suit you just fine. *Well, I won't go.*

Simon suspected that Viola guessed his inner conflict, and that the awful subtleties were interesting to her. Until she went to another job he avoided her, closing down any attempt she made to talk, and allowing Clarice to deal with her. His feelings about her were tinged with a sense of blackness, guilt, unease.

Viola got a job working at the Auckland Museum. Simon had seen her a few times when he was walking to the hospital. She didn't seem to pay him particular attention when they passed each other one evening. She greeted him neutrally; no sign of the mad grin that used to play over her face. That expression of hers, it used to make his hair stand on end. He supposed she'd grown up, calmed down. He assumed the incident with his father was forgotten.

And then one summer, when he and Karen were lounging on the deck of their beach house at Whangamata, Karen had suddenly shaken the newspaper, leaned forward and said in a high voice, 'Simon, look at this.'

The paper had been running a story competition, and was publishing placegetters. There was a full-page story by Viola Myers from Auckland, third-prize winner. It was called, 'The Moneys.'

Karen was making small, indignant sounds. She shook the paper under his nose. 'Read it.'

Simon straightened up unwillingly. Karen thrust the paper onto his lap, went to the verandah rail and stood with her hands on her hips. She turned and pointed her finger.

'I told you you couldn't trust her,' she said.

In the story, Viola had used detail from the incident all those years ago. She had Simon thinly disguised as 'Mr Money', a 'top surgeon'. She had described the young woman based on herself as 'a student'. She had spent a lot of time on the character of the father. Here was Aaron Harris, renamed old Mr Money, in all his drunk, foul-mouthed, raving glory. His 'spittle-flecked face', 'blackened teeth' and 'yellow skin'.

But Simon saw, grimly reading while Karen paced about his deckchair, that Viola's story had managed to transform the Aaron Harris character into a kind of victim. There were romanticised passages about old Money's musical brilliance, some complete invention to the effect that the old man's wife (Simon's mother, how dare she) had been insensitive to her husband's talents, that this might have contributed to his descent into alcoholism.

Worse, Viola's story managed to insinuate that young Mr Money and his disgraceful father were just two sides of the same flawed hereditary coin. Where old Money was 'drunk and damaged', young Money was 'cold and materialistic'. Young Money rebuffed the old man's approaches and retreated into his life of wealth and privilege, content to let the 'struggling old pianist' rot.

It made Simon angry when he thought about it now, the nerve of it: for her to intrude into his private life when she had no idea about him, not a care about the pain she might cause.

Further on, and even more disturbingly, in a scene in which the student was brought back to young Money's 'palatial Epsom dwelling', Viola had cast the young female character in a distinctly ambiguous light. Here, he had to acknowledge, she had been as hard on the student as she had on the Moneys. The student was seen by Mr and Mrs Money to grin, to stare around the room with undisguised interest, to appear not so much traumatised by her experience as diverted and amused and even, at one point, to be enjoying their discomfort. If this was how it really had been, if Viola had just been amusing herself at their expense then she was, as Karen was now saying, an evil little bitch.

Mrs Money was cattily described as a fat blonde with joggling cheeks and blue veins snaking up the backs of her legs. Mr Money's face was 'a florid mask of fury'. At the end Viola had Mr Money bundling the student into his large, powerful car, taking her home to her 'simple rented flat' and pushing her out into the rain, but not before the student had made some sinister observations about 'what this might mean to your social position if any of this comes out'.

This was why, seeing her in the street for the first time since the story had been published, he had dropped his guard and given Viola a look of frank and undisguised loathing. A mistake. The look she had given him was a sudden refocusing, like a cat fixing its eye on a movement in the grass, the stilling before the abrupt flash of claws.

Getting ready for the evening, Viola had her mind on Simon Lampton. She was sure he must have read the story. There could be no other reason for that black look. The way he'd scowled, he'd looked nearly as angry as his father. The story must have created quite an effect. It was daring of her, wasn't it. He must think she was coldly audacious. As a real writer should be. Would he admire her nerve? The way she'd made no bones about portraying the student's attitude as questionable and the doctor and his wife as sheltered and privileged. It wasn't that this represented the truth. But you had to write as if the real world didn't matter.

She leaned close to the mirror. She needed reading glasses, but when she had them on she couldn't get around them to apply make-up, although she did her best, poking the eye pencil behind the lenses. She tried asking her flatmate Kate if her eyes looked all right and Kate looked up briefly from the TV and said, 'Yeah, fine.' Not reassuring. There was no one else to ask.

Grant would be here in half an hour. She was hungry, but there was nothing in the kitchen except some tins of soup, and anyway they belonged to Kate.

She'd been going out with Grant for six months. He worked for a company that carried out polling and market research. He had joint custody of two kids, Sarah and Jacob. Since her parents' divorce, eight-year-old Sarah had got into the habit of having accidents. The first time, she was found lying motionless at the bottom of a climbing frame. She said she couldn't move, and an ambulance was called. After a long wait at casualty, Grant and his ex-wife were told that there was nothing wrong, and that they should take her home. After this had happened twice they began to wonder, and on the third occasion they realised that Sarah was faking. There was a lull and then she did it again. The hospital referred her to a psychiatrist.

Viola sensed Grant watching her when she was with his kids. She knew she was good with them. They were easy to get along with. Sarah's only kink was her fondness for drama and hospitals. Viola had a talent for making them laugh. She could diffuse difficult situations, like long, boring car rides, by making the kind of hammy jokes they loved. Grant was grateful. He said, 'You're brilliant with the kids.'

Viola said, slowly, as if she'd only just thought about it, 'I've never been interested in kids. But now I've met yours . . . '

'Well, maybe one day you'll have one of your own,' Grant said, and she looked at him neutrally, hiding the quick, secret thrill.

There was a small fact that she hid because it didn't matter and did no harm: she didn't feel much for Sarah and Jacob. What she wanted was one of her own. Her kindness to Sarah and Jacob was a signal to Grant as much as it was just that: kindness.

She knew Grant had had other girlfriends. She had secret fits of jealousy and searched his house like a cop when she got the chance, shaking her head and wondering aloud at herself. What am I doing?

She was waiting for him to ask her to move in. But he'd been hurt before. His wife had run off with another man. He was in no hurry. She knew she had to give him time. Without thinking about it, she had grown a kind of shell. Instinct told her to hide what she wanted. She feigned slow surprise at her success with the children. She pretended she'd never cared for babies. She mentioned how much she liked her independence.

Grant was easy-going, but under the surface he was sharp. She didn't know how well he knew her. She couldn't be sure.

He never opened a book himself, but he often mentioned her

writing. At parties he would push her forward, 'This is Viola. She's a writer.' Most people looked neutral, or faintly sceptical. Some asked her if she wrote children's books or romances. Some drew her aside to talk about the novel they'd always wanted to write. She would be embarrassed, 'I'm just starting out really.' But she felt superior too. People who said they wanted to write a novel usually turned out to have only a vague idea about writing. Certain things gave them away. If you asked them what they were reading and they couldn't come up with a single title. Or they mentioned a piece of pulp fiction with innocent reverence. After that, all she could do was nod and smile.

'Your teeth look red,' Grant said, as they stood outside the bar. He and some people from his company had been invited to a party, the end of year celebration for the staff of a Sunday newspaper magazine.

Viola laughed. 'It's beetroot. From the salad.'

He put his index finger gently on her teeth and rubbed.

'Better?' she said, her lips against his skin.

He stood back. 'Perfect,' he said. He was apologising, she thought, for being distracted during dinner.

Her head was already spinning with the wine they'd drunk. She threaded her way into the crowd, and accepted a glass of darkly sticky fizzy stuff from a man who shouted, 'Champagne cocktail.'

The music was loud; her head throbbed and buzzed with each jangling chord.

She took a sip of the drink. It was strong stuff.

It was a fashionable crowd. She recognised a clothes designer, a gossip columnist, some journalists from TV and the papers. She joined Grant, trying to hear what was being said over the noise.

Her mind wandered. Last night she'd dreamed she was walking through a crowd of people under a canopy of huge trees; light angling down through the branches, bright beams of revolving dust. Simon Lampton was walking away, across an open plain. Dry tussock, waving grass. A voice said, 'This is the suede landscape.' She crossed into bright light, following; a gust of wind blew down and bent the tussock into a blonde path. She hurried after him, against the wind, Simon Lampton walking away.

Someone took the glass out of her hand and replaced it with a full one. Viola took a gulp and had the troubling sense that her head was floating up towards the ceiling.

Grant was explaining something to a woman. He gripped her arm and whispered in her ear, and she drew back, giving him a glare of affectionate reproach.

Viola plucked at his sleeve. 'Grant?'

Just perceptibly, he pulled his arm away.

She went to the bar and waited, looking around for someone to talk to. She felt awkward, not knowing anyone. She asked for a drink of iced water.

It didn't matter that he had pulled away from her. It didn't mean anything. She told herself this. But she felt suffocated. Something gnawed inside her, a desperate impatience. If only she could break through whatever it was that was holding her back, things would change. She thought, I won't be able to bear it if things don't change.

She took the iced water and faced the room. Everyone was standing in tight groups, and it would be hard to break in. She knew that if she held her nerve the groups would break up and she'd get a chance to join in. But she was sick of the inner voice that made sensible decisions like this. There was too much putting up with things she didn't enjoy in the hope that something better would come. If I keep going, if I don't panic, if I just keep my head ... She thought of Sarah's 'accidents' — the girl spread-eagled under the climbing frame, the adult world in a flurry of emergency action above her.

Viola felt she had to do something. The only thing she could think of was to put her glass down and walk out into the street.

Outside, the air was blurred with fine, misty rain. She felt better in the fresh air. Her head cleared. She walked under the shop verandahs, heading for the main road.

She would have to walk home. It was too late for a bus. She didn't want to catch a taxi. With her pay from the museum she could hardly afford rent and bills.

It was late and there weren't many people about. Cars flashed by occasionally. The streetlights had haloes of whirling rain and the street was dotted with puddles that looked like bright holes in the asphalt. Viola regretted her shoes, which pinched her feet. Her hair had glued itself clammily to her face. She walked on.

A small, tan car drove past and pulled up just ahead of her with a brisk little squeal of tyres. The driver leaned across and was winding down the window. His face was turned sideways and beaming out at her: gingery hair, a bushy moustache, freckled features. An anxious, rabbity grin.

'Want a ride? ' he called in a reedy voice, bobbing about, craning his neck and hoisting his mouth into a desperate smirk. He was in his fifties, thin, with frail wrists sticking out of his sleeves. Viola hesitated. The wind blew a shower of drops down onto her shoulders. He looked harmless. Not a physical threat. Anything was better than trudging through the rain.

She climbed in.

He said, rubbing his dry old hands together, 'Well, well. What are you doing out in the rain? Has your car broken down?'

There was a strong smell of menthol. He was wearing tweed. Was it tweed? It was checked and thick, with a hairy texture. He had on a jacket with leather patches on the elbows. Camel-coloured trousers.

He stroked his moustache, rigged up the desperate grin again and said with an air of swashbuckling nonchalance, 'Well, well.'

Viola looked at him. What a weirdo. Look at him. Those sideburns. And what was it with the accent? Prince Charles. Sherlock Holmes.

'I'm just trying to get home,' she said.

'Where's that then?' he asked gallantly.

'Grafton.'

'Ah,' he said, working the long, old-fashioned gear stick as if he was stirring a large pot, managing to plunge it into first, then second. The old car groaned deep in its innards and began to chug mournfully up the hill.

'Peter,' he said, and added a surname, something double-barrelled.

He offered a gingery old paw sideways. She shook. 'Viola,' she said.

'And do you have a line of work, Viola?' There was something suggestive in his tone; he gave her a thrilled, pop-eyed grimace.

She shifted in her seat. The old car seat squeaked and groaned. 'I work at the museum,' she said, sounding affronted. They were shuddering and bumping down Symonds Street now; she stared out as they crossed the motorway bridge, above the river of lights streaming out to the south.

'I'm a printer by trade,' he said. He lowered his voice. 'Do you like cricket, Viola?'

'Watching it I suppose.'

'Ah yes. I like to watch,' he said, squaring his shoulders, staring tightly ahead. 'I'm a cricket umpire.'

They drove across Grafton Bridge, the car picking up speed on the flat, snorting along like an old dog with its snout to the ground. The man, Peter, sat up straight and peered out, his nose almost pressed against the windscreen. The short, old-fashioned wipers jerked ineffectually across the glass.

'You can drop me here,' Viola said, pointing to the top of her street. They were on the edge of the Domain, the dark trees shifting and sighing in the wind. Across the road at the hospital, in the white light from a neon sign, a man in a robe was leaning on a drip stand and having his cigarette lit for him by another man, while a woman paced in front of them, smoking and gesticulating.

He pulled over. She thanked him and went to get out. The trees heaved suddenly in the wind. A large wet leaf landed on the windscreen.

'I say,' he said. She paused. He steadied himself with a series of manly coughs and harrumphs, before fixing her with a moist, ardent gaze. 'I say, you do seem very nice. Do you, I mean, would you, be at all interested in an enema?'

She stared.

'An enema,' he said earnestly. 'It's a sort of tube thing, rather thrilling, if you . . . '

'An enema,' she repeated.

He held up his hands, alarmed. 'Look here, it's just a bit of fun.

Quite safe. You do it to one another. Or whatever combination you like really. I just thought you might be interested.'

'Are you joking?'

'No no. Just a bit of fun. When I was at school . . . '

She slammed the door, leaving him bobbing and waving his hands and mouthing through the glass. After a moment the car started, the gears clashed and the car jerked quickly away from the curb. She watched him drive into the dark heart of the Domain, until only the brake lights on the back of the car were visible, and then he shot round a bend under the canopy of trees and was gone.

It was two o'clock in the morning. Viola lay in bed and reviewed the evening. Dinner with Grant, during which he'd been tired and distracted after a bad week. The party: everyone remote and glamorous and uninterested in her. Grant pulling his arm away and flirting. (Was he flirting? Yes, he definitely was.) The walk in the rain, finishing with a ride home in an ancient car and the strangest invitation she had ever received.

Why had she got in the car with a strange man? She could have been murdered. Maybe that was what she'd wanted. To be carried away, horribly beaten, found dead somewhere. Instead he had come out with that bizarre suggestion. She let out a short, appalled laugh. It was idiotic of her to get in the car. She'd got what she deserved.

She turned on the light and sat down at her desk. She opened her diary.

> Chapter two, she wrote.
> When Dr Simon Lampton saw Viola Myers in the street for the first time in two years, he couldn't help himself. He gave her such a foul look that his whole face contorted.

She made herself a cup of tea and got into bed. She went into a deep sleep. Later she dreamed that she had stopped breathing. She needed to draw breath but couldn't make herself. She struggled. She was on a spiral staircase, in darkness. The steps went down and down and there was no end. She thought, no, this is one of those dreams that just goes on and gets worse, I'm not having it, and felt herself bursting out of it with huge effort. She woke up.

There was someone in the room.

She said, 'Kate?'

A man's voice said something. She sat up, clenching her fists, still with fright.

'Your French doors were unlocked,' Grant said. He sat down heavily on the bed.

She remembered. She had left the party without telling him.

'What happened?' he asked.

She couldn't tell whether he was angry or drunk, or just tired.

'I thought you must have gone off with someone,' he said. His tone was joking, no real feeling in it.

'No.' She tried to think what was best to say. 'I felt bad. Sick.'

'Why didn't you tell me?'

'Sorry.' She thought of saying, You were flirting. I didn't think you'd care.

He lay down next to her. He started to stroke her arms and back. She wanted to push him away, but she was responding to his touch.

When he was lying lightly on top of her he said, 'Do you like that?'

'Yes.'

'Say it. Say you love it.'

He whispered this sometimes. *Say it. Say you love me fucking you.* In the right mood she could go along with it; she could put herself in a kind of trance where saying it didn't seem like obedience, like being made to do something that wasn't natural to her, and in that mood it could excite her too. *I love you fucking me.* Wantonness. Lust. But now she couldn't put herself in the right frame of mind.

Say it.

'Oh for Christ's sake, Grant,' she said in a normal voice. He paused, then carried on.

He rolled off her.

'Sorry,' she said.

'It's all right.'

They lay in the dark. She sat up suddenly and said, 'I forgot to take my pill.'

Grant had his arm over his eyes. He said, 'I wouldn't worry about it.'

Viola lay still. A small alarm started inside her head.

She raised herself on her elbow. 'What do you mean?'

He didn't answer.

She said, holding herself steady, 'Do you mean I don't need to worry?'

'Can we go to sleep? I'm tired.' His tone was flat. Cold. Dismissive.

I wouldn't worry about it.

Viola said, 'You meant I don't need to worry. Have you had yourself . . . ' she couldn't think of the word. 'Have you had, what do they call it? The snip?'

He rolled over, his tone suddenly sharp, engaged. 'What does this mean? That you want a baby?'

'No.'

'If you want one let's make one. Come on. Let's go again. You want a kid? Come on then.'

Viola felt cold all over. He was taunting her.

'Say it. You *do* want a baby.'

There was something boyish and loose and vicious in his voice, as if he was thrilled to be entering a place they had always steered carefully around. Was he punishing her for her pretending, her coyness? Throwing it in her face?

She made herself say, 'No, I don't want a baby.'

She thought, what if he'd had a vasectomy? (Could you tell? She had no idea.) 'I want you to tell me exactly what you meant,' she said.

But he'd slipped into a kind of refrain, almost crowing, as if he was finally enormously sick of something that had lain between them.

'Come on then, if you want one.'

They lay in the dark, taken over, engulfed by this sudden scalding bitterness between them.

Say it. Say it.

Simon Lampton got through the week. Nothing happened.

Another uneventful week passed. But Viola was constantly in the back of his mind; a kind of tension had spun itself around him, as if the barometer had dropped and the air was radiantly still, holding itself in check before a storm.

One cool sunny morning, the sky high and hard and clear over the city, he tramped across the Domain, went into his office and began to go through his files. Clarice appeared, arms folded across her chest, one eyebrow raised.

'Guess who rang this morning.'

There was a pause. Looking down he said, 'Who?'

'That hopeless Viola Myers. Remember her? I said I doubted you'd be able to ring her back.'

'Really?' A small tension headache throbbed in his temple, as if he'd been stabbed with a pin.

'She can't be looking for a job. Honestly. What a dimwit. Everything she touched ended up in the wrong place.'

'What did she want?'

'She's left a number. Shall I chuck it in the bin?'

'No. Better not.'

Clarice left the bit of paper on his desk and went out, shaking her head.

His first thought was to ring Karen. He stopped himself. Reading Viola's story, what he and Karen had both felt was hurt. They had done their best to help her, and she had revealed herself to be sinister, ambiguous, nasty. He would protect Karen this time. He would deal with Viola himself.

He got up and stood at the window, nervously clicking his pen. He thought of not doing anything. But that wouldn't be any good. She might persist, come to his rooms, ring the house. (If Karen answered there would be fireworks.) Best to find out what she was up to.

He rang the number and got the reception at the museum. He asked for Viola.

She said, 'Hello?'

'It's Simon Lampton.'

'Oh. You *called*.' She laughed, flustered, pleased. He felt a secret fascist rise in himself, saw himself slamming a heavy cell door in her face. He remembered the old sense of her: frivolousness, self-indulgence, vulnerability, her notion that she could just waft into someone else's life and they would welcome her.

She said, 'I work just across the park from you. At the museum.'

'Really.'

'I've got something to ask you.' She lowered her voice. 'About that incident with your father.'

'Ask away.'

'No, it's too complicated.' Again that silly, nervous laugh. 'Couldn't we meet, just quickly, in the park this lunchtime?'

Meet in the park.

'I suppose I could do that, if it's important,' he said.

'It is, it is. Could we?' She sounded thrilled.

'How about one o'clock, at the garden for the blind?' he said. He looked at his reflection in the window. His expression was gruesome.

'Okay. Great. Bye.'

At one o'clock he went to the garden and sat on a park bench, watching the mynah birds hopping and squabbling on the concrete. The sound of balls thwacking on rackets came from the tennis club. The air was still, the sky bright and pale, with a milky sheen of light around the sun. The palm tree cast short spiky shadows.

She was late. He detested lateness. He felt his anger rising and steeled himself; he must be calm and controlled, assess her like pain, as if from a long way off. Deal with her and be done with it.

He saw her coming down the hill from the museum, taking a circuitous route, as if she was nerving herself up. At one point she veered right away, heading towards the soccer fields. He stood up, prepared to march after her and grab her by the arm if necessary. He wanted this over with. He wasn't going to be driven mad by a whole series of melodramatic near misses and failures of nerve. But she turned back and came down the hill. She was dressed in a black dress, sunglasses and sandals. Her sandy hair was pulled up tight, away from her face.

Simon faced her. She saw him, drew back, laughed nervously

and said, 'Hi.' Her upper lip quivered. 'Shall we sit down here?'

Simon sat on the edge of the seat and stared at the fronds of the palm tree. She sat next to him, playing with her fingers. They both turned and began to speak and lapsed into embarrassed silence. Simon found his mood strangely heightened; he felt more angry and harassed now than he had felt before. He thought of Karen. That nasty description of her. He swallowed.

She said in her breathy, slightly sugary voice, 'I'm sorry to bother you. I've never tried to talk to you since that night. I want you to know I've never told anyone about it.'

She pressed her small fist against her heart: high-minded, self-sacrificing.

Still he didn't say anything, not trusting his voice.

'But I saw you the other day and you gave me such a terrible look . . . ' She tittered.

Simon pressed his fingers to his forehead.

She ran on, 'And when I saw that look you gave me I got an idea. The thing is, last year I wrote a story based on the incident with your father. I did a creative writing course and I've been trying to write a novel, but the story's as far as I've got. It won third prize.'

'Congratulations,' he said as coldly as he could.

'Thanks.' She turned to him, beaming. He edged further away.

She went on, 'When you gave me that look I thought you must have read the story and that it had made you angry. Had you? Did it?' she asked.

He didn't answer.

She rushed on, 'I just wanted to tell you that I put a sort of spin in the story that's not the truth. It's something I made up, the whole thing, about the student being sly and dodgy and the young man being the way he is, cold and rich, and the father being this poor simple musician. I made it all up. It's just fiction. It's not how it was. Really, I was just stupid and got myself into a bit of trouble and you helped me. You see?'

'Yes,' he said slowly. 'I think I do.'

'Yes?' She leaned towards him. 'Do you mean you're not annoyed?'

'Not in the least,' he said.

She clasped her hands in her lap and bent forward, her feet pigeon-toed, like a four-year-old waiting for a present. 'Does this mean it's okay?'

'Sure.'

She turned to him and put her hand out, as if to touch his arm. He drew back.

She said, 'So there's nothing to stop us talking like friends.'

Friends. She was out of her mind.

'Friends,' he repeated. He looked at her. She understood. Her smile dropped. Her mouth went lopsided, quivered. She gave a little squeak and put her face in her hands. There was a silence.

She made a muffled, sniffing sound.

Simon took a breath. He allowed the silence to lengthen. A couple strolled past with a child in a pushchair, a Labrador panting and lumbering behind.

Viola's shoulders were hunched. With his fists on his knees he swivelled towards her.

'Thank you for your concern, Viola.'

She looked at the dog and sniffed bleakly.

He went on, 'The truth is, I haven't read the story you're talking about. I did see you recently, but if I looked out of sorts, it was nothing to do with you.'

She turned sideways, looking at him from behind her hand with one damp, sceptical eye. He straightened up. The oppressed feeling had lifted, as if, in one sudden arc of electricity, power had leapt from her to him.

'As far as your writing goes, you can make up whatever stories you like. I won't be offended at all. How could I be?'

She turned sideways again. Yes, there was wetness, tears escaping under her fingers, blurring the dark make-up. She snatched a handkerchief out of her bag.

'Indeed,' he added loftily, 'writing can be a form of therapy.'

There was a pause as this hung in the air. He felt an evil little laugh rise in himself. Was that over-egging it a bit?

'I'm not *mad*,' she said, with a sullen flounce.

'No, of course not.' He looked down at her black handbag. It was stylish but cheap, as were her dress and shoes. She was pretty. She would know how to make herself look very good if she had the money. He looked at her flimsy shoes. He had an odd sense: sympathy, pity. And then something not altogether different from pity, but worse. Was there a point where pity and cruelty came close, where you couldn't tell which you were feeling?

'What do you do up there?' He pointed up the hill at the museum.

'I'm just an assistant. I haven't got a degree or anything.'

'No.' He nodded, as if to say, of course not. She shot him a startled glance.

'And are you . . . married, living with someone?'

'No,' she said.

'No children?' he pursued.

'No.' The look she gave him now was one of childish incredulity, as if he were a bully beginning to twist her arm in the playground, slowly ratcheting up the pain.

'No,' he said again, softly. 'I suppose not.'

'What do you mean you *suppose not*?'

He waved his hand. 'Oh . . . And are you at all published?'

She said, wiping her eyes, smudging them more, 'No, I'm not published. Except for my story in the paper. Which won a prize. Okay, third prize. I've done a creative writing course.'

'Mmm,' he said. 'Well. Good luck. Perhaps you'll get properly published one day.' He wondered how old she was. Thirty? She had smooth, unlined skin.

He smacked his hands on his thighs. 'I have patients waiting.'

She rose and stood before him, biting her lip and glancing away up the hill. He had the sudden clear perception that she had dressed carefully for this occasion; that she had excitedly planned for it, making up her face, wearing her best, most flattering black dress, perhaps rehearsing her lines. And somehow it had fallen terribly flat, and she stood in the patches of sunlight between the cruel shadows of the palm fronds and regarded him with dumb misery.

'Can I see you again?' she asked, and then winced and closed her eyes.

Simon stood over her. He said, hearty, 'Now that we've cleared this up, there's no need, is there. You get on with your life, which I must say sounds full of terrific possibilities, and I'll just plod on back to mine.'

'Yeah,' she said, nodding, biting her lip, twisting the strap on her bag. 'Yeah.'

As he turned away she made a move forward, in the faint hope, perhaps, that he would make some final gesture. He stepped nimbly back.

'I know my story wasn't any good,' she said. 'It wasn't subtle. I should have done it better.'

He shrugged. 'Really.'

She made a last attempt, twisting the strap in her fingers. 'I'm trying to explain the difference between journalism and fiction. You're angry because you think I portrayed you in a bad light and showed myself to be sinister. But that wasn't anything to do with my real feelings, or the truth. I was just using the detail to make something up. It's fiction. I could have made you Superman and myself a heroine — that wouldn't have represented the truth either.'

He said smoothly, with a hint of iron this time, 'As I said, you can make up whatever you like. I don't have much time to read fiction. My wife Karen does. Karen reads quite a lot. Perhaps she read your story.' He paused, allowed that to vibrate between them.

'Oh God,' she said.

'But I doubt it,' he added.

He said goodbye and went off down the hill.

Viola walked back to the museum. At the top of the hill she felt she couldn't go inside just yet, and walked instead around the outside of the building, clenching her fists, stopping to put her hand to her forehead and wince as a fresh wave of embarrassment struck her. It hadn't gone as she had planned. It had gone badly wrong. When he said writing could be a form of therapy. That was the worst. He was patronising, treating her as mad.

But he was underestimating her. She wasn't mad. She'd been trying to explain something serious: the business of writing fiction. She stopped and looked miserably over the harbour. It was a bright fresh day with clouds casting dark blots of shadow over the sea. Towards the islands there were rain showers, patches of silver mesh on the horizon. He's a doctor, she thought. He doesn't understand what I was trying to do. He said himself he doesn't read fiction. Of course not, he has to bury himself in medical texts. His is a different intellectual discipline.

She would write to him. That was the way to deal with this humiliation. She would put it to him in writing, in a dignified way, what she had been aiming at when she wrote the story, and where he'd got it wrong about her.

She hurried up the steps and into the foyer. She was late, but she thought she'd be able to get away with it, since she was in sole charge of her section that afternoon. She ran up the stairs to the second floor, to her work station in the children's 'Weird and Wonderful' rooms. Here she had her desk among the plaster dinosaur bones and aquariums and drawers full of preserved insects. She took school and kindergarten children on tours around the rooms, explaining the exhibits, and when there were no groups to lead, maintained the collection and worked on the colourful displays. She made the eye-catching signs and banners and charts that were designed to draw children's interest. She had always been good at art. She was the one management came to when they needed a new laminated sign or wall diagram, or materials and ideas for school holiday art activities.

The section was empty except for a couple of glazed mothers, gossiping as their toddlers played on the jigsaw mat. Viola moved a mobile of the planets off her desk. She sat down and got out a piece of paper.

> *Dear Simon,* (Could she call him Simon now? She decided she could.)
> *Just now you said that writing could be a form of therapy. I've been thinking about this. If fiction is written as therapy, it isn't going to be any good. The point is, fiction is produced out of experience, but it has to become something beyond just emotion and reaction. It requires a distancing,*

an exercising of talent and literary skill. This is what I was trying to explain, very ineptly I'm sure, that the source is experience but the true creative process changes the material, changes it utterly (to quote Yeats) and it should become something that is true only to the shape of the composition. Like, for example, Picasso making a sculpture of a monkey out of nuts and bolts — the end result, the composition, isn't nuts and bolts any more, it's a monkey. And even if someone personally recognises those nuts and bolts it doesn't matter, they're not what they were any more. They're a work of art, they are the monkey. Does this sound ridiculous? Not if you're in the monkey business. Anyway, I know you said you'd never actually looked at the 'monkey' (the story I mean) that I was going on about. I also know it might seem strange to acknowledge that one regularly makes things up, and to assert that on this occasion one is making nothing up, but merely speaking 'after hours', when all the tools of invention have been laid down. But that's the case. Everything I said when we met just now was true.
Viola Myers

She read it through, agitated. This was more like it — to engage on a serious level, to impress him with her dedication to her craft. She sat chewing her pen and gazing at the rows of preserved specimens floating in their disgusting formaldehyde. The bit about the monkey, that was good. To call it monkey business — showing she wasn't too solemn and pedantic. She pictured Picasso's monkey sculpture. But was it really constructed out of nuts and bolts? Or was it made out of a toy car? She couldn't remember. She could only be sure by looking it up, and felt knackered at the prospect. Should she just cover herself by changing 'nuts and bolts' to 'bits and pieces'? The whole thing was a bit rambling. It was good to quote Yeats — that showed depth, seriousness. But did a reference to 'talent' matter? Did that sound conceited? And what about referring to herself as 'one'? Was that pompous? As for 'the tools of invention' . . . God.

A door slammed, sending an echo up the stairwell. She heard a voice raised in a foreign language in one of the adjoining halls. She looked up. On the wall in front of her was a section of her latest poster series: The Life Cycle of the Dragonfly. It showed how a dragonfly develops from an egg to a nymph to the beautiful, glittering adult creature.

Next to the photos she had written in large letters:

> *The dragonfly lays its eggs on or under water. The eggs hatch into a creature called a nymph. The nymph, a tiny bullet-shaped creature, has a system of breathing and propelling itself through its own rectum.*

Viola stared at the words, written in her own careful capitals. She thought about her hopes, her ambitions. Talent, literary skill. Yeats, Picasso. Who was she to spout these words, to claim them as if she and they were part of the same grand process?

A system of breathing and propelling itself

And what was the real reason for her high-minded note to Dr Lampton? Was she writing it out of a passion for art? Or was it nothing more than an angle? A cheap attempt to impress a man who regarded her as beneath contempt.

Simon spent his days honourably, did his work well, looked after his patients and his family. He had what she had dismally failed to achieve. He had a decent life.

She felt dazed. How had it happened? She had always hoped for, expected, great things and yet somehow she had found herself in this strange position, shut out, continually looking into other people's lives, wishing for what she saw there, and only able to enter by a series of tricks. Stunts. Acts of disingenuousness.

I have no centre. No self. I am beneath contempt.

A party of small children rocketed into the room, herded by two harassed teachers.

Viola opened her diary in which, that morning, in a mood of wicked expectation she had scrawled: *Chapter Three. Viola messes with Dr Lampton's mind again.*

She looked at the words. She saw herself writing them. She thought about her life. Excitements. Disappointments. The hoping and the waiting. The careful spinning out of days.

She thought, I can't write him. I'm no good. I can't write Simon Lampton down.

A woman put her head over the partition. 'Hi? Hi? We're from Bayfield Primary. Are you our guide?'

'Yes. Coming,' Viola said.

She would never finish a novel. She saw that clearly. She didn't have it in her. If she couldn't put Simon Lampton on the page, then there was nothing else but life. She pressed her fingers against her eyes. She felt herself spinning; something in her head had come loose and was whirling madly round.

The teacher popped her head up again. 'Excuse me.' And then, kindly, 'Are you all right?'

'I've just got to make a phone call,' Viola said.

She rang his home number. Karen Lampton answered. Viola sat in the rowdy room, listening. This lightness. So strange. It was frightening. And yet, it wasn't all bad. She had a sense of having thrown off a burden at the end of a journey; as if, at last, she had properly arrived. I've given up writing, she wanted to tell Karen. I'm facing up to things. It's just me and life now. Here I am.

'Hello? Hello?' Karen Lampton said.

One of the children smacked his head on a glass case and began to wail. Viola looked at him with glittering eyes. She smiled.

'Hello?' the tiny voice buzzed in the receiver.

'Quiet everyone,' the teacher called.

Viola replaced the phone. She rose and went towards the children. She clapped her hands and they gathered around. One of the teachers pulled the injured boy onto her lap and rubbed his forehead. There was a general settling down. They all looked at her expectantly.

'Welcome to Weird and Wonderful,' Viola said. 'All the exhibits are specially laid out for you. You can pick them up and handle them as much as you like. In the drawers along this wall you will find the preserved insects, and on this wall here we have creatures preserved in formaldehyde. Across the room we have some live specimens, and the aquariums. Some of our creatures are shy, so please don't bang on the glass.'

The teacher with the boy on her knee was gently, absent-mindedly rubbing his bruised forehead. Viola looked at the hand stroking the small, soft face.

'We have lots of interesting bones for you to look at.' She swallowed. 'If you'd like to ask me about them . . . '

She stopped and turned to the teacher. 'I'm sorry. I'm going to have to get a replacement.'

In the surprised silence she went to her desk, picked up her bag and her diary and went to the door.

The teacher followed her, exasperated. 'We're booked for a full session.'

'I'm sorry,' Viola said. 'I'm sick. Maybe it's something I've eaten. I'll get you another guide.'

She went into the back room and told them she was sick. One of the other guides, Gavin, put his lunch away, saying he didn't mind taking over. There was some half-hearted sympathy, tinged with scepticism. Viola was quite good at her job, but they all agreed she was hopeless with the public.

There was another adjustment, more clapping hands and quelling of the restless kids, the teachers rolling their eyes, shrugging capably at one another. Gavin launched into his fluent, jokey spiel. There was a sense of relief in the room as Viola left.

She walked down the steps. It was a beautiful, clear autumn afternoon. She turned her face to the sun and closed her eyes, feeling the heat on her face. She had a shivery feeling all over. Perhaps she really was sick.

She thought that she was leaving the museum for ever. She assumed that she would be fired for walking out in the middle of a session. (But they didn't fire her. Two days later she went back to work and no one even mentioned she'd been away.)

She saw herself travelling towards the Lamptons. Here I come. Remember me? I went away but now I'm back. Why? Because words fail me. Because I can't forget you and I can't write you down.

It was a beautiful day. It would take her twenty minutes to walk home. It would take her an hour to walk to the suburb where Simon and Karen lived. She was capable of walking any distance.

She liked ranging through the city. Exercise was a good way to get over things, to pick up your mood and clear your mind.

Over the following days and months, each time she left the building at the end of the day, Viola would pause on the steps to decide. How far would she dare to go that day? Would she walk for twenty minutes, or an hour?

SINGULARITY

Emily sat on the plane. Out the window she could see the endless red desert, stretching away across the curve of the earth. The bright light, angling through the window, made shirred patterns on the seatback, and the man beside her, tugging on a small punnet of water, peeled the foil lid off and sprayed drops across her tray table.

Immediately, involuntarily, she apologised.

'My fault,' he said, in a heavy German accent.

She smiled and turned to her own meal, not wanting to talk.

She had arrived in Melbourne, transferred onto a smaller, more cramped plane, and now they were flying into the centre of the country, over thousands of miles of empty land. To be flying away from civilisation and into nothingness was striking to her, almost frightening. The idea that the country had this space in the centre of itself that was so vast and forbidding, so empty ... In the departure lounge she had read about a sheep station that was the size of Belgium.

She thought of her daughter far away. Her mother soothing little Caro to sleep and outside the rain falling on the trees in the reserve and the lights coming on in the wooden houses. Her father Per in his study staring out at the rain. But she was flying away, into silence, endless skies, parched land. The air hostess came singing down the aisle, 'Tea coffee? Coffee tea?'

Emily could see something shining at the horizon — a mirage or a lake? A silver patch, just where the earth rolled away. She had dreamed more than once of a building so vast that no one knew what was in the centre of it, and in the dream she was always walking in, leaving the known world behind. She thought of Lampedusa's *The Leopard*; in it there was a vast palace of abandoned rooms, 'dark and sunny rooms, apartments sensual or squalid' into which Tancredi and Angelica ventured, further and further, until they risked being lost. And in there they found — she tried to remember the phrase — 'the sensual cyclone'. She wanted to laugh. Beside her the German coughed and dipped his head seriously over his guide book. The hostess walked backwards holding her silver jug aloft. 'Tea? Tea?'

Two weeks ago, in Auckland, her editor Angus had leaned on the edge of his desk and said, 'I've got something good for you. Four nights at Ayers Rock. It's a circle of linked hotels. They fly you over, you do all the tourist stuff — look, you can even go camel riding. Then you write a nice big piece. I'll give you plenty of space.' He took a black pencil case out of his drawer as he spoke, and detached a plastic syringe. He pulled his shirt up, pinched a roll of his stomach and stuck the needle in. He performed this diabetic's ritual as casually as if he were marking corrections with a pen. She'd worked for him for two years. She liked him. He was large, expansive, sharp — he understood everything she said immediately, even though she was sometimes vague and inarticulate. She was fluent where it mattered, on the page.

She said, 'Shouldn't Claudine be doing this?'

'No, you go. You'll enjoy it.' He put his black pencil case away.

'I'll have to get Caro minded. She might not want me to go.'

But little Caro, instead of protesting, had bounced up and down: 'Can I stay with Beth and Per? For long? Will you bring me a koala?'

Only later, in bed, did Caro say, 'Can I come? Will you take me too?' Emily thought, if Harry was around we could all have gone. I could have taken notes and you and he could have played by the pool. But Caro's father was far away — living in Spain, last Emily had heard.

'I'll bring you a koala bear,' she said.

The plane tilted, changed direction. The hostesses moved up and down the aisles. The puddle of silver gleamed at the edge of the earth, then vanished as though it had slid off the world. Emily looked up into a sky so blue it seemed to pulse. Light struck off the wing. They were lower now, gradually descending. The land was red, a Martian desert, without towns, crossed by the occasional road or tiny dotted fence line. The pilot's voice came over the intercom, telling her to look for Ayers Rock — Uluru — out the left side of the plane. There it was, redder than the desert, softly contoured, vast, rippled with black shadows, a great blemish on the face of the ancient land. It was strange, uncanny, beautiful.

Voices along the rows. What a landscape. How about that. I get another coke before we land?

And the hostesses backed down again, collecting headsets. Emily held onto hers, and listened to loud rock music as they came in to land.

They were directed onto a bus. Over the intercom the driver introduced himself as Travis. As they drove into the national park, Emily saw that the landscape, so red from the air, was surprisingly dotted with feathery vegetation, beautifully green and incongruous against the red sand. Travis kept up a commentary: 'Notice the plants, folks? We've had something unusual here in the last few days: a bit of rain.'

But today the sky was clear, cloudless blue. And when she got out of the bus she noticed the silence. Heat and stillness, no cars once Travis had driven the bus away, everything silent and clear and exquisitely sharp, a weird landscape, cut in bright light.

The hotel was a series of little houses set about the grounds. She walked along a stone path, following a golf cart loaded with her luggage. Bright birds flashed about. She was shown to her room, up a flight of steps. The room was big and fiercely air-conditioned, with a balcony looking over the road that wound away across the land. She looked out at the gum trees, the road, the unfamiliar colours. She hadn't expected it to be so beautiful.

The Outback. This was where a dingo had taken Lindy Chamberlain's baby. This was where — somewhere out there, far away along the lonely road — a man in a ute had attacked two English tourists. The man's body never found. Signs in the room said, 'Danger, extreme heat. If you go out into the park, drink a litre of water every hour. Wear strong, closed shoes. Inform others of your plans.' Emily took great pleasure in these warnings. There was a pamphlet displaying a picture of a smiling Aboriginal boy. It invited her to pay a modest tax for the upkeep of the fragile indigenous community — a conservation notice, reminiscent of notices at the zoo: this creature is endangered. Programmes are in place . . . She hadn't seen a single Aborigine since she'd arrived.

Angus, wielding his needle kit, had said, 'Good you've never been before. You've got a fresh eye. If I send Claudine she'll just write about the food.'

Emily unpacked her swimming gear and headed for the pool. Figures lay slumped on loungers in the shade. The sun beat down, hot and fierce; ribbons of white light danced above the pool. The silence and stillness seemed to gather and press down; everything lay exhausted in the heat. She lowered herself into the water and swam slowly back and forth. The people on deckchairs spoke in low voices, somewhere in one of the rooms a woman laughed. A huge wasp zoomed down and hovered above the water. The size of it — it was twice as big as a wasp back home, cantilevered and elegant, souped up, a Ferarri, a sportswasp. On the steps of her room she had noticed ants that were similarly enhanced, their shiny bodies disconcertingly plump. She lay on her back. Another wasp zoomed down, then another. She swam away. And at the end of the pool, peering over the edge and waggling its feelers at her, was the most marvellous, strange beetle, beautifully shiny, its wings a deep, iridescent blue. She imagined showing it to Caro.

Strange, for a moment, she couldn't picture her little girl's face.

She lay on a lounger reading a book she'd borrowed from Angus: The Chekhov Omnibus. The heat. It was like a substance, it turned the air into a force. On the way back to her room Emily forged through it. A man looked out of a doorway and silently withdrew. People were hiding in their cabins, waiting for the evening.

The room was too cold. She fiddled with the air-conditioning.

She looked at her itinerary. That night she was to wait at reception for a bus that would take her to a 'Dinner under the Stars'. She lay on the bed and closed her eyes. She dreamed.

Auckland, a summer Sunday. Tuis squabbling, rosellas flying through the trees. Caro running up the path towards her grandparents' house, shouting. There's something important to tell. 'Per. Per.' She cranes up, bellowing. Beth puts her head out the window. 'Come down here,' Caro demands. The grown-ups not listening but turning away. 'Uncle Larry's down here,' Caro shouts. 'His eyes are closed and he won't get up.'

Per at the window, looking at Caro. He is still, his eyes fixed on her. As still as stone.

Something chimed. Emily sat up. The dinner, she thought. I've missed the bus. And she thought of Angus, disappointed, shaking his head.

There was the pinging noise again. A voice called from behind the door.

Something bad has happened, she thought, lurching across the room.

But it was only a teenage boy with an envelope addressed to her. He put it in her hand and trotted away down the steps. She opened the package, and there was a fan of tickets to tourist trips, courtesy of the hotel, and a letter hoping she would enjoy her stay.

The pamphlet had said to dress warmly. It said: the temperature in the desert drops substantially at night. The tourists gathered in the foyer, holding their tickets. The bus arrived and Travis jumped down and began ushering people on board. Emily watched him. She thought of the 'fragile community' of Aborigines and thought, here is another kind of creature: the predator. He had a hard, watchful face, a cruel mouth. He gripped her arm and looked hard at her as she stepped up into the bus. She blushed.

The sun was setting as they drove away from the hotel, along the highway and onto a rough sandy road, bumping over uneven ground. The light was bronze, and in the distance the rock, Uluru, cast its soft black shadows. Here were the colours she'd seen in

Aboriginal paintings, in the illustrations of the Dreamtime. Emily closed her eyes. She saw Caro, her face lit up with red light. And other faces: Per, Larry. Words chimed in her head. Dream time. Desert time. The line of a poem: *He who was living is now dead.* The bus went over a bump and down into a sharp dip. There were small shrieks from the passengers. Over the intercom, Travis was reciting a spiel: 'You will see the sun go down over the rock. Something everyone must see, once in their lifetime. It is beautiful, so beautiful you will be struck dumb.' Emily sat very still, looking. The red rock and the black shadows and the sun on red sand. Twilight. Silence. Long shadows over the land. Behind the rock, the sky in flames.

And behind her a deep man's voice said, 'You wanted to see it. You've made it. Here it is, mate. Voila.'

Wallah!

They were met by a guide and led to a small hill from which to view the sunset. They were served sparkling wine and nibbles from tables covered in white cloths. A man appeared with a didgeridoo, and blew its eerie drone as the sun went down. The New Zealanders immediately identified the guide and the didgeridoo player as Maori. They started whispering. 'What a laugh. Where are the Abos? Why are they being played by our people?' They knew the answer, they felt smug about it: their country had its problems but it was more equal. Maori and Pakeha got on in a way that Aborigines and white Australians didn't. The poor Abos would be out the back somewhere, hopelessly boozing.

One of the New Zealanders drew the guide into their circle.

'You're right, mate,' the guide said. 'I'm from Otara.'

A man grabbed his companion by the arm and said, 'Look mate. God, that's beautiful.' His was the voice that had said behind Emily, 'Voila.' He stood holding his friend's arm. He was short and squat, the other man was younger, taller and thinner. Emily thought there was something familiar about them.

The sunset had intensified the colour and deepened the shadows. The rock blazed for a moment, lit up with a sheen of evening light. They stood watching the colours change. In the evening Uluru was vast, ancient and strange. They moved closer together and looked across the high grass and stones, to the flaming sky. The red landscape was darkening now, the colours bleeding out. The air was still and hot, but as the sun sank something changed; a violent squall of wind blew up, whirling the sand around and sending the edges of the tablecloths flapping. The wind caught scatters of dry grass and flung it spinning upwards. The waiters grabbed at the napkins. For a moment the air was full of grit and sticks, and then the great heave of wind subsided, and everything was still. The rock glowed with a last weird brightness, and in the final moment before the sun went down its colours were so intense that it seemed to float above the plain. Long shadows moved across the land and the air began to cool.

Now it was time for the 'dinner under the stars'. They were led beyond the hill to a space of cleared land. There were huts for preparing and serving food and tables set about, and a big bonfire redly crackling. It was dusk now, and there were lamps rigged up around the tables. There were no lights anywhere near, and soon the sky began to blaze with stars. After the meal, the guide promised, they would be 'taken on a tour' of the night sky.

They queued for the first course. Emily sat down with her plate. The New Zealanders had stayed in a group, and had been placed together. She was mostly quiet. After the meal the tables were rowdy. The guide rose and shouted them down. The lamps were switched off.

The only light now came from the bonfire. A woman stood up and began a talk about the night sky. She had a powerful torch, and as she pointed out the constellations she directed the beam, and when they followed its light they could discern clearly which clusters of stars she was talking about. The whole sky was studded with silver light. They could see the Milky Way, the spirals of space dust, the close and distant stars, fixed, glittering, still. And every now and then they saw a satellite, moving busily between the points of light.

The man next to Emily had been talking to people across the table. Now he leaned close and spoke to her: 'Guess what? The universe we live in is not the only one.'

Emily turned. He said, 'The universe is a membrane. The Big Bang was caused by the collision of the membrane of our universe and a parallel one.'

Emily tried to make out his face in the dark.

He kept talking: 'The very beginning of the Big Bang is called the singularity. Before membrane theory scientists couldn't calculate back to the moment of the singularity. Now they've realised there are parallel universes, they can.'

Emily repeated the word. The singularity. The dark, mysterious sound of it. She looked up at the stars. Their stillness was strange to her. That they should be so fixed and unmoving. She turned back to the man.

'I know you,' she said.

His voice came out of the darkness. 'A lot of people know me.'

'And your friend . . . '

'Terry Carstone,' he said. He was offering his hand. She shook it. 'Your friend?'

'He's Andrew. Andrew Newgate.'

She hadn't recognised them before. They had faded out of the news back home.

Carstone said, 'We're having a holiday. Little break. Travelling round. Andrew wanted to see the Rock. He had a hankering to see it. So I thought, let's give him the chance.'

Emily said, 'I'm a journalist.' Then she wished she hadn't told him. He wouldn't want to talk to her. But to her surprise he said, 'Really? Great. I'll introduce you to Andrew.'

The woman next to Emily said, 'Shhh.' The astronomy lesson was still going on.

'You working?' Carstone whispered.

'I'm doing a travel piece.'

'Are you here by yourself?'

'Yes.'

Carstone turned and said, 'Andrew. Mate, this is . . . ?'

'Emily Svensson,' she said.

Terry Carstone and Andrew Newgate. They had been famous for a while back home. Newgate, a music student, had been convicted of murder and Carstone, a wealthy businessman, had taken an interest in his case, and had campaigned successfully for his retrial. At the retrial Newgate had been acquitted. He and Carstone had appeared in papers and women's magazines — the victim of a miscarriage of justice and his dashing champion. 'He's like a son to me,' Carstone had said. 'Together we fought for justice, against the might of the State.' After the retrial they'd faded from the news, Newgate to start a normal life and Carstone to new business ventures.

Andrew Newgate leaned across. He and Emily found each other's hand in the dark and shook. His hands were large, dry, rough. His grip was strong. She looked at his silhouette against the stars. The talk finished and table lamps were being lit again, red light on sweaty faces. Andrew looked at her calmly, his glasses reflecting the light. The bonfire was burning down, collapsing in on itself with little showers of sparks, creating black spaces inside the flames. She looked up, into the cold, glittering sky. The dark pressed in around their circle of light. She thought of that word. Singularity.

Terry said, 'Your paper's been quite good to us. Not like some other bastards.'

They climbed back into the bus and Terry ushered them down the back. She sat next to the two men. She saw why she hadn't recognised them earlier. They had been wearing sunglasses and hats, and both had changed. Carstone's face was lined and he had put on weight. Andrew Newgate was heavier too, and he was losing his hair.

'Like at school, eh? Down the back of the bus.' Terry was drunk, voluble. 'Andrew's a composer now,' he said.

Andrew said quietly, 'I work in a shop. But I'm writing music.'

'Tell her,' Terry said.

'I'm writing a piece called "The Mountain".'

'He's amazing. He works all night sometimes. Just sitting in his room. Let's find a bar when we get back.'

They went to a bar in the lobby of the hotel next door to theirs. It was crowded. Terry bought drinks. He said, 'That tour was good. The night sky. I've always had a thing for cosmology. The universe. Andrew was telling me this theory . . . tell her, mate.'

Andrew smiled. 'There's a theory that the universe is made of sound.'

'And the other thing. Prime numbers,' Terry urged.

'Oh well.' Andrew shrugged. 'She might not be interested, Terry.'

'I am,' Emily said.

'I was telling Terry on the plane. Prime numbers drive mathematicians crazy, because they don't have a rational sequence. You can't predict when they'll occur. But then someone thought, what if they're a kind of composition, like music.'

'And the universe is made of sound,' Emily said.

Terry put his arm around Andrew's shoulders. 'He's a good boy,' he slurred. 'Mate, back in a minute.' He went off to the toilets.

Andrew said, 'I have this feeling, when I'm writing music, that it's outside of me. That it's around me in the air and I bring it in. It's not coming from inside me — I'm hearing it.'

His voice was deep and polite. There was a kind of stillness about him. He was tall and thin, with a gaunt face. He'd been accused of killing his friend, a music teacher, but as soon as he'd been convicted there'd been an outcry. The case against him was weak, the investigation bungled. And then Terry Carstone had got onto the case, and had campaigned relentlessly. And after that, there'd been an outpouring of public sympathy when he'd been retried and acquitted.

He said, 'I hear patterns, sequences, and I bring them in. Does that sound strange?' He shrugged again, charming, whimsical, lowering his eyes.

'No, it doesn't sound strange. But if there's no symmetry to prime numbers, then how can they be a composition?'

'Maybe the composition's too big for us to comprehend. And anyway, why does it have to be symmetrical?'

'Doesn't beauty equal symmetry?'

He said, 'The universe is not necessarily beautiful.'

'So,' she smiled, feeling drunk, 'art is an attempt to recreate the universe.'

'Who knows?'

She said carelessly, 'You're hearing the music of the spheres. You're reeling it in and turning it into your great works. Are your compositions symmetrical?'

'Yes, they are.'

'So they don't echo the universe.'

But she felt, suddenly, he was looking at her in a new way. His mouth was twisted and he was staring, really staring at her.

She put down her glass. The music pulsed around them, loud and frenetic. Terry came back and slung his arm over Andrew's shoulder. Andrew didn't move. He was still looking at her.

Emily left them in the bar and walked back to her room. She rang her parents' house in Auckland. All was well. Beth and Per were reading. Caro was in bed.

She set her alarm clock. The following morning she was to climb Uluru. The start time was early, before the desert got too hot. She was apprehensive about the climb — people had told her it was dangerous, that tourists had fallen to their deaths. And the Aborigines didn't like you to do it, although they allowed it to happen.

Angus had said, 'Of course you've got to climb the bloody rock.' And someone else had said, 'Ooh bad karma. You'll be cursed for ever if you do.'

She woke too early. A truck drove past on the road, beyond the gum trees. She couldn't go back to sleep. She made a cup of tea, got Angus's *Chekhov Omnibus* out of her bag, and began to read a story called 'The Black Monk'. She tried to concentrate, dozed, woke and started again.

She read:

> *A thousand years ago a monk, dressed in black, wandered about the desert, somewhere in Syria or Arabia ... Some miles from where he was, some fishermen saw another black monk, who was moving slowly over the surface of a lake. This second monk was a mirage. Now forget all the laws of optics, which the legend seems not to recognise, and listen to the*

rest. That mirage cast another mirage, then from that one a third, so that the image of the black monk began to be transmitted endlessly from one layer of the atmosphere to another. So that he was seen at one time in Africa, at another in Spain, then in Italy, then in the Far North . . .

She looked out the window. There were headlights moving across the desert, into the national park. An image of her brother Larry came to her. She saw him walking through the trench of shadow in the reserve behind her parents' house. His dark eyes, his white face. She had tried to imagine how he'd felt, what he'd seen, in the last hours of his life. She'd imagined a black door, an opening, cut in the sky.

Then he passed out of the atmosphere of the earth, and now he is wandering all over the universe, still never coming into conditions in which he might disappear. Possibly he may be seen now in Mars or in some star of the Southern Cross. But my dear, the crux of the legend is that exactly a thousand years from the day when the monk walked in the desert the mirage will return to the atmosphere of the earth again and will appear to men. And apparently the thousand years is almost up . . . According to the legend we can expect the black monk any day now.

The sun was rising. There were long shadows. She flicked to the notes in the back of the book. The composer Shostakovich was enthralled by 'The Black Monk', she read. He believed it was connected to his Fifteenth Symphony. He told his biographer: 'I am certain that Chekhov constructed 'The Black Monk' in sonata form . . .'

Emily dressed and went over to the dining room for breakfast. A beam of light came over the roof. Alien birds strutted, insects streamed through the morning air, and on the paths the giant ants scurried to and fro.

Terry Carstone waved her over. He said to the waitress, 'Is this trim milk?'

'Trim?'

'Skinny. Skeeny.' He winked at Emily and Andrew. He said, 'We're on a fitness kick. Low-fat diet. Running.'

The waitress looked dully at him, turned on her heel and walked away.

Emily sat down and tried to eat. Andrew was working his way through a bowl of cereal. Terry was puffy-eyed. He ate noisily, talking all the time. 'I've been a sportsman all my life but lately, what with the business, I don't have the time for . . . It's all about time these days. What about yourself, Emily? Into your fitness?'

'I'm going to climb the Rock,' she offered, and felt apprehensive again. Someone had told her, teasingly, 'There's a list of names at the bottom, of people who've fallen off.'

Terry said, 'The Abos don't want us to do it — bad juju — but it's the chance of a lifetime.'

'My editor wants me to,' Emily told him. She wondered whether Angus would want her to work in a description of the people she'd met at Uluru.

Terry was thinking along the same lines. He pointed his fork. 'There's a significance to this place, of course, Emily. Lindy Chamberlain. I mean there was another person basically framed by the State.'

He was talking loudly. People looked over. Andrew calmly worked on his plate.

'There's a sort of hook there, for you, isn't there, Emily. If you wanted to write something about me and Andrew being here. Andrew enjoying normal life, the great outdoors, obviously, but here we are, right next to the camping ground where . . . what was the kid's name? Azaria, was snatched by the dingo. And they arrest the mother; they bring her in and more or less construct a case around thin air.'

The waitress walked past. Terry said loudly, 'Excuse me. Excuse me? Can we have more coffee over here? When you've got *time*?'

'You'd think lessons would have been learned, Emily. I'm not saying we're on some kind of weird pilgrimage. Basically, my business partner Russell Cunningham and myself have had a good year. And I'm taking the kid some places. I've had a few ups and downs, relationship-wise. We both needed a break. I was set for Cairns, Port Douglas, lounge around in the sun, swim, but things changed, and young Andrew, he wanted to see Ayers Rock. He's got a bit of time off from his job, so, voila.'

He paused, stood up and walked over to the waitress. She regarded him silently. 'Excuse me. I think they pay you for waitressing don't they? So could we have a bit of service?'

The girl brought the coffee pot. Terry rubbed his hands over his face. There were heavy bags under his eyes. He looked sallow, unhealthy. He muttered, 'Bit of a headache this morning.'

'I think we're supposed to get the bus now,' Emily said.

Andrew pushed back his chair awkwardly, and upended Terry's cup. Coffee splashed over Terry's arm. He grabbed his napkin, mopping his sleeve, exclaiming irritably.

Andrew apologised.

Terry looked at Emily, nervously shaking the wet napkin. 'The thing is, Emily, people think the story's over. Andrew's free, our battles are won. Interest fades. But it's an ongoing process. It doesn't stop. I mentioned ups and downs. Take relationships. Take my partner, Renell. She's a lovely lady. I'd really thought she'd be a rock in all of this. But as soon as Andrew comes out of prison to live with us, well. She's 'not comfortable'. She's 'having issues'. She's not coming to Port Douglas or anywhere. She's 'visiting her mother'. Then she's on the phone trying to tell me some crazy nonsense . . .'

Andrew said, 'Terry.'

Terry stood up, sighing. 'Yes, okay. The bus.'

Andrew watched as his friend signed for the breakfast.

On the way to the bus Terry leaned on Andrew's shoulder. 'Ah, it's a drag growing old,' he sighed.

There was a large group waiting in the foyer. They boarded the bus, and drove away into the countryside. Travis's gravelly voice crackled over the intercom. Soon Uluru appeared ahead of them, and for the first time they could take in its size. They drove alongside it, looking up at the great cliffs of red rock that formed its sheer sides, the strange hollows, shadows, the eerie distances. There were swirling patterns on the surface. It looked as if it had landed on the surface of the earth, a huge piece of debris flung out of the universe. Above it the sky was hard, bright, clear. They drove into a large, dusty open space and Emily saw the track and a row of posts leading up the side of the rock — this was the path that they were to take to reach the top. It looked impossibly dangerous, precarious, minimal. Her feet tingled at the sight of it.

But there was a chain across the gate, and a sign with a large cross on it. Emily stood looking along the vast curve of the rock. The cliffs cast dark shadows and above them the sky glowed, ferocious blue. Around the base the land was covered with tussocky grass. Green foliage grew in the shade under the cliffs. The wind screamed around the bus, blowing dust and tussock into the air. And Travis, his hair blowing wild in the gale, consulted a guide, gathered the group and shouted, 'There's a high wind warning. It's Plan B, folks. The Rock climb's closed. If we took you up there in this, you'd be blown straight off. Trust me, it's happened before.'

They opted for the walk round the base. It was nine kilometres all the way round, Travis said. Emily went to take a closer look at the tortuous little path up to the summit, and found the sign with its list of those who had died climbing the rock. She sent a prayer of thanks to the wind.

But when she got back to the bus, the group had set off without her. She followed the nearest path, a track that wound close in to the rock. It was shadowy under the cliff. She walked along the sandy red track, under the feathery trees. The wind, rushing over the stone face, made a hollow, moaning sound. Above her the cliff face was twisted into odd shapes, cones and knobs and caves, and there were spaces of deep shadow, sudden blackness, in the holes and hollows. The surface was scored with rippling troughs, running up towards the blue sky. She was alone in the vast landscape, and even the sound of the wind was strange, with a ringing note in it as it buffeted the trees and raced up the giant red cliffs. Where the path was exposed the wind was so strong she could lean against it. It tore her clothes, blew stinging dust into her face. She came to an open stretch of tussock and made out the group ahead in the distance. But the track she was on was turning in the wrong direction. She was on a different path.

She thought of turning back, but the track under the cliff seemed forbidding, too lonely and strange. She turned off the path, climbed a wire fence and hurried, stumbling, across open fields of tussock. The land was difficult to cross, there were bluffs and holes, and places where she sank so deep into grass and sand that it was hard to go forward. She reached another fence and climbed over it.

On the other side of the fence was a large sign. It said that the land Emily had just crossed was of deep spiritual significance to the local Aboriginal people. Since ancient times, important cultural rituals had been carried out there. It was absolutely prohibited to walk on it. There was a five thousand dollar fine for anyone who did.

Emily stood in front of the sign. She looked at the zigzag tracks of her footprints on the forbidden ground. There was no one around except her group in the distance, disappearing along the path into the haze of bright light.

She hurried after them.

When she caught up Travis was showing them another sacred site. It was a shallow cave at the base of the rock. Signs warned them from walking on it. It was a place where rites of manhood were customarily performed. Cameras clicked. People asked solemn, respectful questions. Emily looked into the shadowed place. She imagined a face appearing out of the dark recess. Many black faces, watching her — reproachfully. She remembered the children's book *Walkabout*. Its cover, with a picture of two white children and an Aboriginal youth, a tall, thin black figure standing above them on a red dune. The youth had died in the end, of a mysterious spiritual ailment, something to do with the pointing of the bone.

The path had brought them around into the lee of the wind. The sun was higher in the sky and it was starting to get hot. The red cliff rose above them, crossed with patterns. Here the rock looked as if it had been sliced through with a giant knife, revealing cross sections, layers, segments of geological time. Ancient time, dream time. In that landscape they were tiny creatures, crawling across the giant plate of the earth. Here, Emily thought, it was possible to conceive of yourself as standing on a planet.

She thought, the didgeridoo makes the sound of the wind in the rock.

She heard Travis say, 'Yeah, well. The blacks'll tell ya, it's a no-no, mate.'

Terry had got hold of a stick, and had tied a handkerchief around his head. His face was sunburned and sweaty. Andrew strode along, much the fitter of the two. The group had spread out, walking in twos and threes.

Emily wanted company. She fell in beside Terry and Andrew.

'I walked on a sacred site,' she said quietly.

Terry pretended to reel back. 'Jesus. You'd better not walk next to us.' He laughed. 'Only joking.'

He held out a bag of mints.

'I went on the wrong path then cut across. I was scared of being left behind. Will I be cursed?' she asked, wanting to be charming.

Terry talked through a mouthful of mint. 'Look, Emily, put it this way. When you go to a Maori graveyard, do you wash the tapu off afterwards?'

She smiled. 'Um, I think I do. Just in case.'

He said, 'You're only fucked if you believe in it.' He pointed his stick. 'Point the bone at an Abo, he dies, because he thinks he's going to. If you don't believe it, nothing can touch you. Goes for everything. Shut it out of your mind. Doubts are poison. If you've got the right mindset, you're armour-plated.'

Andrew walked alongside, listening. He looked at Emily.

'Terry's right,' he said.

They came to a place where the path led close in to the rock. They walked in shade, under the trees. They crossed a small wooden bridge. Terry limped, complaining of blisters. There was a big patch of sweat on the back of his shirt. Andrew took photos and talked to Travis in his deep, polite voice. Emily listened.

Travis said, 'The Abos say, if someone points the bone at you, if he *sings* you, you'll die.'

Andrew said, 'Oh, I've heard that, yes.'

'Mind you, mate, some Abos pointed the bone at John Howard, cursed him, and he's still alive.'

Andrew said, 'A failed assassination.'

'Mate, I've lived here for all my life . . . '

'You must know the place very well.'

Emily tried to pin down Andrew's tone. Talking to Travis he sounded automatic, distracted, saccharin, like a parent closing the book at the end of a bedtime story: What fun! Now it's time for a lovely sleep . . .

'Speaking of the . . . "Abos", Emily said to Travis, 'Where are they?'

Travis waved his hand. 'They're over the back. They're happier in their own place.' He laughed harshly. 'It's always Happy Hour over there.'

There was a ranger's truck approaching across the sand. Travis went to meet it and stood talking through the window.

Emily said to Andrew, 'I was reading something this morning, a Chekhov story.' She wanted to get a reaction.

Andrew listened.

'It was about a man who starts seeing a black figure, a monk, who appears out of the air — a hallucination. After the monk's appeared to him a few times the man realises he's going mad.'

Andrew nodded. 'Terry and I've been trying to get some reading done. It's so nice to have some time to relax.'

'This monk's a completely black figure, black robes. Black hands.'

Andrew looked at her with his calm eyes.

She went on, 'A composer, Shostakovich, thought the story was written like a piece of music, that it echoed one of his symphonies. I thought of you. You were talking about the universe being made of sound. And you said you sometimes felt you were drawing music from the air; that it came from outside yourself.'

Andrew said sensibly, 'I did say that, didn't I? I'd had a bit of beer.'

Emily said, 'When the man's seeing the vision of the monk he's insane, but happy. When he stops seeing the monk he's sane, but miserable.'

'Well, what could that mean?' Andrew said pleasantly.

'I suppose it means he needs his madness. It's the only thing that keeps him sane.'

Andrew laughed. She looked at his face. His eyes were very dark, the pupils large.

He waved Terry over.

'Hello kids,' Terry said. 'I think I need a beer.'

Andrew said, 'Emily's been telling me about a book.'

'Oh yeah,' Terry said. 'I'm writing another book myself, Emily. Following the success of my first two, which were bestsellers. This one's about Andrew's retrial, and other issues.' He looked around unhappily. 'Think it's much further? It's fucking hot.'

'People are always recommending books to me,' Andrew said. 'Over the years, I've had a lot given to me. By people, wonderful friends.'

'You've had a lot of help in that way,' Terry said in a soulful voice.

'Oh, wonderful help,' Andrew said. 'I'll see if I can get hold of the book you've mentioned, Emily. Thank you.'

'You're welcome,' she said.

Andrew looked at her. She thought, his voice is a wall. He is somewhere behind it. She sensed a power in him that was not out of place in this strange ancient landscape. It was being made known to her that she had breached some deep rule of decorum; she had been exposed, warned, and forgiven — for now, only for now.

The bus was waiting. They were driven to a tourist centre decorated with Aboriginal art. In a row of wooden toilets set back from the road there was a yellow bin for needle disposal, and beside it a litter of syringes. Somewhere out there, the unseen locals had graduated from booze to drugs.

But there was a pretty, dark-skinned girl at the counter in the café; hers the first set of Aboriginal features they'd seen, and from the kitchen another dark-skinned girl and boy exchanged cheerful banter and insults.

They ate lunch in a faux-rustic shack, surrounded by Dreamtime tea towels, ornaments, mouse pads and coffee mugs.

Andrew said, 'I think it's a bit early for a beer, Terry. Why don't you have a lie-down when we get back, and then we could go for a swim in the pool.'

Terry sighed, 'Okay mate. Maybe you're right.'

Andrew looked at Emily. He said, 'And after that, a bit of reading and then dinner. We'll have to pick which hotel we eat in, won't we.'

Emily said, 'Are you sorry we didn't climb the rock?'

He smiled, although his eyes didn't change. 'No, not at all. The walk, the scenery. It's been wonderful. Don't you think. Terry?'

'Magic, mate,' Terry said. 'Out of this world.' He rubbed his red, pouchy cheeks. His fingers trembled.

'We've got some great things lined up, haven't we, Terry,' Andrew said. 'All sorts of things to look forward to.' He sat very straight, and didn't take his eyes from Emily's face.

'Yes, Andrew,' Terry said.

TRIAL

About six-foot-two, thick-set, strong arms, big head, big hands, freckly skin, sandy-brown hair, direct blue eyes. Nervous.

Emily sat in the press seats and wrote this on her notepad. But this was not the man she had come here to describe.

Ford fidgeted and sweated and looked around for a better seat. He had a pillar in front of him. The place was full; there were no other seats free. There was a low, expectant murmur. The front was packed with journalists. There were rows of the complainant's family and supporters, police, further back were the curious, some students.

The side door opened and Reid Harris entered, flanked by two security guards. He glanced behind, his eyes darting across the rows. Ford found that he was pinching the skin on the back of his hand, hard. He had an odd sense, what was it? A powerful sense of memory where none actually existed, an emotion like yearning, or pity, that seemed to roam over a blankness, seeking somewhere to fix. He looked at the back of Reid Harris's head. Reid leaned and listened to his whispering lawyer, and Ford saw he had a whorl of hair at his crown. His neck was powerful; he was a big, fit man. Ford was close enough to see the blue of a large tattoo through the thin white cotton of Reid's shirt.

The registrar swept in, gathering her robe around herself. At her command all rose and the judge bustled in, making, it seemed to Ford, an excessive effort to appear ingratiating, not 'above himself' — that fussy smile, the fiddling with glasses. He was a swarthy little man with bright eyes and a smooth little helmet of black hair. He sipped some water, nodded in sprightly fashion at the stenographer.

The lawyer was whispering intensely. Reid nodded, casting his eyes behind at the public gallery. There was a blonde woman wearing a gold cross sitting next to Ford; Reid's eyes rested on her for a moment and flicked away. Listen to your brief, Ford wanted to say. Concentrate. But when Reid nodded and sat back there was something assured in his manner, a toughness. He was no novice. He was a senior policeman, had been in court many times before. His big hands were clenched on the table in front of him. Ford wiped his brow with a handkerchief and caught sight of a stain on the front of his shirt. He felt exposed, and was glad of the pillar in front of his seat. He had not expected to feel like this when he had decided, after a night of thinking about it, to head down to the court. It was more difficult than he had envisaged.

In the press seats, a woman journalist was looking at him and writing something in her notebook. She seemed to be paying him close attention. Could she see that he was nervous?

Reid's lawyer rose and began to speak. There were issues he needed to raise, matters of evidence, hearsay and so on. The judge smiled, twinkled, 'Indeed, it seems we'll have to discuss this in chambers.' The registrar rose, there was a collective moan of disappointment. The court would have to be cleared. The jury filed out, the crowd stood, the doors were opened. Ford made for the doors resolving that he would not take this intermission as a chance to escape.

In the café he stood in a long queue. The dusty morning light filtered down. The tables were full, but he found one out in the foyer and sat down. The journalist who had been staring at him from the press seats came out carrying a coffee. She walked towards him.

'There's no seats. Do you mind if I . . . ?'

'Sure.'

She began scrabbling in her bag, took out a phone and sent a rapid text.

'I'm covering the Reid Harris trial.' She named her paper. 'Did I see you in there, or . . . ?'

She had pale-blue eyes, strong features, tangled hair.

There was a silence. Her question struck Ford as disingenuous: she had been staring at him in there. Voices echoed up to the high ceiling; there was a harsh laugh, the sound of a slamming door.

'You in the police?' she asked.

'No, I'm a lecturer. University.'

'Sort of academic interest?' Her phone beeped and she glanced at it, business-like.

'Fuck,' she said. She snapped the phone shut.

Ford sipped his coffee and was glad that his hand was steady. He saw himself at four that morning, in a state of agitation, sitting out on the deck with the cat, Ticket, on his lap. He had resolved to come here, today, to see Reid Harris in court. Why had he come? Because I have lost so many connections. Because I am alone.

'Yes, academic interest,' he said.

'What's your field?'

'History. You're a journalist,' he said weakly.

'Yes.'

'I don't want to . . . ' He was making a mistake. Her face had sharpened, now she looked interested.

'I'm a relative,' Ford said.

'Of the complainant?'

'Reid Harris is my brother.' He felt a tremor of pride at coming out with it.

'Really, he has siblings? I thought he was an only child.' She sat back, regarding him.

'He's my half-brother.' He thought of Reid's face. His hands clenched on the table in front of him. 'I didn't know him, until I was approached by a friend of his mother.'

'Do you have contact with him?'

'Yes, I've contacted him. I don't know if he's seen me here today. But we have met. Quite a few times.'

She looked fascinated now. Ford wished he could stop this, yet her interest made him keep going. He'd been thinking about this for days, obsessing about it really; now here was someone he could tell it to. He hadn't wanted to bother Simon with it. There was no one else.

'His mother is,' she thought for a second. 'Rima Richards. A member of the Assembly of God.'

'Reid and I have the same father.' Ford brought this out with difficulty.

'Really?' There was something in her keen-eyed expression, was she laughing at him?

'Yes, really,' Ford said coldly. He wished she would go away.

'My name's Emily Svensson,' she said and held out her hand.

'Ford Lampton.' He shook her hand, leaned forward and said urgently, 'I don't think I should be talking to you. You're a journalist. I don't want you to harm Reid in any way.'

She looked thoughtful. 'Do you think he's innocent?'

'He doesn't need me interfering, making things worse. And yes, I do think he's innocent.'

'Why?'

'Because of the things he's told me. He did nothing wrong. I absolutely believe him.'

'Your brother . . .'

'Yes, he's my younger brother. Half-brother. And he's on trial for his life. He could get eight years in jail. And you ask all these questions, no doubt you'll write something inaccurate.'

She didn't react, only looked at him, bright-eyed, thoughtful. She held something out to him. 'This is my card.' And then, 'Can I ring you?'

Ford looked at her slender bare arm. His nerves prickled. He steeled himself.

She said steadily, 'I won't write anything you've said. I won't do Reid or you any harm. I'd just like to ring you.'

'Why?'

'Oh, I don't know.' She smiled, sighed.

He said, 'I'm at the university. You know my name.'

'Will you take my card?'

'Yes. Fine.' He took it, rose and walked away, his shoes squeaking on the tiled floor.

Emily watched him leave. A corner of his shirt had come un-
tucked and was flapping at the back of his trousers. He smoothed
back his hair — a nervous gesture.

She took out her phone and wrote a text: Guess what one of half
brothers here at court. Talked to him but not much. Says RH 'not
guilty'.

A text came back. The doctor?

Lecturer. She replied. No sign of the dr.

She yawned, stretched and finished her coffee. People were
moving. The court would be back in session. She followed the
crowd back upstairs, thinking intensely about Ford.

Ford had grabbed a better seat. He turned Emily's card over in his
hands. He looked at the line of journalists in front of him, some
of whom he recognised from TV; pretty, thin women, a young
man with gelled-back hair. Many were furiously texting before the
registrar came back in. The registrar policed the court with gaunt
vigour, threatening to confiscate phones. Ford watched the blonde
woman wearing a gold cross thread between the seats. There was a
quality of stillness about her, something watchful and contained.

The jury filed in, and then the judge.

Emily made herself stop looking at Ford, and watched Reid
Harris.

*Six foot three. Physically powerful, muscular, obviously works on
fitness, body-builds, whatever it takes to get shoulders and arms that
big. Alert eyes, sharp face, wide, thin mouth, an overall appearance of
pumped-up masculinity that will be construed as arrogance. Undeniably
butch, extremely tough, but not necessarily nasty. Neither stupid nor
vicious . . .*

Emily sat back and considered, twirling her pen in her hand.

According to the charges, a young woman had come to Reid
Harris's door with a petition while he was living in a house in
Northland. He was posing as a drug dealer in an undercover
police operation. He was alleged to have dragged her into the
house, sexually assaulted her and raped her. It was a historic
charge, some years old.

The complainant, a tall, slim, attractive woman, had been brought over from Melbourne for the case, and the press had been allowed to watch her give evidence. On that day the glass doors had swung open and shivered back into place and in a sudden rush of activity Ms Charlene Heka, now Mrs Vitali, had swept into the corridor amid a parade of supporters and cops. She had been stationed in an interview room and her husband, Mr Vitali, could be seen roaming to the door, peering through the glass, scanning the hall and veering away again like a predatory fish in a glass tank, while his wife sat immobile at a table, guarded by a woman detective from Melbourne who wore high-heeled boots, had her foot up on a chair and a cell phone clamped to her ear. When she was called as a witness there was a sudden intensifying of police activity, much important marching about, and as she was brought into the court the air seemed to compress, as if the room itself were drawing a long, excited breath. Reid Harris's lawyer swivelled on his chair and stared grimly over his half glasses and the prosecutor rose, held up his hand and nodded to the assorted press, acknowledging the intensity, the fearful glamour of the moment.

On the stand she was likeable and attractive. She had a low, pleasing voice and a way of leaning forward conscientiously to listen to questions, keen to get details exactly right. She paused, thought before she spoke, admitted when she could not remember or when she might have got something wrong. Listening, Emily found it impossible to imagine someone more honest and sincere. She conveyed no sense of melodrama or relish, no shrillness or anger, only a kind of delicate distress at the situation in which she found herself. Details of the actual assault had to be dragged out of her, the prosecutor coaxing, apologising, taking inordinate care to be sensitive. When at last Mrs Vitali had been induced to describe the nitty-gritty of the assault, to name, unwillingly but bravely, body parts and functions, Emily had seen one of the juror's eyes fill with tears, and Emily herself had felt that a kind of violence was being inflicted on this slender, gentle-natured woman.

Reid Harris's lawyer couldn't get anywhere with her. He needed to challenge her, yet he risked alienating the jury, who liked her.

On the other side of the courtroom Reid Harris sat motionless, his hands clenched in front of him.

On that day — it was two days ago now — Emily hadn't fully heard the question, her mind must have wandered, but it was some time in the afternoon as the late sun was slanting in and the air, full of revolving dust, had a drowsy shine to it; the tension of the day had slackened, the jury were glazed and Mrs Vitali seemed wan, her hair awry and her composure dented. Afterwards, Emily had searched the transcript to find the exchange. Q: 'After the day you say you were assaulted, did you seek a pregnancy test?' A: 'I don't know.' Q: 'More than one pregnancy test that year?' A: 'I don't know when I had tests. I might have had lots, I can't remember. I — my boyfriend and I — had a baby the following year.' Q: 'A baby?' A: 'He died of cot death. One week old.'

There was an objection, the prosecutor was on his feet, the jury blinked, looked muddled and dragged themselves upright, refocusing, in their seats. A piece of paper fell off the edge of the registrar's desk and swooped through the shining air. The registrar reached out to grab it and Emily looked past her at Mrs Vitali who was leaning forward and holding the wooden rail in both hands. She had her eyes on Reid Harris and he was looking back. An intense, silent communication passed between them, and in that instant Emily saw that they knew each other. They knew each other well. This could not be what would pass between a woman and a stranger who had attacked her. She thought, he's telling the truth. They have known, maybe even cared about each other. What if this isn't a rape case? What if it's something else?

Emily had a free night on Fridays. Caro stayed with Beth and Per, and usually spent Saturday morning with them.

She sat alone at her kitchen table, drinking a glass of wine, her notebook in front of her, and read over the description of Ford Lampton. She had not stopped thinking about Ford all afternoon.

Emily hadn't been with a man since Harry had left. Caro had recently turned four. At first, Emily had been too busy trying to be a good parent to go looking for a man. But lately the idea had begun to haunt her: I will grow old and die and never have anyone else.

A fierce restlessness sent her pacing around the kitchen. Time was passing, she would get older, no one would want her and life would be over. It had been fine, just Emily and Caro getting on with life; now, suddenly, it was agony. She could not get Ford Lampton out of her mind. Why him? Why anyone, she thought. There was something about Ford (the way he looked, the way he talked?) that had got her into this strange mood.

She picked up the phone book. There was a listing for F Lampton and Dr M Bandaranaike in Grey Lynn. He would be at home with his wife, he would be out at dinner; he would be in bed with his wife (her scalp prickled). She rang the number.

Ford answered.

'It's Emily Svensson.'

There was a long silence. Ford said, 'I'm sorry, I told you, I don't have any comment.'

'I know you said that, but I wondered if we could meet.'

'I don't know any more about the case than you.'

She thought, I want you to come over here, we could go for a walk, we could have a coffee, we could talk about our problem brothers, we could compare family weirdness, we could laugh about the fact that we turned out normal and sane, we could walk closer and closer until your hand brushed mine and then on some street in the sun we would be kissing and go home and get between the sheets and fuck one another blind, because for some reason I like you, strangely you, because time is running out, because the world is going to hell, because all I want to do is fuck you to pieces, now now now.

She said, 'I know you may think it's "inappropriate" of me to call. But I would like to talk, just briefly, about the business with Reid.'

He laughed sourly. 'The business?'

She said, 'I think he's innocent too. There's something I could tell you.'

'So tell me,' he said coldly.

'I realise you don't want to talk to a journalist. I know that.'

'I've read your stuff. Your in-depth profiles. Your reputation for "honesty". You don't leave anything out. Why would I want to end up in one of your pieces?'

She registered this. He knew who she was. His tone was hostile; there was something else, a sadness. A quick perception flashed into her mind: he was alone. She said, 'I didn't mean to disturb you and your wife . . . ?'

'No problem,' Ford said in a harsh voice.

Emily waited. The silence lengthened. She held out.

'My wife is dead.'

Emily stifled a sudden laugh. She got up and paced around the room. She was struck with an exquisite, private sense of comedy.

'Dead?'

'Yes.'

'I'm so sorry,' Emily said, and squeezed her eyes shut. She put her hand over her mouth. What was she doing?

'She died in a car accident.'

Emily took a reckless swig of wine. 'Really?'

'Yes. Last year.'

'Look, I'm sorry. I shouldn't have bothered you.' She winced, willing him not to end the call.

'She was a doctor. An anaesthetist. I don't know how I've got through the year without her. She was the most beautiful, talented, charismatic person I've ever known.'

Emily, the phone clamped between her shoulder and cheek, stuck her head in the fridge, drew out the wine bottle and said, 'Go on?' A milk carton tipped up and spilled, she grabbed, missed and it sprayed across the carpet. She threw a tea towel on the floor and stamped on it vigorously, filling her glass at the same time.

Ford said vaguely, 'She was driving on the northwestern motorway. I should have been with her. She was badly injured, didn't have a chance.' He sighed, a lost sound.

'Can we meet?' The words shot out. She couldn't tone down the abruptness.

His voice went flat. 'I've told you, I don't have any comment.'

She should have let him go on more about the wife. Now she'd sounded cynical, impatient. She'd lost him. She tried to think quickly. 'Have you spoken to Reid today?'

'Yes, I have,' he said.

'What about?' No no, wrong question. She closed her eyes, clenched her fists.

'None of your business,' Ford snapped.

Emily picked up the milky tea towel and whirled it round in frustration. 'I don't just want to talk about the case. Honestly, if we met it would be more just a social thing.' She grimaced, waited.

'A social thing? Since when does a journalist just want to have a social thing? It'll be all very cosy and chatty and then I'll pick up the paper and the whole thing will be there, transcribed. No thanks.'

She said desperately, 'What if I promise not to talk about Reid at all?'

'What's the point of that?' He sounded amazed.

'Then it would be purely a social thing.'

'Look, Emily, I'm sure you play these kinds of games all the time.' His tone was final.

She wanted to tell him, I do play around with subjects, I do interview people, I do write about them, but I'm straight about you.

'I'm sorry to have bothered you then,' she said brightly.

'I admire your tenacity.'

'Oh well, back to business. Life goes on, and so on,' Emily said surreally.

'You must have a very interesting life.'

'Yes. It's fascinating,' she said.

She hung up, fell face down on the couch, and lay there for a long time.

The next morning at the first adjournment, Emily sat down next to Ford in the court café. He put his newspaper down and looked at her, long-suffering.

'I can't write anything about Reid now, it's *sub judice.*'

'Yes, but you're here with a view to writing something after the trial, aren't you,' he said sarcastically. 'Otherwise you wouldn't be here.'

'No. Okay. But I wanted to tell you. I saw Reid and Mrs Vitali looking at each other and I could tell they knew each other. It was when she said she'd had a baby that had died. The baby could have been his.'

Ford winced. 'Well, he is supposed to have raped her.'

'Yes, and you couldn't prove now that it was his, and even if you could it might only say something about dates — that they were having sex after she says he attacked her. But the baby's dead, so that's not helpful. The point is, when she mentioned the baby she looked at him, their eyes met and I could tell.'

Ford looked weary and troubled.

'Tell what?' he said in a flat voice.

'That they were communicating. That they had a history. That more had gone on between them than just one "attack".'

'I see.'

She looked at her fingernails, considering. 'My editor wants me to do an interview with Reid, to run it if he's acquitted.'

'And you want me to help you.' Ford crossed his arms and assumed a grim can't-fool-me expression.

'No, that's my job. I don't need your help,' Emily said sharply.

He folded his paper and slapped it down on the table. He pursed his lips, haughty, high-minded. He picked a thread off his sleeve. 'Are you the sort of person who derives enjoyment from other people's pain?'

Her expression changed. She leaned forward. 'Yes,' she said. 'I'm a sadist. That's it. I'm just here taking an interest, telling you these things because I'm a sadist.'

He stared.

'Forget it. I've been awake all night thinking about you, about this case, I mean, about your brother, and I've got a few ideas about it, and I'm just doing the job I get paid for and it's not necessary for me to talk to you. It's just not necessary.'

She put down her cup. Near them, a man in a suit rose from his table, flipped open his beeping phone and said intently, 'Yeah yeah yeah yeah.' The glass doors opened, a baby wailed, and a woman walked across the foyer grappling with a heavy child, the sun making long dusty shafts of light through which she staggered, the child flailing, the mother's face averted from the little fists.

Ford, his knees locked together, swivelled awkwardly on his seat, his hands clenched on his thighs. 'Emily.'

'Forget it.'

He held up his hands, looking around, wanting to quell this sudden alarming surge of intensity. His face was creased with consternation.

She stood up and walked off, leaving him at the table. She went into the ladies, looked at herself in the mirror and laughed. She thought again, what am I doing?

Late morning, the next day. In his office, coffee mug in one hand and a folder in the other, Ford ran his eye down the list in his inbox. He stopped abruptly at the name. Emily Svensson.

He lowered himself into his seat. Good God. Now she'd got into his email. Like a stalker. But it was what journalists did, stalk people. Follow them, find out about them, write about them.

He opened the message:

Now I can't concentrate! Is this case rather distracting or . . . Sorry, if I've bothered you recently. I need to get back to work don't I. I have a deadline and I'm just so uncharacteristically . . . distracted.

That was all. Ford looked at the words, trying to hear her saying them. She sounded girlish, playful, apologetic: sinisterly so? That 'distracted'. It was like saying, 'I've been thinking about you.' Not asking for anything specific, but definitely inviting further talk. The time of the email, he noted, was 1am. Last night. She'd been sitting up late then, trying to work but her mind straying. To him. Weary, frustrated, oppressed by her deadline, she had fired off, on impulse, a quick message to the person who was distracting her.

No. She was playing games. He must not reply. She was drawing him into communicating; she would try to worm out information about Reid, about their family, or, heaven forbid, their father. He would not fall into a trap. Of course she would pretend to be interested in him; this was probably her *modus operandi*.

Ford exited the email, rolled his shoulders toughly, whistled between his teeth and went to work on a paper he was writing for a journal. The traffic roared under his window, the department secretary glided noiselessly past his door. *It is important to note, however . . .* Ford typed. He paused, sipped his coffee. *In this case it is important to note that . . .* He scratched his chin. *It cannot be overlooked that . . .*

With a tsk of irritation, he went back to the inbox. He frowned over Emily's message until he found he'd lost the sense of it. He sat vacantly tapping his pen on his teeth. He clicked on Reply. He tried: Yes, you need to get back to work. Ford. Then deleted that and wrote: I am also 'distracted' — by a large workload. Ford. He deleted that and played around with: Get out of my inbox. Ford. Then, Are you a stalker? Ford. Followed by, Fuck off. Ford.

Jo Allen poked her head around the door. 'We're going for a coffee, Ford. Are you coming?'

With his finger on delete he said, 'No, I'd better get on thanks. I'll get something later.'

He hunched forward and banged out: Are you trying to FLIRT with me? What if I take you up on it? What if we get together and I GIVE YOU ONE until you can hardly

He stopped. He thought of Reid. This woman (and who was she really, where had she come from?) had been assigned to write about Reid's trial for the titillation of a very hostile, very interested readership. Anything he did could become public very quickly. It could compromise his brother, damage his own standing at the university. What if she made some kind of allegation against him, Ford?

He deleted the last sentence and sat back. His shirt felt too tight; he was sweating. His colleagues trooped by his door, heading to the café.

Nice Jo Allen, a divorcee, had asked him to go to a film with her next week. Life goes on. There are even things to look forward to. No need to get involved in nonsense with strangers. Jo, who was brilliant, always stood very close and once, bold and tipsy after a departmental dinner, had toyed childishly with a button on his jacket. Looking down at the top of her head Ford had glimpsed the pink tips of her ears poking out of her shining blonde hair and a vision had floated in his mind, of his own beautiful May, savagely laughing. He'd flinched and stepped aside. This had only aroused Jo's interest further; she thought he was 'gentlemanly' and 'shy'. If she only knew how the inner Ford roamed the halls like a wounded savage clawing at the unfindable wound, how, since May had died, he had dreamed of violence, smashing a fist into a face, or his own face beaten by an invisible fist. How grotesquely his mind worked at departmental meetings too. In his tranced reveries Jo Allen fellated the departmental head, danced naked on the table, flopped down on the floor and gave herself a handjob. But he didn't want her, didn't fancy her, no, not at all.

He clicked on Reply. He wrote: I am rather distracted myself. But I have a lot of work to do. Good luck with your writing. I do appreciate your considerateness. Ford.

Driven by his steady finger, the cursor travelled to Send. He clicked.

Ford saw in his mind his message flying away, a scrap sucked into the ether. He rose, went to the window, and stood looking at the backs of his hands.

Emily dropped Caro at kindergarten. In the terraced, leafy playground, with its ropes and sand and bright cuboid toys, the little girl turned and gave Emily a considering look. 'Can Beth pick me up today?'

'What's wrong with me picking you up?'

'Beth said we can make a cake or a sword. Or a cake shaped like a sword.'

'Well. We'll see.' It was hard to argue with that. Emily kissed her and walked away, and then came back and kissed her again. She went home through the reserve. It was a windy day, the sky crossed with flying tatters of cloud.

In her room, she turned on the computer and stared out over the tops of the trees. The machine roused itself with soft whirs and clicks, until the inane surge of electronic notes (what were they supposed to signify: stars, fountains, inspiration, hope?) announced that it was ready.

She opened the email. Had he? Yes. Ford's name appeared in the inbox.

There was also a message from Angus, her editor, which she opened first: i hear you've been talking to reid's brother - take him for a cup of tea. get him to open up - why not might as well see what you can get out of him

She opened Ford's message: I am rather distracted myself. But I have a lot of work to do. Good luck with your writing. I do appreciate your considerateness. Ford

The night before, Emily had stayed awake, thinking about Ford. At midnight she had got up, turned on the computer and sat staring at the screen. She had written, rewritten, deleted. How to approach him? It wasn't possible to tell the truth, that for reasons she couldn't explain she had taken a liking to him. The circumstances couldn't be less propitious. He wouldn't believe she was sincere. He had much more pressing things on his mind. And he would feel vulnerable.

She'd gone out onto the balcony and looked at the sky all streaked with black cloud over the city. The idea had come to her: a 'deadline'. To set the scene: herself labouring over her work, her late night distraction, the 'impulse' of sending him an email. She'd waited until it was good and late: 1 am, written a scrappy message and sent it. Then she'd gone to bed and lain awake again, until the light was glowing softly around the curtains and the first birds were stirring in the reserve.

Now she stared at his message. Had he fired it off straight away? Had he hesitated, worried? He appeared so worried, so tormented all the time. He also looked highly intelligent. Why would he risk having anything to do with her? Why would he necessarily want to? She had the sense that she was balancing on a thin wire, that if she made the slightest false move all would be lost.

She got up and paced. Now she *was* hopelessly distracted. I do appreciate your considerateness. What did that mean? Was he thanking her for saying sorry she'd bothered him? Or did he mean he would appreciate further considerateness, i.e. I would appreciate it if you would go away and not make any more out of this?

She felt exhausted; up all night scheming over the email and now no further. She hadn't had time to shower or eat before getting

Caro off to kindergarten; she felt grimy, shabby, hollow, and yet there was a kind of exaltation at the edge of her mood. This strange, difficult game: it was the opposite of boredom.

Another email flew in from Angus: ps kate says have the cup of tea in a crowded place - he might have the rape gene

Emily laughed. Two rosellas burst suddenly out of the trees in the reserve, their wings sarcastically clapping.

She sat down, went to Ford's message, clicked on Reply and wrote out rapidly: Sorry — mind wandering in dead of night — these deadlines always a drag — have to work sometimes after putting my daughter to bed — joys of being a solo mother — but you're right, no point in you and I talking re Reid — was nice to meet you briefly. Haven't mentioned to anyone I've talked to you — best wishes, Emily Svensson.

She pressed Send.

Terrible. Weaving in that you're a solo parent. That you're alone. Cynically planting these hooks. But it's not cynicism, she thought. I like him. Is that bad? She stopped to consider. How could she like him? How did it happen that all the men you met were unacceptable and then suddenly one was interesting? At least interesting enough to want to find out more. This didn't happen to her often; in fact it hadn't happened since Harry, and before him she'd been very picky.

She looked up Ford on the internet. There was a picture on a departmental website. He was not conventionally handsome. But the deep eyes and the contours of the face expressed power, a kind of voraciousness even, and yet good humour too.

She flicked back to the email. No reply. She sighed and felt stale, bored and flat. These bouts of passion, these feverish nights — why couldn't she just settle down, let life come to her? All this over a man she didn't know and had barely spoken to. Ridiculous. Lately she seemed always to be prowling around, wanting, with the sense that she was standing outside life. Always the feeling that something vibrant, exciting and colourful was just out of reach, and that she could not find it, no matter how she tried to drive her life, to bend it to her shape.

Emily was in the court café sending a text to her mother. She looked up and saw Ford circling warily, holding a tray. He hesitated, approached. His coffee cup slid across the tray, clattering in its saucer. He had chosen a large triangle of cake with a cherry on it. He coughed, grunted a hello and carefully set down the tray. Emily sat very still. The cake with its festive cherry struck a poignant note: Ford keeping his end up, consoling himself with a childish treat. He plunged a knife into it and it broke up messily.

He had the look of having spruced himself up; a clean shirt, his hair combed. He sat frowning at the cake, a few locks falling over his forehead. What was so affecting about a bowed head, hair falling on a forehead, a shaving cut on skin, clumsy hands? The way he seemed to possess physical power and yet to struggle through the physical world.

Her phone buzzed.

'Did you get your thing finished?' Ford asked cautiously.

'Oh, yes. I banged it out in the end.' Her face went hot.

'I've been busy too, trying to finish a paper.' He ripped open a sachet and sugar sprayed over the table. Emily watched, her eyes lowered. Those big hands.

She looked down at her phone. Beth's reply appeared on the little screen: Ys c@n pike uppp Caro seeee yu& after%.

She laughed. 'It's from my mother. She's still getting the hang of texting.'

Ford sipped his coffee and flinched. He squeezed his fingers over the bridge of his nose.

She said, 'You know I'm going to interview Reid and his wife? They've agreed.'

Ford looked away.

'What's his wife like?' she said.

'Angela. They met when he was in the Far North. Then they got together later in Auckland. She's got some kind of graphic design business. They're a tight couple.'

Emily said, 'You know what I admire? You sticking by your brother. Because I think I somehow abandoned mine.'

She started gathering up her things.

'Your brother?'

'He's dead.'

Ford rose and stood slightly crooked, one shoulder hunched.

'Dead,' he repeated. He stared, his forehead creased, as though he were labouring through some intense calculation.

She said, 'I'm going. There's some kind of delay. I don't need to be here.'

He stepped sideways, knocking against the chair. He seemed to be casting about for something to say.

Emily felt a wave of frustration and irritation so strong she stood on tiptoe. She frowned and snatched up her bag. 'The context makes it impossible,' she said.

He raised his hands, palm up, helpless. 'Makes what impossible?'

'For us to talk like this. As if we're friends.'

'Friends?' he said, wondering.

She walked away, out through the glass doors and into the polished light of the afternoon. It was a day of wind and agitation, clouds racing across the sun, moments of glare followed by abrupt dimming of the light. In the park across the road the trees heaved in a sudden roar and rubbish blew up and whirled around and settled. She was crossing the courtyard away from him, her body tilting slightly against the rush of air. Ford followed. He called to her to wait. She stopped and scowled, passing a set of car keys from hand to hand. His shirt billowed out in the wind. She had put on a pair of sunglasses and he looked at twin reflections of himself, his hair on end, his face distorted. He took hold of her arm and leaned close to her.

'Nothing's impossible,' he said.

Emily laughed.

He let go of her arm. 'Seriously,' he said.

She stepped away. 'You mean you want to be friends?'

'We could step outside the context, as it were.'

'As it were,' she repeated. Her eyes were bright. She looked amused, conspiratorial. 'So, do you want to come to my place?'

The hair lifted on Ford's scalp, his nerves flared. 'Okay. Yes, sure.'

They walked in silence to her car. She drove him to Parnell and parked in a dead-end street outside a white stucco house with peeling paint. They crossed the yard: an untended garden, some old white iron furniture, a child's tricycle. In the hall he looked at large black and white photos, film stills. There was an actress he recognised.

'My father's a film director,' she said. She led him along the hall, pointing out scenes from films. He looked at studio scenes: cameras, cables, an actor being instructed by a wiry, intense man in a plaid shirt, the man holding a clipboard, and pointing away from the camera, the actor deferentially frowning.

There was a picture of a young man. There was something wrong with his smile. It was too wide, too much.

'My brother,' Emily said.

They passed a child's bright bedroom, toys strewn on the floor.

He sat at the kitchen table. She went to the sink, putting the kettle on. She paused, laughed, put her hands up to her face.

'What's wrong?' he asked.

She rested her knuckles on the bench and looked out the kitchen window. Her shoulder blades stood out under her thin shirt. The shirt rode up; he could see the bumps of her spine. With her back to him she said in a remote voice, 'It's sort of astonishing.'

'What?'

She turned, leaning against the cupboards, one arm folded against her stomach, her hand cradling her elbow. 'To get what you want. I wanted you to come here. I tried to shape it, to make it happen. And here you are.' She threw herself down in a chair and slouched across the table. 'That email I sent you. I did it deliberately. I didn't send it on impulse, I planned it, I was trying to get you to come here.'

'Because of Reid.'

'No. Nothing to do with Reid. Because of you. I don't invite any old person here. I don't invite any men. I live like a hermit. Caro's — my daughter's — father lives in Spain. He's never coming back.'

She looked directly at him. Faint blue veins on her bare arms. Tangled dark hair, pale-blue eyes, strong jaw and wide mouth.

Clean white teeth. Faint smudges of shadow under her eyes.

He absorbed the words: because of you.

Silence. Outside, the trees in the reserve tossed in the wind. A branch scratched on the window, the kettle boiled and clicked off. Ford stood up and went around the table, took her by the arms, pulled her up, and as he was kissing her had a sense of dry cool skin, dry skin smooth against dry skin, his nerves flared to such a pitch he was all nerve, like walking too near a cliff, feeling sliding dust near the edge under bare feet, exhilaration and fright and the blood racing under the skin, and she walked backwards down the hall and up the stairs, still kissing him, led him to a double bed under a sloping attic roof, the windows looking over the reserve and across to the city, and they fell down on top of it, the wooden bed head letting out a groan of protest as they landed; she was on top but then he turned and pinned her down, bore down on her and looked into her eyes, because he wanted it to matter, to move her, because he wanted it to seem like love.

Ford went into a deep sleep. He dreamed he was on an open plain somewhere dry, wild and barren, surrounded by hundreds of people. They were all moving slowly on their feet and chanting. It was early morning, bright, golden light. Slow chanting, bright light. He woke up and saw Emily sitting at a desk, her bare feet splayed on the wooden floor, the square of a computer screen glowing in front of her. Outside the sky had turned a dull, bruised colour. It was raining; he could hear the drops drumming on the iron roof.

He moved. She looked over her shoulder and exited the screen.

'Checking emails,' she said, coming over, pulling a robe around herself and lying next to him. 'My editor sends me all sorts of mad stuff. He's a funny guy.'

Ford was remembering the atmosphere of his dream.

She said, 'I'm getting my daughter minded for the night. Do you want to stay?'

'What's the time?'

'Four o'clock.'

'God.' He sat up.

The city skyline was draped with heavy cloud and the dark smudge of a rainstorm was advancing up the suburb. There was a rush of wind and the fat drops splattered against the window.

'Will you stay?'

He was silent, struggling with the feeling that May, the spirit of May who lived in his house, would roam through the rooms, wondering where he was.

'Yes, sure,' he said.

Later, when she was downstairs in the kitchen, he listened to the pots banging and smelled the warm smell of food; he looked out at the rain falling over the wooden houses, and thought again of his own house, Ticket prowling the perimeter looking for him and the dark rooms and the silence, and the absence. He got up, swiftly crossed the room and touched the keys of Emily's computer. The screen flickered up, bright in the dark room. He clicked on the emails and scrolled down. There was his own. Then one from an Angus Ferguson: i hear you've been talking to reid's brother - take him for a cup of tea - why not - might as well see what you can get out of him

Further up, he found a p.s. from the same name: ps kate says have the cup of tea in a crowded place - he might have the rape gene

He stared. He felt the blood swarming through his body, a surge of nerves. He exited the screen and began looking around for his clothes. He stopped, considering. He sat down on the edge of the bed with his shoulders bowed, his shirt crumpled in his hands. After a moment he dropped his clothes on the floor and stretched himself gingerly out on the bed. He lay staring at the ceiling until she came in with a tray of food.

Her face was flushed, she was grinning. 'I've even made you a salad,' she said, sticking a piece of basil leaf on top of each plate. She angled the tray across his legs and sat down, wriggling in next to him.

'How lovely,' Ford said.

He picked up his fork, moved closer to her. 'When are you interviewing Reid?' he asked.

'Tomorrow evening.'

The dark outside, the two of them in the yellow electric light. Rain drumming on the iron roof. He felt like a terrible old man, full of terrible secrets, telling a bedtime story while the throb of some other, hidden life beat an urgent drum in his head. The rape gene . . . He didn't know whether Reid was innocent or not. But he wanted, he willed it to be so. She turned happy eyes on him. But they're not innocent eyes after all, he thought. Brief wretchedness. The desolate feeling threatened his self-control. He steadied himself. Slowly, 'thoughtfully' (I'll tell you a little tale my dear, let me think, oh yes) he began to talk about his half brother. Everything he knew and had recently discovered about Reid. Reid's life of service. His courage and loyalty. The fundamental goodness of Reid.

Ford kept his answering machine on. When he heard Reid's voice he picked up the phone.

'We've done the interview,' Reid said.

'How did it go?'

'She was fine. Angela liked her. I was careful. It can't do me any harm. She seemed well-disposed.'

'You can't tell with journalists.'

'I know, but I was careful. I stated my case, that was all. She met the kids. Patted the dog. Said nice things about the house, how Angela's done it up so tasteful. Angela got in everything she wanted to say. It was pretty friendly. She asked a bit about you. I said you and I got on well. That we were pleased we'd met.'

Ford leaned down absently to stroke Ticket, who was circling around his legs.

Reid said, 'They won't run it if I end up in jail. They'll write a different sort of piece.'

'No doubt,' Ford said grimly.

'Will you be there tomorrow?'

'I'll be there,' Ford said.

Early morning. Another easterly storm battering the city, purple sheet lightning flashing over the buildings. The air was full of whirling rain. Ford rode the bus into town, looking out at the sodden city, people wrestling with tattered umbrellas, leaning, coats plastered to legs, into the sudden blasts of wind. The air was warm and so full of moisture that it seemed to toss and swirl before his eyes. Walking up through the park he heard the trees roaring overhead and felt as though he were walking on the bottom of a lake; above him the agitated air slopped and broke, heaving with currents.

He met Angela and Reid in the spot they'd agreed on. Angela smelled of smoke and peppermints. There were dark loops under her eyes. Reid was silent, grim-faced, fidgeting with his tie, breaking off his sentences to stare somewhere above their heads, as if some unspeakably horrible vision floated there. They waited, drinking coffee and not saying much.

In the courtroom Emily waved, threaded her way over and whispered hotly in his ear, 'Where've you been? I rang you. I've interviewed Reid.'

'How did it go?'

'It was good. Look at all these people. I'd better grab my seat.'

The court was packed. They all stood. The judge came mincing in, angled himself into his seat and straightened up with a peppy little bounce. Ford sat through the summing up, unable to focus. Angela ate peppermints, plunging her hand vengefully into the crackling packet. He could hear her steady crunching. The summing up went on for a long time, until finally the judge gave a little sigh of satisfaction, picked up his papers, shuffled them into order, smiled sweetly at the jury and nodded to the registrar. They filed out, and the waiting began.

Ford looked out a window and watched a seagull riding the wild air, making little twitches of adjustment as it kept itself aloft. He drank four coffees in a sitting. When he couldn't stand being indoors any longer he walked around the perimeter of the courthouse, down the sheltered side and then out into the wind as he crossed east, the trees roaring above him, the air getting under his umbrella and tipping it away. The harbour was grey, full of chop. The parked cars were strewn with piles of twigs and leaves.

The hours dragged by. Looking down from the mezzanine floor

he saw Emily standing with a group of journalists, nodding and listening and at the same time moving her thumb rapidly as she sent a text. A trapped feeling came over him; he felt bound and gagged; he yearned for some kind of violent blow, to deliver it or to receive it. He thought of the emails on Emily's computer. He thought of May and was disturbed to find he couldn't picture her face; he couldn't bear to think that she was fading from his mind. In a bad moment he yearned for her, his eyes burning. He rang Simon and was told he was in theatre. Once, emerging from the toilets, he heard Emily's voice; as he opened the door a crack she passed, laughing, with one of those skinny, coiffed boy journalists from TV. He stayed out of sight.

He was coming in from a circuit around the court when he saw people at the café tables all rise at once, grab their belongings and head in a rush to the court. He joined the crowd hurrying up the stairs. People called up and down the stairwell. Yes, it was certain, the jury was coming back in. There was a crush around the doors as the crowd squeezed in; all the seats were full and people were still threading in, standing in the aisles, even sitting on the carpet in front of the press seats. The registrar, in a state of suppressed excitement, strode about the room, her robe flapping, delivering rebukes and directions. He saw a woman laugh and put a hand over her mouth; it was the heightened atmosphere of a school hall before the appearance of the magician. Even the journalists were fighting down excited expressions, sitting two to a seat.

Reid had an odd, unfocused look in his eyes; he stood still amid the agitation, as if separated by an invisible wall. In the harsh neon light Angela's face was strained and haggard. She sat next to Ford with her head held high, pressing her arms against her chest, her feet crossed neatly under her seat.

The judge bounced in, sighed, took off his glasses and polished them. With apologetic smiles, with excessive delicacy, as if it were unseemly to sully the exquisite tension of the moment, he replaced his glasses, turned and asked the jury whether they had reached a verdict. The foreman replied that they had.

The registrar rose and read out each charge, and as the replies came back the crowd reacted with moans, gasps, harsh exclamations. Then they were all on their feet; it was chaos in the small room, Reid was standing, he turned, pushed back his chair and met Ford and Angela as they came forward. Ford felt it in his heart, in his soul, wherever it was that deep emotions rested, that Reid put his arms around Ford as well as Angela. 'Thank Christ,' Reid was saying. 'Thank Christ thank Christ.'

In the blur that followed, the pushing, shoving, shouted questions, the surge out of the court, down the stairs and out into the rain, Ford kept his hand clamped on Reid's arm. He saw Emily, intent, looking for him, bobbing around the shoulders in front of her. She fought her way to him. Reid had turned away and was speaking. She said something Ford couldn't hear. But she was shouldered away and Reid pulled Ford forward; he saw her again behind him, trying to catch up, and as they got in the car hers was one of the faces in the crowd that surged after them, falling away raggedly as they bumped off the curb and sped out into the traffic, Reid urging the driver, 'Go, go,' and sitting back and turning to Ford with an expression of triumph and relief, the first time ever that Ford had seen him smile.

Ford sat out on the deck and read Emily's article. A prism of sunlight danced in Ticket's water bowl. A seagull had landed on the rail of the deck and was shifting along it on its red feet, eyeing him. He laid the article aside, then took it up again, trying to see it as others would. Spread across an entire page, it was a generous portrait of Reid Aaron Harris, fallen from grace, freshly acquitted but future career uncertain. There was Reid at home in the suburbs, surrounded by his loyal family. His good-looking children, his attractive wife. His hobbies, his homely pursuits. The dog he loves, the garden he tends. The big colour photo was flattering. As public relations, as damage control, it was perfect. You couldn't say that Emily hadn't been useful.

Ford thought of her bedroom. Rain drumming on the roof, yellow light, the view of the wild sky over the city.

The phone rang. He picked it up. Emily said eagerly, 'Ford?'

'Yes.' He closed his eyes, pinched the bridge of his nose.

'Have you read it? What do you think?'

'It's good.'

'Will you come and see me? Will you ring me? I've been ringing but you're never home.'

'I've been spending time with Reid.'

'Well. He probably won't get his job back.'

There was a silence.

'We do appreciate your considerateness,' Ford said.

'What?' He heard her grappling with the receiver. 'What do you mean by that?' Her voice rose. 'That phrase. What does it mean?'

He didn't say anything.

'Does it mean you don't . . . ?' She stopped.

Ford screwed his eyes shut. He put his hand to his forehead.

She said, 'You don't care about me.'

There was another long silence.

'I care about my brother,' Ford said.

Emily driving. Light rain made blurred loops around the streetlights. She was supposed to be driving home, but at the last minute she had turned and gone a different way. It was Friday night. Caro was staying with Beth and Per. Emily had been out to a film with Jack James from work; afterwards he had charmingly worked on her, trying to persuade her to go for a drink. She'd refused. She was avoiding going home to the empty house.

She drove up Queen Street, onto Karangahape Road. Past the Owl Bar. Onto Ponsonby Road, towards Grey Lynn. The empty streets were washed with rain. She passed Ford's road, stopped and did a U-turn. She parked and got out, walking beside sodden hedges, wet lawns, wooden fences. A dog threw itself against a fence with an explosion of barks; in her fright she lurched sideways, turning her ankle. She kicked the fence angrily and the dog stuck its snout under, hysterically yapping, the mutt.

The gate was open at Ford's. She hesitated only a moment before walking quickly down the side of the house. There was a thick clump of bushes against the window. Gingerly she angled herself in among the wet branches and looked through the screen of leaves.

The kitchen was unlit. Beyond its space of intervening darkness

Ford, Reid and Angela were grouped at the wooden dining table. A hanging light cast a soft, cone-shaped glow. Angela was wearing a loose shirt and a string of beads across her delicate throat. Her face, framed by curtains of blonde hair was sharp and foreign; she had a look of sideways laughter, grace, quickness. She was leaning on Reid's shoulder, her elbows on the table. Reid's elbows were also on the table, his hands joined at the knuckles of his clenched fists. He was resting his chin on his fists and smiling.

Ford, in jeans and a faded sweatshirt, had risen from his seat and was leaning across, putting a plate in front of Reid. He had shielded his hand from the hot plate with a tea towel. He screwed the cloth into a ball and tossed it away into the shadows behind them. The way he threw the cloth, the little comical flourish — how happy he seemed. He sat down and passed a bowl to Angela. The three of them sat talking, intent, close, in the circle of light.

Emily turned away. A branch bent back, released itself and scratched her face. She stumbled and her foot struck the tin side of a meter box. It reverberated with a hollow bang.

She hurried back along the path, embarrassment flaring in every nerve. It was not possible they hadn't heard the sound. Sure enough, as she reached the gate the front door began to open, and as she sped away up the road she heard Ford's voice, 'The cat? I don't think so.'

She drove. If only she could drive away from herself, leave this body behind. Nothing was enough; there was only wanting, yearning and never getting. Life would not be shaped or controlled; it ran on its own cruel lines.

At one-thirty, out on the Southern motorway near Otara, the orange light began blinking on the petrol gauge. A rare, thick fog lay over the southern suburbs. The roofs and treetops rose from the seething ropes of cloud and the streetlights flared, garish and strange, above the empty highway. A dark figure crossed the motorway bridge followed by a loping dog. There was a smell of burning in the air. Emily turned the car towards home.

The fog had come up the street from the sea; now the city had disappeared, and the only trace of the skyline was a dirty brownish orange glow. She entered her walled garden, walked past the blurred shapes of the iron garden furniture. Sounds were muted in the damp air; the roar of the port had softened to a low hum. Nothing was stirring. The streetlight shone into the garden, making radiant, billowing shapes in the fog.

Emily saw something in the corner of her eye: a dark shadow rearranging itself, passing the white chairs under the tree. Away from the tree, with the glow from the streetlight behind it, the figure expanded, grew tall, many-armed. Light rippled across it; it was made of rings and shadows of itself. It came towards her, a black figure in the sloping mist.

She ran back to the street, scrabbling for her phone.

'It's me,' Ford said behind her. 'Emily. It's me.'

'Ford.' She leaned against the wall.

'I didn't mean to scare you.'

'You were just this black shape. The shape of a man, but huge.' She tried to explain the magnifying effect of the fog.

'I've been waiting for you,' he said.

He leaned against the wall beside her, running his hand nervously through his hair. He turned and faced her. 'Can I come in?'

She squeezed her hands together, feeling her heart pulsing, the blood racing under her skin. It took all her effort to maintain her self-control.

She gazed off for a moment, as if taking time to consider.

'Yes, sure,' she said.

May used to tell Ford about her patients at the public hospital. The injured and sick, women in labour, children. The intellectually handicapped who needed their teeth fixed or growths removed — these people sometimes had to be held down. They didn't understand what was happening to them. Some were large and strong and had to be chased around the room. Her colleagues called this part of their job 'sporting anaesthetics'. May had partaken of the black humour of her profession; she had the thick skin doctors needed in order not to be shocked or repelled, to act with compassion.

She told Ford about people with autism and Asperger's

syndrome. These patients were born without the ability to understand social interactions. If they were intelligent enough they could learn to get on in the world, to behave like people.

The memory of this came back to Ford.

Ford and Emily went to a café for breakfast. Emily told him about herself, her life, her daughter. He thought about the Asperger's people who didn't understand or feel emotion. They had to learn intellectually what other people know by instinct. They learned to ape human behaviour.

All the months he had spent without May, missing her and learning to live without her, had armed him to do what he was doing. It armed him against the possibility, which seemed unlikely to him now, that Emily wasn't sincere. He felt he was the outline of a man. Inside him was the black shape, the absence of May. But he didn't want to live alone. He wanted to live, not die. It was easy to make Emily believe that he cared about her. He felt her affection for him. He sensed it was real. He was comforted by it, he drew strength from it. It was enough.

He would find his way back to feeling. He would be pierced by jealousy, passion, fear of losing her. This would not happen for a long time. In the meantime he made a new life. He lived well. He wanted to behave as a decent human being would.

He tried, and mostly succeeded, in this.

DRAGONFLY

They sat in the departure lounge, Larry drinking coffee, Leanne blandly flicking through a magazine, and the two teenagers whispering to each other, fidgeting, getting up to cruise in a predatory way around the shops, legging it back and sprawling in their seats. The boys were both seventeen. Lynx was Maori, with silver studs running up his ears, dyed hair cut short at the back and long on the top, and a thin, wiry body. He couldn't keep still. Slade was also Maori, although paler than Lynx and much bulkier, his face sprinkled with brown freckles, his eyes hazel and slightly misaligned. He had a line of shiny black fuzz on his upper lip, and an air of sly intelligence.

Lynx pushed his heels against the floor, levered himself up the seat until he was almost sitting on the back of it, and fell down with a thud.

The boys were cousins. They came from Otara, and had won a film competition that the company had run for high-school kids, finally announcing last month that Lynx Jones and Slade Rupapera were the winners of the grand prize, a package of video equipment for their school and a chaperoned trip to Los Angeles, where they would visit a film studio.

They had made their winning film during English classes, using equipment provided by the school. When he'd first met them, Larry had assumed that Slade was the creative genius and that jittery little Lynx was just the sidekick, along for the ride. But Lynx, it turned out, had come up with the idea for the film and had written the screenplay. Among the hundreds of entries the film stood out for the intensity of its tone. It was simple — they were only kids — but they had achieved an atmosphere of dreamy ambiguity, half-menace, half-nostalgia, that suggested real talent. The film was called *The Clothesline Man*. In it, a man, played with brilliant restraint by Slade, came to put up a clothesline in a woman's back garden. The woman was a solo mother living in a state house, and was played by one of their classmates, a Tongan girl. The clothesline was the classic New Zealand rotary model with a pole and rotating spokes, the kind that everyone remembers occupying a central place in the backyard, the sheets snapping in the wind, the kids climbing up and swinging round on the spokes. In the film the clothesline man does his work and goes away, but rings the woman with extra instructions about its use. There is a pin she can use to tighten the cords, and so on. He notes that she doesn't have a man in the house to do this for her. She is charming at first, but starts to rebel and mock when he rings her again.

The dialogue was good: subtle and nuanced. And Slade put in a top performance, managing to alternate soft-voiced, controlling, macho bossiness with sudden consternation when his character realises he's being laughed at.

Lynx had made full use of the visual potential of the clothesline — there were dreamy shots of children whirling round, coloured clothes blowing in the wind, figures appearing suddenly behind sheets as the clothesline turned. A dark figure, the clothesline man watches the woman hanging out washing in the yard, the linen dancing around her. The tone was ambiguous: is the man charmed by the scene or is he all menace and thwarted male feeling?

Larry and his boss, Ezra, picked the film. Their favourite shot was of the clothesline man picking up one of the woman's small children and walking towards her as she turned to face him, the linen blowing up into the air, as if the clothesline was throwing up its arms — in horror or celebration.

Ezra said, 'It's miles better than the others. And that fat kid can really act.'

He said, 'Leanne will do the babysitting, but you can go too, and we'll set up some meetings. You can look after business while she does the kids.'

On the plane the boys were subdued. They'd never been out of Auckland before. Leanne got them to relax. She had hit on the right way to deal with them: jolly but bossy. She was able to get their attention, call them to order. Larry was too shy; he could hear himself sounding strained and over-polite.

'I thought your film was brilliant,' he told them.

Slade puffed himself up, nodded, and made some sort of gangster gesture with four fingers. Lynx just ducked his head and grinned. Larry thought they were laughing at him. He was happy to let Leanne take control. She was a tough woman with a sharp face and a short crop of dyed red hair. Already she and the boys were laughing together, swapping food out of the airline meal, arguing about which films in the movie menu were crap and which were good. Having ripped through their dinner, the boys settled down to watch a big budget bloodbath, while Leanne sensibly donned earplugs and a mask, and dozed off.

Larry was trying not to drink.

He had a list of people he had to meet in Los Angeles. If he started drinking he wouldn't be able to stop. Ezra would fire him. He had already had a serious warning; Ezra had made it clear that any repeat of last year's incident would mean the end. Larry had got so drunk and stoned at the Christmas party that he had passed out, ripping down a line of coloured lights and knocking over a table laden with glasses. They called an ambulance for him. He was conscious but unable to stand. The memory was excruciating. Afterwards he pleaded exhaustion and overwork; he produced a doctor's certificate to say that he'd been on antibiotics that had caused him to react badly to alcohol. Ezra knew this wasn't true, but accepted it. And now he'd sent him to Los Angeles. It was a test. He couldn't mess it up.

He'd watched Leanne drink her mini-bottle of chardonnay

and then just switch her focus, to the boys, to the movie screen on the back of the seat. How was that done? He sighed and wriggled. Not drinking was as hard, as exhausting, as drinking. And how could he last without a joint to calm his nerves? He couldn't show up at LA airport with a stash of dope in his bag. He felt a surge of anxiety. The trip seemed impossible, beyond his strength. He sipped his Coca Cola and tried to focus on a movie.

They landed at night, the great city spread out below them, static lights and the highways running through them like glittering veins. The terminal was chaos; whole sections of the airport were being renovated and they queued beside hardboard barriers, under temporary, hand-scrawled signs. There was a querulous, exasperated atmosphere. Those who strayed into the wrong place were herded back into a place by aggressive personnel: 'Sir. Ma'am. Where you think you're going?' The security gates were under-manned, by two slow old guys who seemed to take pleasure in their slowness, the queues patrolled by snappish women who snatched up passports and rapped out orders and redirections. There was a mood of dull unease and dislike in the aliens' queue, everyone feeling the atmosphere of American officialdom, American paranoia. A mother said to her sons, 'Remember, no jokes. Don't make any jokes.'

Larry arrived in front of one of the old guys, who took a long time before looking up. He asked laborious questions. Larry answered, dry-mouthed and shifty. The security man photo-graphed him, Larry expecting the camera to jerk back affrontedly at the flaming condition of his eyeball. Slade and Lynx glowered and smirked and stared at the armed security guards. It was the land of guns and Americans, the real world of TV.

Outside the terminal a raddled black man with a clipboard loped up to them and said, 'Where you going? I'll take you. Leave those bags to me.'

Leanne mentioned a taxi. The man said, swaying, tugging on her suitcase, 'I'll take you. Ma'am, wherever you wanna go.'

'No,' Larry said.

The man looked up furiously, holding the clipboard against his

hollow chest. The cords stood out in his neck, his expression was
hyped up, frantic.

'We'll take the shuttle. Thanks.' Larry pushed Leanne's suitcase
back towards her with his foot.

The man held onto the handle for a moment. Then he thrust it
away. 'Fuck yo. Hey, fuck yo, man. Take yo ass where you fucking
like.' He lurched away, waving the clipboard, veering up to another
group.

They took the shuttle, gliding round the long airport strip as
the automated robot voice announced the stops. They trundled in
to the foyer of the Marriot. While Larry and Leanne waited at the
desk, Slade and Lynx drifted away, checking out the Starbucks, the
diner, the restaurant with the garish seventies-style lights, like a
series of flying saucers. They were fascinated; it was all foreign, all
familiar from TV.

The boys had a shared room, Larry and Leanne had one each.
They dumped their bags in their rooms and went down for a meal
in the foyer. The waitress was sexy, tiny, in a tight uniform. Her
name tag said Molly. She was from Ecuador. Slade and Lynx
mumbled their orders and stared. She brought the boys cokes
with ice.

Leanne asked Larry casually, 'Do you want something to
drink?'

'No.' He wondered what Ezra had told her before they left.

Leanne ordered a gin and tonic. She drank it fast and a flush
crept up her neck and into her cheeks. The food came in enormous
portions, all fatty, creamy, slathered with mayonnaise. Slade ate all
of his and half of Lynx's. The boys ordered another coke each.
Leanne asked for a second gin. She said to Larry, 'Sure you don't
want a drink?' The waitress paused, her notebook ready.

'No.'

'A wine, maybe?'

'No.'

'Well, there's always the mini-bar in your room.'

A look swelled in her face. She put her hand lightly to her chest,
as if at some secret pleasure. He tried to place her expression, to
define it. The bitch. What was she was doing? He was tired; his

head felt fuzzy and heavy. He glanced up and saw Lynx watching them. The boy sitting very still. Those noticing eyes.

They went to their rooms. Larry lay on his back, one arm over his face. He thought he was tense and wide awake, but then he was waking up. He drifted, remembering. Last week, in Auckland, he and Raine in the supermarket. There was a commotion in the aisle. A shoplifter had been collared by a store detective and was trying to argue his way out of it. He started to bluster and shout. Tins dropped out of his coat, and he tried to gather them up, pushing the woman aside. Then uniformed trolley boys and storemen were galloping into the aisle. The man fell over and struggled on the floor, hitting out. He was tall, raw and skinny. His glasses, strung on a plastic chain around his neck, got trodden on and bent out of shape. One of his sandals flew off. Larry looked at the skinny old ankles. There was a yellow puddle underneath him, and a dark patch on his jeans.

It was horrible, the skinny body writhing on the floor, the trolley boys in their sweaty serge kneeling over him, their faces lit up with excitement. Raine stood still and watched, her hand held lightly to her chest. The look in her eyes — avidity, heat.

He woke with a dry mouth. It was morning. He went to the window. Below, there were people lying on deckchairs around the pool. A uniformed black man was on his hands and knees reaching down into a manhole while another stood above him talking. The kneeling man sat back on his haunches and said something emphatic, the other went into a pantomime of hilarity, staggering and slapping his thigh. Behind the building, planes flashed past, the light catching their metal underbellies. Rings of light on metal. No sound but the sigh of the air-conditioning.

Larry went down to the foyer and checked his emails. There was one from Raine:

You've caused more trouble than you realise. Tim thinks I've put up with enough. I think he's right.

He logged off.

Raine had been angry for a week. She'd refused to drive him to the airport. It was because of Evelyn.

Evelyn was Raine's aunt. She'd been a successful businesswoman, a member of the city council, and still sat on the board of a few companies. Her husband was dead and she lived alone in a big villa in Herne Bay. Evelyn had a lot of money and no kids. She was going to leave her money to Raine, to Raine's cousins the Westons, and a small percentage to Tracy, the Maori girl Evelyn had taken under her wing.

Tracy's mother had been Evelyn's cleaner. She had seven children to five different men. She lived in chaos, on welfare. She used to bring Tracy over to Evelyn's while she did the cleaning. Evelyn took an interest in Tracy and eventually paid for her to go to a private school. When Tracy left school, Evelyn got her a secretarial job.

At a Sunday lunch at Evelyn's, glazed and steadied by a joint beforehand and a series of drinks through the meal, Larry had joined Tracy out on the deck for a cigarette. She was a pretty, melancholy girl, with a round face and tangled hair.

She said, 'I'm pregnant.'

He said, 'Fuck, how'd you manage that?'

She looked at him. They both laughed.

They turned and leaned on the rail. Inside, Raine and Evelyn were sitting at the table. Raine's churchy cousin, Tim Weston was holding forth.

Larry nudged Tracy's shoulder. He liked her. They were outsiders. They both felt it, their separateness.

He said quietly, 'You'll be all right, mate. You know you're going to inherit. Fifteen per cent of Evelyn's pile.'

Tracy stared. She said, 'No.'

This had been Larry's crime.

He had disobeyed Evelyn's edict, pressed upon Raine and through her, on Larry. Tracy was not to be told about the share she was getting from Evelyn's will. Evelyn wanted Tracy's affections to be sincere. She was emphatic about it. She didn't want Tracy to act out of what she called 'cupboard love'.

When he was given the order by Raine, 'Tracy's not allowed to know', and the reason, Larry recoiled. He hated the expression, 'cupboard love'. The low insult of it, the coldness. He expressed his distaste, clumsily, hopelessly. (He was completely pissed at the time.)

He blustered, trying to find his way to what he meant. 'If it's a gift it should be unconditional. Given out of affection. To honour someone. Why anticipate something squalid. "Cupboard love" — doesn't that just partake of the squalid? I mean, if you want to give, to honour a lifetime's association, isn't everything that's passed the reason for giving?'

He said these things, while Raine coldly ignored him. He thought to himself: Evelyn. The power-crazed old woman. All the secrets, the cold withholding. All that disgusting reverence for money. The elevation of it over everything, over love.

'You're drunk,' Raine said. 'Don't you interfere. It's none of your business.' And added, 'Just keep it to yourself.'

He had done, until that Sunday afternoon, a week and a half ago now. And he couldn't remember, he honestly wasn't sure, whether he'd told Tracy on purpose or whether it had just slipped out.

That same afternoon, Tracy mentioned the will to Evelyn. They were in the kitchen. Evelyn was making coffee. Tracy made a clumsy attempt at saying thank you. Evelyn looked over the girl's head at Larry, just looked at him. Her eyes like stones.

You had no right.

Ah, to hell with you. That was what he told them, silently, in his head.

In the driveway Tim Weston made a sorrowful face.

'Fuck off, Tim,' Larry said.

Later, he said to Raine, 'Evelyn has to forgive me. She's said it herself: every time she thinks badly of someone she has to repent.'

'Don't be so sure,' Raine said.

But now Larry couldn't stop himself. Something had been let loose. He started raging again. 'It's like when you and Tim start talking about "Asians" and what a menace they are, Evelyn can't tell you what racists you are, because then she'd have thought ill of you and she'd have to repent. She'd sit around while people were planning the Holocaust and not think ill of them, because then she'd have to repent. It's the perfect moral cop-out. Say nothing, do nothing. Don't think ill. Badness all around and she puts on that smiling, do-gooding face.'

'You're sick,' Raine said. 'No, you're really sick.'

'Why do you care about Evelyn's bloody machinations? Maybe *you're* all cupboard love.'

She threw him out then. Or rather, she threw things at him until he went to the pub, scored a lot of dope, and blasted himself out beyond caring.

He looked at the hot, gritty LA morning. He rang Leanne from his room. She sounded brisk and efficient. She'd been to the hotel gym and the boys were in the pool. She was going to take them to breakfast and then they were to be picked up and taken on one of their scheduled outings. She mentioned Disneyland. Larry wasn't listening.

He located Slade and Lynx down there in the plastic blue pool. They were resting their elbows on the edge and watching a woman in a short dress who was unloading a trolley of towels. Behind the hotel, the planes flashed past. Bursts of metallic light. The sky was clear, with a hazy rim of brown.

He thought of Raine and Tim, discussing him. Raine's email. Tim's opinion (when did that prick lose an opportunity to offer it) that Raine had suffered enough. No doubt she had. For years he had up put a chemical barrier against her. Without it, she flayed him.

He shaved, checked his bag, got himself ready. He went downstairs, ordered a cab, and shouldered out into the blinder of the LA day.

The first meeting was in a house in Santa Monica. A maid showed him in and he waited by the pool. His contact emerged through a creeper-covered archway. They talked, and the maid served Coca Cola. Larry's head was clear. He was doing well. The cold drink made his brain ache.

At lunchtime they cabbed downtown, and there was another meeting in an office tower, more difficult this time, Larry casting his eye down the list he and Ezra had drawn up, making sure he stressed what Ezra wanted him to say, and feeling a surprised thrill when, about two hours in, he got a concession that Ezra hadn't expected him to get. And then the little breeze of doubt — were they letting him have this because they were going to deny him something else? These Americans were so friendly and casual they were inscrutable. They were all white teeth and veneer. Maybe there was something he hadn't thought of.

He could see a highway jammed with cars, far below. The man opposite him, Ed Talley, had light grey eyes and brown, pockmarked skin. He never left off eye contact. There was something feral about him, a coiled quality. A shaft of cold air blew constantly down on the top of Larry's head. He had to get over wincing at the sound of his own accent. He sounded strained, too polite. Behind a glass wall a girl in a tight pink top slouched back and forth, pushing a cleaning trolley.

The meeting finished. Larry sat back, absorbing the fact that he'd got what he'd come for. No one had come in at the last moment and taken it away. He felt triumphant, then superstitious. A twitch of anxiety. But he couldn't think of anything wrong with the deal. It was what Ezra wanted. He'd stuck to the plan and pulled it off.

He was left alone with Ed, the man with the grey eyes, and Don, one of the young vice presidents.

Don slapped Larry on the shoulder and said, 'We could use a drink.'

Through the glass, Larry watched the girl in the pink top blow a balloon of gum out of her mouth. She was carrying a wastepaper basket. Outside, the city was all flash and glass and glancing afternoon light. Tiredlight. Whitelight. He felt how high up he was, how far away from home. There was a dark blot on the horizon, summer fires.

Use a drink. The words glowed in his head.

Ed put a bottle of white wine and three glasses on the table. Larry heard the ping as the glasses clinked together, and he saw the sound, a pure, sparkling droplet.

With the first chilled sip something went off in his head. There was a cool tide, a wash of sensation, and he was swept with it, marvellously free, his limbs light, his head full of soft sound. The world was a place of clarity, beauty.

'Whoa,' Don said. 'Another, my friend?'

He was out in the street, clutching his bag to his chest. The hot blast of street air hit him. For a moment he looked back, down the tube of time. He had the memory of the day running smooth and clear through its hours, before the abrupt crumpling of the evening, when time compacted like a train smashed head-on into a wall. Jumbled fragments flew off the wreckage. Ed telling a story. The second bottle. Don throwing open a drinks cabinet. At some stage they were wedged into an office kitchen, leaning against the cupboards while Ed mixed cocktails over the sink.

Don whistled up the girl in the pink top. She left off emptying bins and sauntered over. Her name was Jacinta. They offered her a drink. Later, Don danced with her round the boardroom table, his hand on her arse. She was drinking out of a plastic cup; liquid spilled as he twirled her around. Beyond the glass wall the offices were emptying out. Over the freeway, shapes hung, black against the orange sky — were they birds? The lines of cars flowed like a jewelled river, through black gorges studded with light. The sky in flames. Larry stood with his forehead against the glass. He saw lava flows, molten rivers, bleeding through the iron land. The glittering freeway. Freeway: even the word shone with light. Desolation. Blackness. Flames. Everything was beautiful. He felt power, energy, he was lit up with love.

Now in the street, the hot wind blew papers and grit around him. He looked along the neon strip, wondering where to go. He turned and the girl in the pink top was standing beside him.

She was thin, brown and sexy in her tight clothes. She had a stud in her nose and split, sore-looking lips. Her skin was rough close up, and her eyes were ringed with black kohl. She didn't smile. She said, 'Hey.'

'Hello.'

She said, 'You going home?'

'Back to the hotel. But I don't want to.'

She looked at him, considering.

He said, 'Shall we go somewhere.'

'Where you from again?'

'New Zealand.'

'How about you take me there one day?'

'Why not.'

She shrugged ironically. 'Well. I'm going home.'

He said, 'Can I come with you?'

She looked startled and gave him a considering look.

'Sure. Why not.'

He followed her, his eyes on her arse in the tight pants. She turned and said, 'You *sure* you want to come with me?'

She told him she was going to take the bus. He could have paid for a cab, but said nothing. He was following her into the iron city. He wanted to go into the black deeps of it, to be lost.

A man pushed a shopping trolley past them. He had five radios strung on it, each blaring out a different station. He was shouting and crying to himself. Beggars lay along the pavement beside their stinking bundles. At the bus stop a middle-aged woman in expensive clothes worked the line, begging abjectly for change. She said she was sorry, so sorry. A man walked past carrying a live lizard on his head, its claws clinging to his hair, the long reptile tail bumping down his back.

The bus was filled with crazies, tattooed gang bangers, the weary poor with their bundles. An obese mother heaved a toddler onto her knee. The boy's hair was cut in a Mohawk, his ears pierced with rings. A woman had an ancient radio stuck to her ear with masking tape. She nodded and winked at Larry, as though they were agreeing, secretly, about what she could hear. A black woman wore a plastic bag over her dreadlocks. Larry looked at the people festooned with bits of city rubbish, like primitive tribesmen, decorated with scraps of their concrete terrain.

Larry sat opposite Jacinta. She had a scab on her lip and a dark bruise on her neck. She gave him a sexy, unfocused stare. She smelled of bourbon. They swayed, looking at each other. She twirled the silver stud in her ear. Outside the lights floated past and turned into ribbons. There was a smell of burning in the air.

They were in a liquor store. The lizardy old Korean behind the counter watched Larry with cold eyes. A sign above his head promised, 'Armed Response'. Jacinta bought a bottle and they swigged it walking down the road.

She led him to a block of apartments that looked like a motel. There was waste ground next to it, strewn with junk and old cars. Larry heard voices raised in the distance, a sudden scream of tires.

Jacinta unlocked a battered door and they went inside.

He sat on a couch. Through the ranch slider he could see a patio lit by a green light bulb, and beyond that, quite close, a section of freeway curving away, and a bridge over it, criss-crossed with metal bars. Across some open ground there was a house with its windows covered by iron mesh.

Jacinta disappeared. He heard a man's voice coming from one of the rooms. When she came back she was holding a lighter and a glass pipe.

She sat down next to him. When she smiled her eyes turned to slits of black kohl. She said, 'Okay. You relax. You put your bag down there. You ready to get high?'

He wondered about the man in the next room. But he was so drunk that the thought whirled away. He saw Raine's face. Soon she would leave him. She had suffered enough. There was the thing with Aunt Evelyn. And he was going to lose his job. The strings that tied him to the world were unravelling. He was almost floating free. He saw how beautiful and peaceful that was. He'd tried to keep life together and now, in a single shunt, the world had released him, pushed him out to the other side.

He took the pipe from Jacinta and breathed in. A great swoop in his head, a moment of frozen time, nothing but little bubbles and screeches, bat-squeaks in his ears. Then the hot slam in his chest, the stars in his eyes blowing outwards, exploding in streams of light.

He wondered whether he would die in this room. He felt himself pass through time and thought he was dead already. Jacinta in her pink top, her face crossed by ribbons of smoke, held her glass pipe aloft, leading him on. Her eyes rolled up in her head, she licked her dry lips and moaned. She leaned close; her breath was sharp and sour. He watched the smoke curling and twisting from her mouth.

Fires in the distance. Iron city. He saw himself walking through a trench of blackness, beside the freeway, by the river of jewels.

Emily had a dream about Larry. He was saying something to her but she couldn't hear.

She woke up. She was in her sister's house in London. She was staying for four days before flying back to Auckland. She thought she'd heard Caro. But Caro was at home with Beth and Per.

It was 3am. There was a thin wail, Marie's baby. She turned and slept.

The following morning Emily went on the train up to Oxford. Her editor, Angus, had sent her to interview the New Zealand vice chancellor of the university, who was creating controversy with a new and unpopular regime.

When she got back to London it was late, and Marie was getting ready to go out. Her husband was away for a week, working for the bank in New York. Marie had tried to get Emily into the work party she was going to, but had been firmly told, no guests.

'Are you sure you don't mind if I go?' she said.

Emily didn't mind at all. She'd offered to look after Marie's kids, but Marie had arranged a babysitter, in case Emily wasn't back from Oxford.

When the babysitter arrived, Emily went out. She took the Tube to Euston Station. She walked to Oxford Street and bought some clothes, a pair of shoes and some presents for the family. As she roamed through the streets she fell into a trance of pleasure. There was nothing to tie her down, no Caro to attend to, no immediate deadlines, just the city and herself absorbing it all. Everything about London pleased her, the crowds, the rush, the drama of security announcements, the fact that a bomb could go off, the crazy wish that a bomb *would* go off, not too close but close enough to hear and see: these were secret pleasures in the private roaming hours. It was only possible to feel like this when you were alone, in the streets, in a foreign city.

Hours later, when she arrived worn-out at Euston Station, her train was cancelled, and after she'd waited for the next one, it was cancelled too. She realised she didn't need to go back to Marie's, and the freedom made her happy. She went to a newsagent and looked at a *Time Out*. There was a film on in Tottenham Court Road. She walked there, buying a filled roll and a drink from M&S on the way. She ate the meal in the cinema and watched the film, and thought it was the closest you could get to pure happiness.

Not that she didn't want ties. Not that she didn't love Caro, her family. But to be alone, outside time, to make decisions without having to consult anyone: it was bliss.

She got back at 1am and let the babysitter go. She was making tea in the kitchen when Marie came rocketing through the door, wearing a short dress and long boots. Impossibly glamorous, hilariously pissed, she lurched around the kitchen trying to get her boots off.

She said, 'It was a terrible party. There was hardly any food. It ran out. They'd booked a place that was too small, and they told half the junior staff they'd have to go to the pub down the road. There was only booze, and everyone got pissed and then the CEO stood up and made this appalling speech. It went on so long that people started yelling at him. Some woman next to me was shouting, *Get him off*. People are going to wake up in fear tomorrow. They're going to get fired.'

She got one boot off and toppled against the wall, standing on one leg. 'What have you been doing?'

Emily said, 'I took the train to Euston. I went shopping, then the train was cancelled, and I went to a film. I bought this bean roll thing and ate it in the movie. It was brilliant. I loved it.'

'You loved a bean roll?' Marie tugged at her other boot. It flew off and hit the wall.

'Everything, the bean roll, the city, freedom. And strangeness, the unfamiliar streets.'

Marie started laughing. 'A bean roll. A film by yourself. Anyone would think that was a bit bleak.'

'Bleak?' Emily paused, surprised. 'No, it was great.'

Marie cracked up. 'A lonely bean . . .'

'No, it was brilliant.' Emily didn't want Marie to think she was putting a brave face on a dull evening. That would spoil the real pleasure in what she'd felt.

'It was fantastic. Especially the bean roll,' she added, to acknowledge it was maybe a bit strange. When Marie started laughing everything seemed funny. Anyway, it wasn't likely she didn't understand. Marie was the sharpest person Emily knew.

Marie said, 'I wonder how Larry's getting on in LA.'

'It's great how he's staying sober.'

'Mmm.'

They thought about their brother.

The phone rang.

'Who's that, so late?' Marie said.

She came back into the kitchen. 'It's Caro, missing you.'

Emily grabbed the phone. She and Caro talked for half an hour, and for a long time after that, as Emily lay awake in bed, the distance between them seemed unbearable.

Larry opened his eyes. There was a man standing over him.

Jacinta said, 'This my brother. Manuel.'

Manuel was tall and thin, with high, round cheekbones and dark loops under his eyes. He looked like an owl.

Jacinta put her arms around his neck. 'Manuel, can you drive us to Mr Vaughan's?'

Manuel's owl eyes went anxious and resentful. 'No way,' he said. 'That asshole.'

Jacinta started pleading. Her voice went high and whiney. Larry studied the brown checks on the couch. Nausea rose in him and then fell away. He tried to rest his elbow on the arm of the couch, missed and fell over sideways.

Then he was up and moving, Jacinta pushing him. They went out into the hot noisy night and lurched along the balcony. Larry looked through a window at a man in a singlet. The man came towards the glass, eyes furious. Larry turned away and the lights froze in a long stream of colour before his eyes.

He let Jacinta guide him. They crossed a courtyard and then they were in a car, Larry slumped in the back seat and Jacinta and Manuel arguing in the front.

Larry lay on his back and watched the lights flash past, the trail of colour they left in the air. He sat up when the car stopped moving. They were parked outside a small house with green fairy lights strung over the front door, and ornate white grilles on all the windows. Jacinta was out there banging on the door.

Manuel lit a cigarette. He said morosely, 'This Mr Vaughan's place. He was her high-school science teacher. Then he got fired.

She been fuckin' him since I don't know when. They been experimentin' since she was a good little girl in school.'

The door opened. Light spilled out. A fat woman stood behind a security grille. They heard shouting. Jacinta put her hands on the bars and rattled them.

Manuel said, 'Uh oh. That's his daughter.'

'Don't come here,' the woman was shouting. 'Take your sick ass *out of here*.'

Jacinta stumbled off the side of the porch. She tried to throw a cigarette through the grille. The woman danced around behind it, yelling. 'You get nothing here. You don't come round here.'

'Fuck you,' Jacinta screamed. She gave the security door a last slam.

She came staggering back to the car.

'He's at work.'

'Oh man,' Manuel sighed. 'Can't we go home now?'

'No. Please Manuel. I need money. You need money. Come on.'

Larry's stomach lurched as the car swerved out into the road. Jacinta threw something out the window. There was the sound of breaking glass. When Larry looked back he could see the figure of the woman jumping and yelling against the light from the doorway, her hands on the metal bars.

'She look like a dog,' Jacinta said.

They were on the freeway. Larry looked at the cars drawing alongside, falling back. Bridges rose ahead and fell behind. They veered across the lanes and rocketed off in an incensed blast of car horns, past dark warehouses and closed shops. Around the corner was a street of restaurants and bars.

Manuel drove into a carpark. Larry got out. The woman shouting behind the grille had roused something in him. He felt the pulse of something like rage. Hot waves broke in his head, he saw the point of violence, the happiness of it. He had been swept into a stream of energy; he was enormously strong. A sudden lightness made him stumble into a pile of cardboard boxes. On a billboard above them, lit up with chemical blue radiance, a woman dived naked into a pool.

He followed Jacinta across the carpark to an open door. Inside he could see the white glare and bustle of a big commercial kitchen.

She put her head in the door and hollered something in Spanish. Someone shouted back. They waited. A man came out.

'J,' he said.

He was middle-aged, paunchy, tall, with a sallow, handsome face and greasy black hair.

He lit a cigarette. 'You know I got no money,' he said.

'You owe me.'

'You know that's not true.'

'You know it is true.'

'You're wired and fried. I bet you don't remember the last time you came down here. It was two nights ago. You got to stop this. You hear me, you got to stop this.'

Jacinta's shoulders hunched. She put her hands over her face. Then she flew at him, scratching his cheeks. He fought her off. He put his hands on her shoulders and started to shake her. Spit flew off her, her hands pawed and her feet thrashed.

Larry hit the man in the side of the head. The man lurched sideways and let go and she fell into a crouch, gasping. The man looked down at her. Then he turned with a thoughtful look and punched Larry full in the face. Larry heard the smack of bone on bone. There was a gap, nothing but wheeling sky, stars turning, cool blue light, a woman jumping naked into a pool.

He woke up. Mr Vaughan was watching them from the doorway of the kitchen. He was walking away, held up by Manuel. Jacinta was ahead, hunched and sobbing. They got in the car and drove.

Later, down a side street full of vacant lots, with Jacinta passed out on the back seat, he remembered the name of his hotel. The Marriot. It came to him, on a hot wave of the dope he was sharing with Manuel.

The Marriot.

Manuel, holding smoke in his lungs squeaked, 'You want me to drive you?'

'Please. Please.' It was all he could say.

He came into himself again in a hushed empty corridor of the hotel. He had no idea how he'd got through the foyer, or how he had found his way to this floor.

He sat on the carpet, panicked by the identical doors, the lines of numbers. Then he remembered his key.

He found his floor and his room, but the key didn't work. The electronic light stayed red, no matter how many times he shoved the card in the slot. He kicked the wall.

The door beside his opened. Lynx stuck his head out. Larry looked at him wordlessly.

Lynx's eyes opened wide. 'Fuck.'

Larry propped himself against the wall.

'What happened?'

'Mugged.' The word came out like a sob.

Lynx took the key and slid it in the slot. The light went green. Larry staggered into the room, Lynx behind him. He looked at himself in the mirror. Both eyes were ringed with black bruising. His lips were swollen. His face was not his own any more. His eyes were wild and frightened, as if his real self was a creature, some raw, wriggling, half-formed thing, peeping out from behind the mask of alien flesh.

He turned, saw Lynx's expression and was struck by the variety and richness of it: glee, horror, mirth, revulsion, pity.

Lynx said, 'You lie down.'

The boy brought a towel and carefully washed Larry's face. He cleaned the blood away from Larry's neck and ear with warm water, then soaked a flannel in cold water and laid it across Larry's face. He took off Larry's shoes, and washed his hands where blood had dried in a brown smear. He put a pillow under his head, dragged the sheets out from under him, and covered him up.

'It's nearly light,' he said. He brought Larry water and made him drink it.

'You sleep,' he said.

Larry caught his arm. He croaked, 'Let's not tell about me being mugged.'

Lynx looked down at him.

'Best if we don't . . . '

Lynx's voice was patient. 'You stink of piss. You stink of drugs.

When you're steady, you have a shower. Okay?'

Larry reeled. His whole body was filled with pain. He slipped towards a ledge. He plunged down, into black.

Around eight in the morning Lynx came back. He got Larry up, supported him to the shower, and stuffed his dirty clothes in a plastic shopping bag. The drugs still in his system gave Larry their last prop, the strength to get over the edge of the bath and stand in the shower. He was a quivering mess of pain. His legs trembled. With Lynx standing over him he vomited repeatedly into the toilet, naked, sick beyond endurance, wishing he could die.

Lynx picked up the stinking bag of clothes. He got some clean boxers and a T-shirt out of Larry's bag and helped him put them on. He turned the air-conditioning higher and left. Larry stared after him. He lay writhing in the silence, in chilled air of the brown room.

A woman unlocked the door and called musically, 'House-keeping.'

He managed to croak, 'No thanks,' and she sniffed and retreated, saying something condemnatory in Spanish. The pain receded enough for him to turn over, but the sickness came again and he vomited into the wastepaper basket. He smelled his own smell, and it seemed as though his body must be rotting.

Faces swam through his mind in sick waves. Jacinta, Manuel, Mr Vaughan. Little Lynx, with his steady eyes.

In the late afternoon Lynx came back from his outing. He kneeled on the bed and offered Larry a sandwich in a brown paper bag. Larry shook his head. Lynx brought him a cup of water.

The boy said, 'Leanne's going to be looking for you. You better ring her and say you don't want dinner.'

'Lynx. Thanks.'

'No worries.'

Larry practised speaking. His mouth was dry, his tongue huge. *Hi Leanne. How's it going? I've got a meeting . . .*

'How does that sound?'

'Fucked up,' Lynx said. He grinned. 'Like you got a tennis ball in your mouth.'

'How about you say I met you in the foyer and I said I was going to a meeting?'

He thought about it. 'Okay.'

Lynx tilted his chin in farewell. But as he opened the door he gave a grunt of annoyance and surprise. He backed into the room, with Slade's meaty hand on his chest.

'I been looking for you,' Slade drawled happily, swaggering into the room.

He stopped and stared. 'Fuck man. What's happened to him?'

'He got mugged,' Lynx said quietly.

Slade leaned close. Larry struggled, pulled away, nauseated by the boy's foody breath.

'Leave him alone,' Lynx said.

But Slade paced at the end of the bed, hands on hips, looking at Larry from all angles. Larry watched him strutting up and down, all brute fat and hammy showmanship. He would be good on stage. A natural actor. The expression on him, he looked like a Roman emperor. He made Lynx seem like a frightened little kid. It occurred to Larry that Slade was gay.

'Wow. That's a fucked-up face, bro. Have you told Leanne?'

He pulled a phone out of his pocket and took a picture.

Lynx tried to grab the phone. Larry just lay there. He lay and thought of nothing while the big boy and the skinny boy wrestled and argued and hit each other at the end of his bed.

Slade pushed Lynx off, angry now. He leaned down and took a picture up close, of Larry's face.

'If he's been mugged you need to ring the cops,' Slade said. 'This is evidence.'

Larry closed his swollen eyes. A memory came back to him. Himself on the back seat of the car. Manuel leaning over him. Jacinta looking over the seat back, eyes intent.

She said, 'The cash. Just take the cash.'

Manuel hissing and swearing at Larry, holding him down, hands in the pockets of his jacket.

The boys went off to dinner. Downstairs, Slade would be showing his picture gallery to Leanne. Leanne would ring Ezra. He thought of Raine. Tracy. Cupboard love. Strange what brings you to the end of things. If he hadn't blabbed to Tracy, if Raine hadn't decided it was the last straw, would he be lying here, sick and beaten, while young Slade put the final nail in his career? Would he have stayed sober, done his job, gone home?

But he saw how it really was. You could blame the things that pushed you; you could say it was someone else's fault. But really it was yourself that let go. You stopped hanging on and the world gave a shrug and shunted you free.

In the end, it was only you.

Leanne got housekeeping to let her in. She stood at the end of his bed. She put her hands lightly to her chest and looked at him. An expression swelled in her face.

He turned away. Nothing was said.

There were eight phone messages for Larry from contacts in the city. Notes were pushed under his door. There were questions, and requests for rescheduling of missed meetings. He answered none of them. He stayed in his room until it was time for the four of them to leave.

In the teeming chaos of Los Angeles airport Emily and Larry came close. She was in transit, London to Auckland, behind the wall. She was on a different flight. They didn't see each other.

At the airport Larry drew out five hundred American dollars on his credit card and offered the money to Lynx. The boy took it, then tried to give it back. Larry gave him his expensive new watch and his phone. Lynx stood holding them, uncertain. Larry squeezed the boy's arm and walked away.

He got himself a separate seat on the plane. The woman next to him asked if he was all right. He asked if she would order a drink for him. The air hostess had stopped serving him, saying she believed he'd had enough. The woman got him one drink, but after that, she refused.

At Auckland, he picked up his bag and walked out into the cold dawn. It was five in the morning; the sky was streaked with red clouds. The air was soft and there was a smell of grass and cows.

He took a taxi to Ponsonby and knocked on the door of a house. When there was no answer he went around the back and got in through the window. Max was still asleep. Larry stood out on the deck watching the sun coming up. He waited.

He paid Max in American dollars. Max liked the idea of this. Larry threw in an extra couple of fifties. Max gave him a cautious glance. 'You all right?'

Larry shrugged.

They lit a pipe then and there.

Afterwards, in Max's bathroom, Larry upended a bottle of pills and held them in his palm. He juggled them lightly, before washing them down. In the kitchen, he found a bottle and poured himself a drink. He felt nothing.

He was walking through grassland. It was hot and still and the track stretched ahead, broad and overgrown and pitted here and there with the hoof prints of cows. Along the track were green pools fringed by waving stands of native reeds. There were green frogs, motionless and watching in the water. The cicadas made a racket so loud that you thought you could see it, a shimmering, glittering wall of sound. The track ran by the side of the river, and the toetoe waved in the air like spears against the blue glare of the sky.

Then he could hear the sea roaring, and once he'd crossed a bridge he was looking up the slope of a giant dune of black sand, so black it had a blue sheen to it. He was climbing the slope, the sand hot on his feet, and when he reached the top there was the great curve of the coast stretching away north and south. Across a mile of sand was the sea, fringed with wild surf. He turned and turned and the black desert was a roar of violent motion. Heat shimmered up off the sand, the toetoe waved, the sea roared against the grey cliffs.

He crossed the back of the monster dune, and reached a patch of grass under the cliffs. He lay down under the cabbage trees. Everything was huge. The air had size and weight. Above him, the sky was expanding.

He turned on his back and saw shapes hovering above his face.

They were dragonflies, colourful, glittering, darting and zooming in the bright air. He reached out, wanting to touch the light, quick, beautiful things.

A light shone in his eye and something touched his face.

There was a green curtain, and behind it, a voice. It came to Larry, over the sound of the sea. 'My nephew made me take him to the Observatory yesterday. He told me about supermassive black holes. Did you know there's a giant black hole at the centre of our galaxy? In three billion years time we're going to collide with the next-door galaxy, Andromeda. He tells me this will throw us into the black hole. The end of the Earth.'

He heard a jingling sound.

'So I thought I'd ring you,' the voice said.

He was moving. A door banged open and closed.

Someone said, 'It's chaos in here. May. May. Sorry, can I grab you? We've got three at once. Can you intubate this one?'

The dragonflies, flitted, sparkled, zoomed away.

He was on the sand, walking away from the valley, towards the sea. Far away, he could see people walking in a line against the waves. Little black figures against the dancing, glittering water. The heat rose and made mirages, great puddles of silver on the sand. The cliffs boomed behind him, the iron sound of the wind in the stone.

He saw Emily standing on the dunes. She was small. A kid again. She had red stains on her mouth.

They walked together through the hot iron landscape, along the back of the black dune, beyond the toetoe spears and the waving reeds. There was a circle cut in the rock, with light at the end of it.

Something black rose out of the sea and whirled in the air. Larry and Emily stood together as it came towards them. It swelled and swelled and made a sound like birds.

In the sky there was movement and panic. A voice shouted in his ear and an object was pushed into his throat. His body was moved around. He felt tiny pricks in his arms.

A great jolt crashed against his chest. Then another. But he turned towards the sky.

Emily looked at him. He said, 'This is my dream.'

She stared into the black shape that was coming across the sea. It was colouring the sky around it, turning the blue into bright streaks of purple, blue, starry green.

'It looks like a migraine,' she said. The black shape was getting closer, swelling, with the noon glare behind it.

They went on together, over the iron sand. The tunnel was ahead of them.

At the end of it he saw Per, standing in the circle of light. He kept sight of Emily until the black thing was above them. He wanted to stay with her. He was afraid.

She said, 'It has been decided.'

The black thing was made of dragonflies. She was absorbed in it and flew away.

He understood. He crossed out of his dream. There was darkness all round him, and tiny frozen stars.

Opportunity

Charlotte Grimshaw

OPPORTUNITY

A man confronts death after an operation, a devout Christian encounters a man who hurt her long ago, a secretary uncovers her boss's secret shame. And in a house in Auckland an elderly woman is writing the last book of her life, one which, she says, contains all of her crimes. How are the characters connected and who is writing the stories?

Each of these astute stories is an inspection of motive, rich in vivid insight into a diverse range of lives. Together, they form a unified whole. *Opportunity* is a book about storytelling, about generosity and opportunism; above all it is a celebration of the subtleties of human impulse, of what Katherine Mansfield called the LIFE of life.

In 2007, *Opportunity* was short-listed for the Frank O'Connor International Prize and in 2008, *Opportunity* won the Montana New Zealand Award for Fiction, along with the premier Montana Medal for Fiction or Poetry. Charlotte Grimshaw was also awarded the 2008 Montana Prize for Book Reviewer of the Year.

In their report the Montana judges praised *Opportunity* for its stories 'packed full of drama, surprising turns and compelling characters.' The judges considered *Opportunity* 'the most structurally sophisticated book of fiction submitted . . . Its stories offer reflections on the art of writing and storytelling, its structures and its self-awareness don't compromise the traditional pleasures of fiction . . . In its structure it resembles the work of Tim Winton; in its stylistic compression it shows hints of Jorge Luis Borges; like Virginia Woolf's *Mrs Dalloway* it offers an uncompromising but tender portrait of a city.'

REVIEWS OF OPPORTUNITY:

'Charlotte Grimshaw's *Opportunity* is one of the most gripping books of short stories I've ever read . . . Grimshaw's imagination and vision is astonishing. Her prose is spare and amazingly expressive. *Opportunity* is a book to read compulsively and re-read for its subtlety, penetration and sheer brilliance.' *Writers' Radio, Radio Adelaide*

'Grimshaw says *Opportunity* is a novel with a large cast of characters . . . Each story stands by itself and adds to the larger one . . . Grimshaw isn't interested in being virtuous — the opportunity to explore the LIFE of life gives her writing a taut energy . . . A darkly glittering achievement.' *The Dominion Post*

'A writer with impressive command of style and subject . . . Do take the opportunity to read *Opportunity*. It's riddling and rewarding. Appreciate its skill. Acknowledge its depth.' *New Zealand Herald*

'This is the most enjoyable New Zealand collection of short stories I have read since Emily Perkins's *Not Her Real Name*.' *Christchurch Press*

'*Opportunity* is beautifully crafted, colourful and hard to keep to yourself. A sense of detail, vividly narrated, gives the whole book a richness that belies its simplicity of structure . . . Never heavy, always one step ahead of the reader in terms of black humour and unexpected outcome, *Opportunity* deserves to be read aloud.' *Capital Times*

'Charlotte Grimshaw just keeps getting better and better.' *Next*

'The best Charlotte Grimshaw stories combine her unflinching eye with real emotional insight.' *New Zealand Listener*

FOREIGN CITY

Anna Devine, a young New Zealand painter living in London, has two chance encounters that set her on a search for answers. Can she really 'see' her new city properly? Can she reconcile family life and art? Her search leads her into past mysteries of her troubled family and her brother's death, and towards future complexities: infidelity, dangerous freedoms, and a whole new eye on her foreign city. In Auckland, in another time, Justine Devantier is reading a novel in order to find out about its author — and possibly about herself. And in a fictional city a man looks for a woman he knew long ago. At the core of this intricate plot is British novelist Richard Black, who may hold the strands that bind all the protagonists together.

Grimshaw's brilliantly drawn characters walk through her foreign cities in different guises. She gives us a 'true' story, a fiction, a love story, a story of family connections lost and found, and a dazzling ride through the creative process — its practitioners, its casualties.

REVIEWS OF FOREIGN CITY:

'She is terrifically good at building cities out of words.' *New Zealand Herald*

'Smart and readable, *Foreign City* not only cements Grimshaw's already considerable reputation, it marks her out as exceptional.' *Dominion Post*

'A swarming energy pervades every page she writes . . . her descriptive writing has always been of the highest order. Most of it would work just as well as poetry.' *New Zealand Listener*

'She's world class.' *North & South*

'Grimshaw builds enormous narrative power through her use of structure, which keeps us guessing, concentrating hard, to the last page.' *Herald on Sunday*

'Like Dickens, Grimshaw makes characters of her cities. Her evocation of the British capital, especially, is superb.' *New Zealand Books*